THE MERMAID THEATRE

By H F Burgess

For my husband, family, and friends, both
dippers and panto stars, with love.

PROLOGUE

Life was somewhat transient in Seabourne, a small town on the South-east coast of England. In 1976 holidaymakers still flooded into the area for a day or a week, or for as long as their particular workplace had shut down, enjoying the relatively sedate seaside attractions, as they had done each summer for as long as they could remember. It would not be long before the pull of cheap flights to the Mediterranean changed all that.

Permanent residents fell neatly into a number of groups. Middle-aged and married couple, Dot and Rob Baker were part of the 'lets move away from our problems, and live by the seaside' collection, as were dad, Samuel and daughter Isabella Williams, with her own daughter, Lizzie.

Longstanding Seabourne folk included Lady Clara Harrington who lived in a vast Edwardian pile, becoming more unhappy and brittle as the years stretched out after receiving the news that her beloved husband had been killed in the war. Her nephews, Jack and Paul, tried occasionally, but could never fill the huge hole left in her life. The estranged Turner family were still keeping their hardware shop running, now almost into the third generation.

Benjamin Solomons, his mother and grandmother had moved here just as the war was starting and felt like it was home now. PC Will Johnson was also moved here as a child and never knew a different life, like most of the inhabitants of Seabourne.

The sea was generally taken for granted and there was little community spirit here. People just got on with their days, until a couple of local people thought how nice it would be to go for a dip.

PART I - THE SEABOURNE DIPPERS

DOT BAKER

It was not even eight o'clock in the morning in early June, 1976, and the sun was already beating down by the time Dot was at the water's edge, chucking her kit off with gay abandon. This was day fourteen of her morning swims, and she couldn't remember enjoying anything so much in ages, not least because it washed away all the uncomfortable sweating that she seemed to be doing every night lately. It made her feel old, unfeminine and a bit stale. She guessed this new symptom was part of the change of life, which she had been reading about, and she really hoped that it wouldn't go on for too much longer. She could just about cope with the mood swings, and the headaches, but the hot flushes were a pain in the backside. Swimming felt like the only pleasure she had at the moment as the change had swallowed up her enthusiasm for all the things she used to like to do.

Dot rushed into the crashing white waves and gave herself wholeheartedly to the flow of the water. Immersed in the rejuvenating sea, she felt she could be in California or somewhere fancy like that. A huge wave came crashing over her head and knocked her into a washing-machine spin. She emerged, spitting out salty water, grinning and smoothing her short, greying hair back from her face. *My God, moving here last year was the best thing she and Rob had ever done.* She vowed she would swim every single day now, even through the winter, if she could. There wasn't much actual swimming to be done today but the feeling of jumping the fizzing waves took her straight back to childhood days spent on the beach at

Broadstairs in Kent. Happy memories.

As Dot was enjoying the water, she glanced over at the old theatre on the pier, the sunlight was catching the window panes which seemed to be winking at her, and she casually wondered when the last play or pantomime had been staged. *Now that would have been worth seeing,* she thought, and her mind went back to a trip to London in February 1935. Her parents had taken her to The Lyceum in London, to see Dick Whittington. She couldn't think who was in it now, but she remembered the smells of the old theatre; smoke from the gentlemen's cigars and pipes, ladies' perfume with just a hint of moth balls. This, however was not the strongest memory of that evening. The Duke and Duchess of York had been there with their young daughters, Princess Elizabeth, who was now Queen Elizabeth of course, and the lovely Princess Margaret. A glittering evening, she would never forget, even though she was only eight at the time.

Dot realised she spent a lot of time reminiscing these days. It seemed now that her happiest times were all behind her, even though she was only 49. She knew that Rob, her husband of thirty years now, was worried about her and that he just didn't know what to say or how to help. She used to be so creative and busy but this last year she felt as if life was treacle and that she was slowly wading through it, on her own.

Rob was a quiet, kind and unassuming man, who had worked for many years with John, an old army friend, running a building business in London. When John had died suddenly, of a heart attack, Rob was heartbroken. They had shared everything; games of cricket, the odd half pint of cider down the pub and most importantly, war memories; both the horrors and better times. Although Rob loved and valued her immensely, Dot knew she could never fill the significant hole John had left. She had been as supportive as she could when John died, and had finally suggested that they start a new life a long way from London and all the memories, just picking the coastal town of Seabourne out of a hat. It had been the right decision for both of them. Rob had started a new building company and had picked up more work than he could cope with during this first year. Dot loved living by the sea but just hadn't found the energy to find her niche. The kids, Jim and Margaret, stayed in London. They were both single, with very busy jobs, apparently.

Recently, her sea swimming felt like a lifeline out of the spiral that was dragging her downwards, and she was damn well going to cling to it.

There weren't many people about yet, but Dot suddenly felt that tingle you get when someone is watching you. She turned and waved to be friendly and then the youngish man came bounding down the beach towards her.

'Is it nice in?' he called out in a London Jewish accent. He had very dark, longish hair and was really rather chubby, but with such gentle brown eyes and a kind face that the overall picture was quite attractive. He looked, somehow, as though he could do with a motherly cuddle. Dot snapped back into the moment as she could see Rob's amused face in her mind at the thought of her eyeing up a much younger man. No, of course it wasn't' like that, he just looked a pleasant chap.

'It's divine. Really fresh and so enlivening,' she replied, feeling her cheeks go ever so slightly pink.

'That's all the encouragement I need then.' Leaving his jeans and shirt on the pebbles, he dived into the water, making that funny noise that only men seem to have to make when entering the sea.

As Dot was deciding on whether she should 'make conversation' or sort of casually move away a bit, he splashed over.

BENJAMIN SOLOMONS

Benny had seen the approachable looking, middle-aged lady in the sea on a number of mornings now and was plucking up the courage to ask if he could join her. He thought she looked like a very happy seal as she twirled through the waves and swam about, as if she couldn't give a damn about anything. She didn't look slim exactly but she was obviously fit enough to enjoy the water. He wished he didn't constantly look at other people's size and compare himself to them. He hated his appearance, his stomach, everything really. He had to lose some weight. Every single advertisement on his TV said so. *Could he pinch more than an inch*? He could pinch about six flippin' inches if truth be told. He had always enjoyed his food too much.

Born in Germany in 1936, to Jewish parents (Matilda and Jacob), sadly his father was killed early on in the war. His mother and grandmother had been unbelievably brave and made the perilous journey to Britain just in time to save all of their lives. Matilda would, at Benny's request, re-tell the story of the heart-stopping and frightening trip across Germany, France and The English Channel, with a tiny baby, finding safety and peace in the very quiet town of Seabourne. Benny had lived with them for most of his life. Their love of cooking and indulgent food had both inspired and spoiled him. Although he had lived in his own flat for some years now, old habits die hard and he badly needed a new regime.

Working in the Planning Department of the local council

didn't really help. He was behind a desk for most of the day and got very little exercise. *Perhaps regular swimming would do something, well it couldn't hurt.* He liked the water and could actually swim quite a long way. The following morning, he decided to literally take the plunge. He rummaged about and found an old pair of trunks, they'd do. He threw on his flares and a baggy cheesecloth shirt, grabbed some cake and tea and he was off. New beginnings.

He watched the lady swimming for a short while and then gathering up some courage, splashed over to her and introduced himself.

'Benny Solomons,' he offered his hand in a rather formal manner, seconds before another huge breaker, rolled the pair of them to their knees.

Gathering herself from the turmoil of the water, 'Dot Baker,' she extended her hand, laughing so much at their formality versus the irreverent, crashing wave, she was almost crying. It was then that they both noticed the blood coming out of her hand and elbow.

'Oh, my word, you're hurt, let me help you out of the water.' She'd also cut her knee and was starting to shake a little bit. They sat on the shoreline and he offered her some tea from the flask he'd brought. The warm, very sugary drink tasted comforting and after cleaning up the cuts with her towel, they were not nearly as bad as they had first looked.

'Er, Dot, would you like a piece of Victoria sponge?' Benny asked, getting a surprisingly huge piece of cake out of his bag.

'Thank you, that looks delicious,' Dot replied, feeling that the situation might be getting a little awkward; this man was a good ten years younger than her and she had known him for all of ten minutes, now she was sharing cake with him.

'I'll cut and you choose.' He halved it and they chatted whilst they ate. Dot soon felt more comfortable, Benny was just so easy to talk to.

'Are you a professional baker Benny? Because if not, you jolly well should be.'

Dot congratulated him on the lightest cake she'd eaten in a long time. *Crikey, my cakes are nowhere near the mark,* she thought.

'Thank you, but I just work in the Planning Department at the Council offices, it's very boring but it pays the mortgage. I do love baking cakes though, as you can probably tell,' he patted his stomach with a sad smile. 'My neighbour, Isabella, tells me I should sell them and then I wouldn't eat so many. She's fairly new around here as well and could do with meeting some people, she's really sweet.'

Benny could see Dot's eyes immediately light up. He quickly realised she was matchmaking, when she couldn't stop herself saying:

'Well why don't you invite her down here next time you're coming?'

'Maybe I will do just that,' Benny replied, but again with that slightly sad smile. *Isabella was adorable but she was just a friend.*

He hadn't actually done any swimming at all this morning but it had been enjoyable meeting Dot. He would work much harder tomorrow. The morning's fun had come to an end and they parted company, both saying they'd be back the next day. Benny thought Dot's idea was a good one and so he popped a little note through Isabella's door, asking her to come along for a swim one morning.

ISABELLA WILLIAMS

Isabella and her six-year-old daughter, Lizzie, lived next door to Benny. Isabella loved it there and felt very lucky to have a new, bright and airy apartment with a view of the sea. Dad had been so generous in helping her with the deposit for her first home. With her two jobs at the school, she could just about afford the mortgage and keep afloat generally. Previously they had lived in the only family home she could remember, a charming old rambling house in South London, but Dad had sold it so that they could both move away and have their own space. It suited Samuel, Isabella's Dad, to leave behind the memories of his beloved late wife, Vera, Isabella's mum. She had died of breast cancer, nearly ten years ago now, and Isabella missed her every day.

Isabella was considering Benny's invitation. There was always so much to do in the morning; get Lizzie ready and take her to school, prepare the singing and dancing lessons for later on in the day, all the housework, and then think about tea. It was really kind of Benny to ask her to go swimming but could she really spare the time? On the other hand, here she was, day after day on her own with Lizzie, apart from Dad popping by, and she really needed to get out and make some friends. Benny was already becoming the kind of friend you didn't want to let go of; he was simply so kind and thoughtful.

Integrate more, that's what she needed to do, according to Dad, who had views and opinions on everything, and was rarely wrong. Accordingly, she tried on her old red swimming costume and glanced at her reflection. With her corkscrew hair falling down her back, her natural copper skin and a few freckles, she was a striking young woman, although she didn't seem to be remotely aware of this.

One only had to meet her father, Samuel Williams, who had arrived in England on the *Empire Windrush,* to understand her good looks. Samuel had an easy West Indian charm together with an athletic frame and a devastatingly handsome face. Little wonder, Vera had fallen for him at Tilbury Docks where she had been working in the canteen, in June 1948. She and her friends had been watching the young men walking off the boat and when Samuel came in for a cup of tea, it was love at first sight. This, however, had been no one-sided love affair. Vera, with her gentle southern Irish accent, glistening auburn hair and green eyes, had knocked him sideways. They had made a stunning couple, and turned heads when out dancing. She was just eighteen when they met, and only thirty-three when she died. Samuel had soldiered on through this incredible shock and pain and brought up Isabella as best he could. He hadn't looked at another woman since Vera's passing. He'd met the love of his life, and she could never be replaced. Isabella had encouraged him to find someone to spend his life with, but he was adamant and seemed content with his lot. He doted on his daughter and granddaughter and said they gave him all the happiness he could wish for.

So, as the blisteringly hot day melted into a crimson and purple night, Isabella put a very sleepy headed Lizzie to bed, and decided to knock on Benny's door and accept his invitation. Before she even reached his flat, she could smell delicious fragrances of cinnamon and brown sugar seeping under his front door, and smiled to herself.

He pulled open the door with his customary over-enthusiasm, which she was beginning to find very engaging. T Rex greeted her with "I love to Boogie", and Benny was soon dancing around the kitchen with floral apron and matching oven gloves.

'Try a piece of this, a new recipe I'm experimenting with, it's just come out of the oven.'

'This is exceptional.' Isabella was trying to speak and eat hot spicy cake at the same time. 'I'd love to come along tomorrow. I'll pop in for a swim on the way back from dropping Lizzie off at school.'

Benny was pleased, as although he had only just met Dot, he felt that Isabella and Dot would get along a treat, despite the difference in ages. 'I'll bring tea and this cake for afterwards.'

The following morning, which felt hotter than ever, Isabella was making her way back from the school when she heard Benny's voice reach out to her from the sea.

'You can't have cake unless you've done at least twenty minutes swimming.'

'Hello yourself,' she called back with a wave. She was sure she remembered Benny saying another lady was going to be there. No sign of her at the moment.

LADY CLARA HARRINGTON

Her morning cup of Earl Grey was only just about adequate. Mrs Jackson probably hadn't warmed the pot properly and definitely not put the cosy on. Even so, she still rallied herself as she did every morning to get immaculately dressed, *coiffured,* and made up in order to do battle with the steps of Rutland Manor, and the little coastal town of Seabourne. As usual she walked through the misty gardens and down to the seafront. One could set Big Ben by Clara's morning walk.

Looking back at her Edwardian villa, peeping just above the sea mist, she had a rare, short moment of pleasure, as who could look at those colours and not be instantly transported somewhere exotic and Mediterranean? She nearly decided to congratulate her long-suffering gardener, but thought better of it, just in time. Rubbing her gloved hand along the lemon balm, she thought of Peter, as she often did at exactly this spot. After all these years, his lemon scented cologne still came to mind. But as always there were notes missing. Notes of him. Freshly planed wood, that unmistakeable smell of welded metal and a workshop full of old tools, oil and Swarfega. Clara vaguely wondered if men still used that odd smelling, green hand-cleaner these days. For several minutes she was lost to the past. A joyful shriek from the sea reached her ears. Dammed tourists!

Refusing to be deterred from her chosen route, by this racket, she grasped her treasured cane with the intricate silver mermaid handle and strode forward with intent. These empty headed, irritating holiday makers were not going to spoil her quiet promenade. Even though she'd selected her lightweight linen suit for this morning, the already scorching sun was almost undermining her façade of icy serenity. She would need her parasol for tomorrow. The summer was proving to be a hot one so far.

Occasionally, Clara, added a stroll up and down the pier to her morning walk, and she started down the weather-beaten boards towards the theatre. With the sun glinting off the windows and a gentle wind blowing the old curtains through some of the broken panes inside the foyer, one could imagine the place was still happy and alive with people and performances. This however, both upset and irritated Clara today. She made an abrupt about-turn and picked up her speed for the solitary walk home. Some days she almost enjoyed reminiscing, but mostly her sadness still felt so raw; she could have lost him yesterday.

There was more sea mist the next morning with an even hotter day expected. Clara decided on a very lightweight pale blue silk dress, for which she had a matching parasol. The outfit had been in her wardrobe these last forty years and still fitted as the day she had received it, packed with layers of tissue paper, from her dressmaker. She admired the trim shape reflected in her mirror. Just right. *Someone in Seabourne needed to maintain standards,* she thought, as she descended the gardens to the sea. She could barely tell the boys from the girls these days, and the music! That did not bear thinking about. She enjoyed music generally however and recalled the sounds of her youth. She and Peter had been quite contemporary with their gramophone records; Louis Armstrong was one of her favourites. Peter had particularly enjoyed the big band sounds but she preferred jazz. Memories of these tunes then kept her company for some minutes until she found herself nearly level with the pier, where a couple of people seemed to be making an exhibition of themselves in the sea again. They looked much too old to be cavorting about in the waves. *Ridiculous.* Above the sound of the sea came shouts of 'good morning' and 'lovely day, isn't it?' which she ignored as she went on her lonely way.

Clara needed to make a couple of purchases in the town today, that she couldn't trust Mrs Jackson to deal with properly, and noted how cheap and down-market the shops seemed to be getting lately. She had loved 'Hulbards', the upmarket department store that used to take pride of place in the High Street. The classic building had been carved up into several nasty little units. Curtess Shoes, *goodness how did young women walk in those heels and platforms?* Clara walked on a little further. 'Good gracious,' she actually said out loud, whilst passing a shop called Athena, which, apparently without shame, had a huge poster of a young female tennis player, scratching her bottom, without underwear. *Whatever next?* Clara made a note not to come back into the town if she didn't have to. She wondered what Peter would have thought of 1976. He had always been a little more broad-minded than her, but even so! By the time Clara reached her front door, it had become unbearably hot for mid-morning in June.

The following day was her bridge afternoon and without meaning to, Clara did actually look forward to playing. Although mostly irritating, one or two of her fellow players could, occasionally, hold an intelligent conversation. There appeared to be few capable of that these days.

Clara heard the doorbell chime. Unusual, especially this early in the morning. Mrs Jackson would deal with it, but who was it? She peered out of her bedroom window to see her two nephews, Jack, and Paul, at the door. Goodness, whatever did they want? The eldest, Jack, looked straight up to the window, beamed, and called a cheery 'good morning, Aunt Clara.'

Clara was momentarily taken aback. She had not seen Jack, who was now thirty-five, for quite some time. He had always resembled his uncle, but today, with his wet hair swept right back, he looked so very much like the husband she had lost in the war, all those years ago. Lieutenant Peter Harrington was on board HMS *Boadicea,* on an escort mission to France, just prior to returning home on-leave. Clara could hardly dare to dream about his homecoming; she was so happy and excited. On 13th June 1944, his ship was one of the last to be bombed by a German aircraft. HMS *Boadicea* went down just twelve miles South-west of Portland Bill, less than fifty miles from Seabourne. Clara returned to the present and before she could command otherwise, Mrs Jackson, the daft woman, had invited them in for some fresh lemonade. Well, there was nothing for it. Manners needed to be observed. Luckily, she was almost ready for her promenade, and so she wiped her eyes with her delicate lace handkerchief, and swept into her drawing room, her graciousness only slightly overpowered by the sharp aroma of 4 7 11.

'Jack, Paul, this is a surprise. To what do I owe a visit from you both?'

Jack, who was never one for formality, just rushed up to his aunt, lifted her off her feet and twirled her round. Clara did her best impression of being cross, but secretly felt rather flattered by the spontaneity of her favourite nephew. He was a gentle young man, creative, intense and frequently a little impetuous.

Paul, born eighteen years later, was an unplanned surprise and unfortunately his mother, June, had complications with this rather late birth and tragically died a few days later. Paul was quieter, and more reserved, but equally attractive, even if his hair needed a jolly good short back and sides. Clara always thought the absence of a mother had made Paul shy, vulnerable and close to his brother, Jack.

Their father, Peter's younger brother, Dennis Harrington, having lost both his brother and his wife far too soon, had struggled with the demands of living, and developed dementia at a very early age. He now lived in a care home further along the coast. Clara visited him regularly, even though he didn't recognise her at all these days.

'We decided today was a very fine morning for a swim and a picnic breakfast with our favourite aunt. We have a flask of steaming hot Earl Grey and some breakfast rolls. Please say you'll join us Aunt Clara?'

'Thank you for the invitation, however not today gentlemen. It's rather short notice for me.' Clara looked at their faces and they seemed genuinely disappointed and so she decided to soften the blow, 'perhaps tomorrow then, Jack.' This cheered them up and they went off merrily, followed by the sounds of the waves and squawking gulls.

DOT BAKER

Through her kitchen window, Dot could see the sun was rising in a glory of pinks and oranges, and she vowed to never take this for granted. She smiled to herself, and realised that smiling made you feel better, and actually she was feeling a bit more human this week and the sea was calling her. As she was just walking out of the door, the phone rang. *Bother.* She wasn't sure who was calling at this early hour, but she was looking forward to swimming very much today. She was hoping to see Benny again, this time with his friend, Isabella. Dot suddenly realised how empty and perhaps even lonely her life was beginning to feel, that these two strangers meant so much to her this morning. She was considering letting it ring when Rob called out from the bathroom that he was brushing his teeth and could she answer it? *Okay, it probably wouldn't take long,* so she picked up the receiver.

'Oh Mum,' it was her daughter, Margaret, and she sounded a bit upset. Blast, now she was definitely going to miss her dip. *Oh well. She rarely rings and never has time to talk when I call,* Dot thought, and immediately felt guilty, focussing on what her daughter had to say.

Margaret was thirty now, and had worked her way up to Sales Manager at a big London company. She was overcome with worry as she'd heard on the grape vine that the General Manager wanted to see her and a higher-ranking colleague had said it didn't look good. Margaret had just taken on a huge mortgage for a swanky flat in the city, and was afraid she was going to lose everything if she lost this job. Margaret had been feeling tired lately. Did Dot realise how high-pressured her job was? Dot sympathised. Margaret reminded Dot that she had never had a proper job in her life and as such, had no idea of how Margaret was feeling. After a further ten minutes of Margaret, Dot attempted to tell her how well she was doing and calm her down a bit in a positive way, but Margaret wanted an argument with someone and after telling Dot that she'd been no help whatsoever and what a useless mother she had always been, slammed the phone down.

During this time Rob had drunk his tea, grabbed a bit of toast and was out the door, on his way to work, blowing Dot a kiss, totally unaware of the toxicity of the call.

Once the guilty, angry and finally, sad, tears had stopped, Dot just stared out the window again. Her fairly short-lived attempt at pulling herself together this week dissolved and she decided to get on with the much-needed job of cleaning out some cupboards. It was incredibly hot work but she felt both a release and a small sense of achievement once the job was finished.

Dot liked getting jobs done and went on to do a lot more cleaning, a huge batch of baking and even a bit of mending. Her day had been productive and she was looking forward to Rob coming home. She'd made a corned beef pie and mash, one of his favourites, and felt she had really turned the day around, when the phone rang…

'It's me again. I've been promoted to Sales Director! How about that? Ken was only joking when he said things weren't looking good. Anyway, no time to talk, going out to Ronnie Scott's tonight *with all my friends* to celebrate. I've just got time to get a slinky new dress, bye.'

As the phone was put down again, Dot managed a 'congratulations darling, so pleased for you.' She was just shaking her head in disbelief when Rob walked through the door, carrying a small bunch of flowers.

'Thought these would cheer you up, you've seemed so

down lately, he said, giving her a hug and a kiss. After the rollercoaster of a day, she just held on to him silently, both of them a bit messy from their labours, and it felt wonderful.

The following morning, she took the phone off the hook, brushed her teeth, got her stuff together quietly and headed off to the beach.

BETTY AND SINDY TURNER

'Come on Nan, let's get you up and dressed. Who do you think you are, lying about in that bed until six o'clock in the morning, Greta Garbo?'

'Sindy, baby, you've no idea who Greta Garbo is, have you? And I'll bet she didn't spend fifty years of her life working in a hardware shop.'

'You know it was all about you making eyes at those tasty builders and plumbers who were lining up down the street, waiting for you to serve them with your pretty smile and sparkly eyes,' Sindy joked. She liked to make her Nan laugh, it was easy and her face lit up when she smiled. Soon, with Sindy's quiet determination and gentle care, Betty was up, washed and dressed and in her wheelchair ready for the morning jaunt along the front which they all, including Diesel the ancient black greyhound, enjoyed very much.

'This blinking thing's got a mind of its own' Sindy laughed as they paraded down the gardens, towards the lively sea, perhaps a little too fast, with Diesel, happily loping off in front.

'Are you working today love?' Betty asked, wondering if perhaps she had more exciting plans. She was such a sweet girl. Betty wished Sindy had some friends and a bit more fun in her life.

'Yeah, just ten until four, I'll be home in time for tea. What shall we make tonight?'

As they were discussing the best use of some left-over roast lamb; Betty was all for shepherds' pie but Sindy wanted to try something different, like a curry; they saw a few people jumping about in the waves.

'That looks fun,' they both said at the same time and laughed.

'I reckon I could make it down there one day for a dip' Betty suggested. She wasn't wheelchair bound, but couldn't get around for very far without it. Her legs just weren't up to it anymore.

'Nan, that's a brilliant idea. Let's wait until the sea is calm and we'll try it together, shall we? How about tomorrow? Perhaps even silly chops here will come in and have a splash about.' Diesel looked doubtful.

After passing the swimmers and the pier, they turned up towards the busy little town of Seabourne. Betty had lived here for most of her adult life and she had seen quite a few changes. Turners, the hardware shop that she had owned and run with Ted, her late husband, still looked depressingly the same with its grey and black paintwork. Prison colours for her. For some reason, the ugly face Ted used to pull while he'd scolded her for mistakes he'd generally made, pushed its way into her thoughts and reminded her of the odd slap or pinch he'd so often felt it necessary to dish out. *Christ, he'd been a nasty piece of work. Why did I put up with it for so long?*

'You're not thinking about that old bastard again, are you Nan?' Sindy's voice broke into her thoughts.

'Sorry honey, yes I was, actually.'

'Well, I wish I knew the name of the bus driver that managed to run him over in London, because I would give him a gold medal. It's a pity he didn't take out the fancy piece he was with at the same time.' Sindy replied.

'She'll be better off without him. It's all a long time ago now Sindy love, and you're right, I have a lot to be thankful for now that he's gone.'

They both burst out laughing at this and decided to pop into Tesco's, as they were giving out double green shield stamps that morning. They parted company then, Sindy to work at the hardware shop which her mum and dad ran now, and Betty went the short distance home, pushing her chair, closely followed by Diesel.

'Hi Dad, can I come in about an hour later tomorrow please?' Sindy asked, as she started opening up Turners Hardware, putting extra baskets of beach toys to the front of the shop, as the holidays had begun. 'I'll work an hour later in the evening and Fridays are always busier towards the end of the day.'

Sindy's dad frowned. 'That means me and your mum will have to open up, it would have been nice to have a lay in.'

'Oh, please dad, there's something me and nan really want to do, and I do open up every morning.'

'Well, if her Ladyship needs you, that's got to be your main priority,' he replied, without any humour reaching his face.

'She's 82 Dad.' Sindy was rapidly getting irritated. Her dad knew what a bully and a scoundrel his own father had been and how he'd made Betty's life so joyless, but Pat Turner could never face the reality of it and accept just how hard it must have been for his mother. Nowadays he just tried to change the subject, if it ever came up, and pretend Betty had imagined or exaggerated most of it. Sindy adored Betty and chose to live with her grandmother, as she simply couldn't bear the way things were swept under the carpet at home. Eventually Pat agreed (to his credit), as even he realised how much Sindy helped everybody out and how little she asked for in return. Now that he had said yes, Sindy was praying that the wind would drop, and that tomorrow would be a good day for Betty's swim.

As luck would have it, the sea was sparkling, clear and calm the following morning. *Brilliant,* Sindy thought as she got everything ready for Betty. A big fluffy towel, a changing robe that she had found in the Oxfam shop and swimming shoes so that her nan's feet wouldn't hurt on the stones. Betty was really excited and on the way to the front, they chatted about the long-gone seaside days of her youth, including knitted swimming costumes, which Sindy really couldn't understand, and trays of tea for the beach (which the little café by the pier did still occasionally sell). Diesel was enjoying the heat of the sunshine on his old bones. He was quite happy with this hot weather.

They were making progress towards the front when Sindy noticed two young men, larking about in the waves. She immediately recognised Paul Harrington, the snooty boy from school, who was also the main subject of too many sketches in her rough book. He was always so aloof and the more he ignored her, the more she wanted him, although she hadn't realised the extent of her crush until now, looking at him literally glittering in the sunshine and the waves.

CLARA

Almost as soon as Jack and Paul had skipped off down through the gardens, Clara regretted her decision. The essence of their youth and optimism was still hanging in the air in her sunny morning room, along with dancing motes of dust. She pictured Peter's querying face, wondering why on earth she hadn't taken up their offer and enjoyed some company. *When did I become so unhappy and cross with the world?* She wondered. The day that pitiless telegram had arrived thirty-one years ago. She was clinging on to that piece of paper, but perhaps as they said these days, 'she needed to let go'. *Rubbish*. She had never 'let go' of anything in her life! Even so, something was nagging in her mind. Perhaps it was time to change, just a little. After some hours of unaccustomed indecision, Clara made up her mind to accompany the boys when they arrived tomorrow morning.

She and her partner, Victor, won easily at bridge that afternoon which was genial and uneventful; he was not the best player however, and

her mind drifted to Peter, who had been brilliant; so clever and measured. As she walked home from the town, she planned tomorrow's outfit in her mind, right down to her shoes and matching handbag. That evening as she watched Angela Rippon reading the news, she considered how much the world was changing. Was she in favour of this new young lady newsreader? She had liked Richard Baker, always correctly turned out and well spoken. Thinking more on this subject, Clara realised that part of her wanted women these days to be able to achieve so much more than she had done, but another part of her was resentful that these opportunities had not been there when she was young.

All in all, she'd had quite a thought-provoking day. As the evening cooled slightly, Clara went to bed unusually tired, but with a glimmer of anticipation for tomorrow's outing.

The following morning Clara was up before the sun. She had laid everything out carefully in her dressing room and spent extra care on her *toilette*. Clara rarely wore any shade of pink these days, it had been Peter's favourite colour for her and it now felt both frivolous and pointless. However, there was a dusky pink, Japanese silk dress in her wardrobe. She had bought it when travelling with Peter and he had insisted on the matching shoes and handbag. She recalled only wearing it once. Both the fabric and style were just right for this incredibly hot weather and it felt luxurious on her skin. She dressed with care, had an early cup of tea and waited, whilst reading The Times, in her morning room.

Mrs Jackson knocked, and Clara rose to meet her nephews, although she hadn't heard the bell. False alarm. Mrs Jackson was just offering her a second cup. Never mind. She settled herself again on the window seat and waited and watched for the boys.

Birds began singing, gulls crying and the ordinary sounds of the morning came and went. Clara read the newspaper from cover to cover and then completed the crossword. The ticking of the clock seemed to be inordinately loud now, but it was only when it chimed ten thirty that she looked up, thinking it must have gone wrong again. She would have to ask Green, the gardener, if he could take a look. Then she checked her wristwatch and realised that she had, indeed, been sitting there for over three hours.

She got up slowly, as her back and legs were rather stiff now, left the room with as much dignity as she could muster under the circumstances, and made her way back to her bedroom.

Once she had closed the door, she cursed herself for behaving foolishly, took off the beautiful dress and put it carefully back on its matching silk hanger. She had let her guard down, just once, in thirty years and humiliation was the result. Mrs Jackson was probably in the grocers laughing at the ridiculous sight Lady Clara Harrington had made, waiting at the window.

Damn them all, this would not happen again and confirmed her belief that she was just a lonely old spinster whom no-one cared about. She had been a fool to think otherwise. Jack should apologise for his lack of courtesy. If Peter had been here…. But he wasn't.

DOT BAKER

Dot recognised the young girl and the old lady in the wheelchair, just ahead of her on the promenade and she quickly realised they were all heading to the sea with the same intention, as they were carrying an enormous bag of beach stuff. Their faces were familiar although they hadn't really said hello before. The black greyhound that was with them noticed her and bounded up to make her acquaintance.

Dot laughed and gave him a pat. 'He's a friendly dog, what's his name?'

'Morning, dear, he's Diesel, I'm Betty and this beauty is my granddaughter, Sindy.'

'It's nice to meet you. I'm Dot Baker, I think I've seen you around quite a bit. We moved here about a year ago, but you don't see so many people through the winter, do you?' They chatted for a few minutes and then Dot saw Benny with a beautiful young woman, having a glorious time in the enormous mill pond that, today, was the sea. It was one of the things that Dot loved. It could change in half an hour and she could never tell what sort of sea it would be from one day to the next.

Dot was so pleased to see the new, happy faces, it lifted her mood from the turmoil of yesterday. They walked down to the tranquillity of the water's edge, which was so incredibly still it felt quite spiritual. Benny and Dot shared the introductions. Isabella chatted about her job at the school. She was a dancing and singing instructor and took classes each afternoon for the little ones. Dot was impressed but felt a bit guilty, as she didn't have a job, having spent the last thirty years caring for her family and keeping house. It didn't sound very impressive when she said it out loud. However, no-one seemed to be judging her here.

Betty was clearly very proud of her grand-daughter, and rightly so, Dot would have been too. Sindy was taking so much care with Betty. As they approached the sea, Dot quietly offered Sindy a hand which she gratefully accepted. Their care was more than repaid by the grin on Betty's face; she was having a ball in the water. She told Dot that she hadn't been properly in the sea for years but the gentle action of swimming came back to her as if it was yesterday. The water felt so soothing, making her feel weightless and wonderful.

'Look at me, look at me,' she shouted out to any passers-by. 'Do you know, I'm eighty-two?' She called to a rather dull looking middle-aged couple. They seemed fairly impressed. The simple happiness of the old lady, wasn't lost on Dot, she was an example to be followed. After a while the 'sea-powered' Betty realised that it was time for dry land and once dressed and back in her chair, she thanked Benny, Isabella and Dot for their company. She said she'd enjoyed every minute of it, and she would be back down on the next calm day. As Betty, Sindy and Diesel left for home, Dot noticed they were all beaming with happiness. Dot, Benny and Isabella lingered a bit longer, enjoying the feeling of the warm sun and the salt drying crisply on their skin.

'It's been really lovely meeting and chatting with you, Isabella. Will you come down again?' Dot was hoping that she would, as they all seemed to get on rather well. They'd talked about the latest films, Benny and Isabella said they both wanted to see the new one, Taxi Driver, with Robert De Niro. It sounded a bit violent for her and Rob. Dot said she was more of a theatre person and was wondering whether to try and persuade Rob to go up to London to see the new musical, 'Jesus Christ Superstar'. Some of her old London friends had been;

apparently it was a bit different, but really impressive. She'd chat it over with Rob, perhaps it could be a birthday treat? She was fast approaching her fiftieth.

While she was walking back home, thinking how agreeable the morning had been, the attractive young men who'd been in the sea further down, wandered along, looking fairly dishevelled, and she couldn't help overhearing their conversation:

'That was such a laugh last night, we must go out together more often Jack, some of your mates are really fun for their age.'

'Sure kiddo, and thank you for the compliment! Paul, how much is your head aching today, because mine is splitting?'

'That's because you're way too old to be doing this sort of thing mate,' replied the younger one, who didn't appear to be in too much discomfort at all. Dot smiled. *Oh, to be young,* and although perhaps that carefree and abandoned lifestyle was in her past, she didn't miss the hangovers.

MRS JACKSON

Ruth Jackson had worked for Lady Clara Harrington for nearly forty years. She had witnessed the tragic transformation of an incredibly talented and kind young woman into a devastated shell, and then further on, through the years, to a bitter old lady. She had never thought them to be friends but would have done anything for the high-handed old dragon that Clara had become. Ruth had been down on her luck when Clara had offered her a position and a home and she would always be grateful for that kindness.

Yesterday morning she had watched out for the boys with equal, if not greater, anticipation. She realised exactly what it had cost Clara to accept their casual invitation but was pleased to see the spring in her employers' step. It wasn't long after 8 o'clock when Ruth realised that they had probably forgotten, but she also knew that to speak her mind wouldn't help Clara, and would simply make the humiliation worse.

Ruth was going to put this as right as she could manage. She'd watched both Jack and Paul grow up into fine young men, but this slip was going to cost the Harrington family dear. If something wasn't done quickly, Clara would never forgive them. Ruth had a note of Jack's address in her diary and decided to pay him a visit.

Walking smartly along the front, she spotted the two of them larking about on the sand, clearly having had a swim, chatting and laughing, and she thought about the contrast with how Clara would be feeling. As soon as Jack saw her, Ruth could see in his face the realisation hitting him. The invitation yesterday. They had both completely forgotten. He looked devastated and she knew Jack wouldn't have intentionally upset Clara for the world.

'I'm so sorry,' Jack started, he knew what it must have felt like for his aunt. Paul agreed and added his apologies. 'What on earth are we going to do Mrs Jackson?'

The three of them sat down on a bench and tried to work out the best way of apologising and making things right. In their own ways they were all very fond of the prickly old lady.

Eventually they decided that Jack should write a letter. Mrs Jackson thought Clara would hopefully, read it, mull it over, cool down a bit, and then the boys should come over with a generous bunch of sweet peas, which were Clara's favourite, and perhaps a box of chocolate rose creams certainly wouldn't hurt. The rest was up to them.

BENNY

That evening, while the apology plan was progressing the other side of town, Benny was experimenting with a dark and rich chocolate cake. He'd used some evaporated milk and lots of cocoa in the recipe. It had risen nicely and now that it was covered with milk chocolate icing, it really did look tasty, and smelled even better. He decided to take it down to the beach tomorrow.

It was Saturday morning and Isabella asked Benny if she might bring her daughter, Lizzie, down for a swim. Benny had met her lots of times and thought this would work well; they got on like a house on fire. On the way to the sea, Benny chatted with the little girl, 'If you're brave enough to have a dip in the water, you might get the biggest slice of cake afterwards.'

They found Dot and Sindy already in, diving through the waves which had risen with the sun. The sea was a bit too rough for Betty today and so she enjoyed watching from the promenade bench, noticing, for the first time, the intricate mermaid shaped cast ironwork on each side of the seat.

The two youngish men were again in the sea, a little nearer today, and Benny noticed that Sindy had scarcely taken her eyes off one of them, and he felt for her, as he was also transfixed by the beauty of the older of the two.

'Benny, BENNY!' He suddenly realised Lizzie was shouting his name. He rushed over to see what the matter was, to find her pointing further out to sea.

'What's that in the water, leaping in and out, Benny?' she squealed with excitement, as she had probably already realised what they were.

A pod of dolphins leapt past, not too far from the shore. Dolphins were not unusual on this part of the coast, but their magical aura, as they dived through the waves, entranced onlookers each time they visited. Benny was thrilled that Lizzie had seen them for the first time, and told her this was a sign that today was going to be special. People on the beach were moving to the best vantage point. The young men swam up towards Benny and Lizzie, also enjoying the free marine show. Benny felt it would have been rude not to say hello and so, although the cat seemed to have unusually got his tongue, he tried to make some polite conversation.

'What an amazing sight, we are so lucky to have seen them this morning.' *Heavens, what am I saying? Pull yourself together and make a proper introduction.* 'I think I've seen you down here a few times, are you chaps local?' *This is just sounding like a cheap chat up line. Help!* Benny was uncharacteristically panicking. Thankfully, Dot, who had put two and two together pretty quickly, came to Benny's rescue.

'Hi, guys, weren't they marvellous? I see you're both enjoying the waves, would you like to join us this morning?'

Paul looked a little cross and embarrassed, but Jack thanked her and said that was kind, they would love to. Benny finally found his courage and introduced everyone in his elegant, if rather old fashioned, style.

'I'm Jack. Jack Harrington, and this is my brother, Paul. It's great to meet you all. Yes, we are local, lived here all our lives.' The group talked about the extremely hot weather and how fortunate they had been, to see the dolphins so close. Jack mentioned it was his birthday tomorrow and thought perhaps it was an early birthday treat. Paul was very quiet and Benny noticed Sindy marching out of the water, changing and arming herself with a large hat and sunglasses. Even from yards away, Benny could see the problem, which was as clear as day. The two youngsters obviously held a candle for each other, but at the moment, it looked very much like the complete opposite. Benny smiled and realised that even young conventional love was complicated, so how was he, in his forties now, ever going to find someone? His thoughts were interrupted by Lizzie demanding chocolate cake now that she had been in the water.

While the dippers were getting changed, Benny cut up his cake. He saw that Dot had brought a big flask of coffee and Isabella had tea, so there was plenty for all. They gathered around Betty who was sitting on the bench, watching the group with considerable interest. While the sun was rising and rapidly gaining power, everyone said that today would not be a one off, and that they would meet, whenever they could, at this spot and take advantage of this remarkably good weather. Benny was pleased to see everyone enjoying the cake; conversation had given way to eating until, relaxing on a sandy spot on the beach, a generous piece of the delicious cake in his hand, Jack joked: 'so, who is the maker of this, and when can we get married?' Thinking he was addressing Dot or Isabella or perhaps Sindy.

Benny coughed, choked on his tea, laughed, felt delighted, and wanted to die with embarrassment, all at once. Isabella helped out, realising a little later than Dot, that Benny was attracted to Jack.

'Benny is wasted in an office. He should be running his own bakery, his cakes are amazing, it's such a pleasure living next door to him, the aromas coming from his kitchen are incredible.' Isabella knew she should stop talking, but couldn't seem to. 'They are all his own recipes.' Benny could feel himself blushing but could do nothing to stop it. Betty, sitting quietly but not missing a trick, hadn't lived all these years not to spot a good thing developing when she saw it, interrupted. 'Jack, why don't you ask Benny if he'll make you a cake, as it's your birthday tomorrow? I'll bet you wouldn't find another one as light within fifty miles of here.'

This time, it was Paul who answered with: 'yes Jack, I reckon that would be a grand idea. His favourite is coffee and walnut. I'll pay for it and it can be your birthday present, as I had completely forgotten, sorry mate.' Everyone, except Sindy, laughed, and Paul agreed to pop by tomorrow morning and collect it. Benny noticed Betty grinning and looking pleased with herself. He, also couldn't help smiling.

CLARA

Clara had resumed her morning walks and today she was wearing a tailored lilac suit with matching lightweight hat. She was just on her way down the steps when she saw Jack and Paul, turning the corner and making their way towards her. She wished she had still been at home and then Mrs Jackson could have sent them away but there was no turning back now.

She had read Jack's letter of apology. It was heartfelt and touching. However, she really couldn't let herself appear so vulnerable again. *What am I thinking?* As she watched them leap the steps two at a time (exactly like Peter used to do) she realised that they were just a couple of youngsters who had drunk too much one evening and forgotten a casually made arrangement. As she was still deciding on how to play this, Jack ran up the last couple of steps and produced an impossibly big bunch of sweet peas from behind his back, their sugary fragrance enveloping her completely.

'Aunt Clara, we are both so very sorry. I know this was incredibly thoughtless of us, but as it's my birthday today, please forgive us just this once and give me a birthday kiss.'

And Paul cheekily interrupted with 'because no-one else is going to.'

Even after everything that had gone on, Jack was rather difficult to say no to, and to her complete surprise, the words 'Happy Birthday' came springing from her usually downturned mouth. Jack took one more step towards her and gently put his arms around her tiny shoulders, whispering that he wouldn't let her down again. Paul shyly produced the chocolate rose creams that she liked and she realised she had lost the battle with her own moral high ground. These two precious boys were her only family, now that her brother-in-law was so unwell, and she would be cutting off her nose if she didn't hang on to them both.

Jack, the crafty lad, took advantage of her wavering; he sent Paul up to the house with the flowers and chocolates and then turned on his heels and guided her down the steps, towards the glittering sea. Unbeknown to Clara, Mrs Jackson was watching from a front window and although she couldn't hear what they were saying, she could see the outcome was favourable. The boys had done well. *Thank goodness.*

On the way down Jack was explaining that he had met a group of local people who all enjoyed swimming in the sea and said he really wanted her to meet them. Clara wasn't wholeheartedly convinced; however, she conceded that Jack was on a winning streak and so went along with him. After a while, Paul went off to pick up a birthday cake and very soon after that, they almost bumped right into Mrs Turner from the hardware shop (in a wheelchair now Clara noted) with a young girl, who must have been about the same age as Paul.

'Hello Betty, Sindy, I'd like you to meet Lady Clara Harrington, my aunt.' Jack was pleased to see them again.

'Good morning, Mrs Turner, I haven't seen you in a very long time, I trust you are well,' Clara said, thinking that Betty Turner must be getting on a bit now and was clearly a lot less mobile than her. Also, she seemed to recall something seedy about her husband. *Poor woman.*

'Hello Lady Harrington, yes, not too bad considering. Sindy here, is my granddaughter, she lives with me now and looks after me. Heaven knows what I'd do without her, she's an angel.' Betty said with a grateful smile towards Sindy.

'Yes, these youngsters today are so kind and thoughtful.' Clara replied and looked over at Jack with a wry smile, who at least had the decency to look embarrassed.

'I think it's probably about time that you called me Clara, as we've known each other for most of our lives,' Clara joked. She and Betty shook hands, introducing themselves once more. They all chatted and walked on, deciding that just to the left of the pier was the safest place for Betty to have a dip today. Clara was steadfast in her decision to remain on the seafront bench.

BENNY

It wasn't many minutes before they were joined at the bench by Benny and Paul, carrying a spectacular looking birthday cake. Benny approached Clara in his usual style:

'Good morning, Madam. May I introduce myself? Benjamin Solomons, at your service and, if it's not too forward, may I compliment you on the loveliest shade of lilac I have seen in forever?' Benny saw Clara smile at his flattery and was secretly pleased that she seemed to like him.

This time, it was Jack who appeared to be tongue tied and so Clara introduced herself, extending her gloved hand, 'Clara Harrington, and I believe you have already met Jack, my nephew.'

'Delighted,' Benny beamed and shook hands with both of them and he noticed that Jack took a second longer than necessary with his hand.

'Hello again Jack and Happy Birthday!' Benny suddenly felt a little foolish and looked round for someone to save him again. *I am generally confident with conversation. Why, when this man is around, do I go to pieces?*

Benny was pleased to see that Dot and Isabella had now arrived at the beach, exclaiming what an amazing cake Paul was holding. He was more than grateful to be able to chat about the ingredients and his recipe.

Benny finished off the introductions and they all got ready for their dip. Benny left his big baggy 10cc T shirt on, saying that he didn't want to get sunburn. There were a few gentle waves today but Benny was pleased to see that Betty was going in for a second time. He held her hand, Sindy took the other and they were just walking into the water when Benny noticed Jack, with one of those new polaroid cameras, taking photos of them. Up until that moment, Benny thought that maybe, just maybe, Jack might be interested in getting to know him a little better, but once he had seen just how fat and whale-like Benny actually was, he'd change his mind for sure. *There was a photo coming out of the device, Oh no!*

However, he forgot about his problems immediately, on hearing Betty's laughter and enjoyment in the water, listening to her and Sindy guffawing at the thought of someone called Ted, who would be turning in his grave, because of Betty's abandoned joy and childlike pleasure. *He didn't sound very kind,* Benny thought as he got out of the sea and quickly dressed. Everyone seemed to be getting on so well, and he thought that this was starting to feel like something special, although he couldn't exactly put it into words.

Clara was chatting with Isabella. 'What a striking young lady you are, would I be right in guessing that your father is the very stylish gentleman, I see in the town sometimes?'

'You can't miss him, he's a six-foot three West Indian and wears the most outrageous colours for a man,' Isabella said, laughing. Everyone smiled at this and Benny suggested it might be time for Jack to cut the cake.

The slightly embarrassing, but essential, ritual of 'Happy Birthday' was sung by one and all and as they tucked into his coffee and walnut confection, Benny heard Jack talking about his photos: 'I'm going to call this collection Sunshine and Frivolity,' he was saying to Dot. The others were looking at the photos and commenting on how he had made them all look like film stars. Benny doubted this would be the case with him, until Jack walked up, lightly touched his shoulder, and showed him the whole collection. Benny was speechless. Jack had captured the sun and the sea brilliantly, using the backdrop of the old theatre. He'd also taken close ups of people's faces, and they were really professional. But what Benny was most amazed by was how alluring he seemed to be in the pictures, he didn't notice his fat stomach, just how his eyes shone and that his long hair looked rather good, wet and casually swept back. Jack had used unusual angles, taken snaps of Benny emerging from the water, shaking droplets from his face, it was incredible. He realised in an instant, that what he couldn't put into words about the group, the photos had captured. Friendship.

People were drifting off now, all commenting on the amazing cake. Jack was thanking Paul and Benny for it and saying he should go professional when Clara interrupted: 'Well, young man, I would happily pay you to bake a cake for me each week. My housekeeper's baking leaves much to be desired.'

'Thank you, Lady Harrington, I'd be thrilled to do that for you,' Benny managed to say, whilst carefully avoiding contact with Jack's delightful, sea-green eyes.

SINDY

Another blisteringly hot day in the making. The peace of the seaside mist was quickly replaced by blazing sunshine and the buzz of people seeking fun, refreshment and above all, the cooling bliss of the sea. Sindy popped down for a quick dip before what was going to be a very hot day at work. Turners were selling more buckets and spades than they had ever done. Deck chairs ran out quickly, and knotted handkerchiefs were in abundance. For the holiday makers at least, there was a luxurious feeling that this weather was going to last forever; an endless summer.

Sindy liked all the swimming group, but she particularly admired Clara, Paul's aunt, who came occasionally to watch and always with Jack or Paul, who both came along nearly every day now. She realised that little by little, she and Paul had been chatting quite a bit lately. When they were at school, they had been too attracted to each other to utter a word, and she had interpreted this as him not liking her. The swimming group and the summer holidays however, had changed that. Conversations seemed easier when you had a shared interest.

One morning, during a particularly fun swim, when the waves had been too much for Betty to go in, Sindy and Paul had a race to the pier. They both swam well but Paul won easily and plucked up the courage to ask her out: 'Hey, they're showing *Rocky* at the pictures in town, do you fancy coming along tonight?

'Yeah, ok, why not?' She tried to sound casual but was secretly about to explode with excitement. *What am I going to wear?* She was happy wearing her bikini every day with Paul, because that was for swimming, but what on earth would she wear for a date? Perhaps she could find something in the Oxfam shop or Nan's attic. A date! She couldn't wait to tell Betty. 'Race you back to the others.'

Sindy's long day at work went by in a flash. They had arranged to meet at seven, at The ABC in town.

The evening was a success. Isabella had lent Sindy her new purple, Oxford-bags, the checked trousers which were really in fashion at the moment. Sindy had been reading about which pop stars wore them in her Jackie magazine and there was a poster of Marie Osmond wearing a pair. Sindy could never have afforded them and was really grateful. She had teamed these up with a plain t shirt and a silk scarf that Betty had given her. With a bit of purple eye shadow, from Woollies, Betty had said she looked fabulous. Paul was clearly taken aback by how amazing she looked, all done up. They had both enjoyed the dark and secret closeness that they shared in the cinema. Sindy didn't care for the film much but holding Paul's hand was something else. Feeling his arm around her later during the film made her tingle. They had both been a bit embarrassed the following morning at swimming with Betty winking at them and everyone else giving them 'knowing' smiles.

Sindy decided to be bold and show the rest that there was nothing for them all to be grinning about, 'Hey Paul, do you fancy a coffee later at Morellis?'

'Sure, what time works for you?' Paul tried to sound more casual than he felt. They decided one o'clock which was Sindy's lunch hour, would be the best.

It was such a busy morning at work, Sindy could see that asking for a lunch hour was going to be tricky, but she really wanted to go, 'Dad, would it be okay if I popped out for a bit at lunchtime today?'

'Are you joking? Have you seen the stocktaking I've got to do later? No Sindy. I need you to work right through to six today.'

Pat replied, without even looking up from his ledger.

Sindy was not surprised and knew it would be pointless arguing, and she certainly wasn't going to tell him the reason. One o'clock came and she pictured Paul sitting with his frothy coffee, looking for her down the high street. *Damn.* She really liked him and this was going to spoil everything. They were barely even boyfriend/girlfriend and this was the end of her first real relationship. She was, unusually, close to tears with frustration, whilst serving the many suntanned customers, when the shop doorbell went once again at one-thirty.

It was him, with a mug of coffee and a cheese roll in his hands. He grinned. She laughed and gestured that her dad was out the back. He plonked them on the glass cabinet, between the windbreaks, chairs and picnic sets. They spoke quietly and she explained the situation. Rather than being sulky, he just said they should do it another day and that he'd brought her a 'take away' lunch, saying he hoped he'd see her tomorrow.

BETTY

Betty was pleased to see that Clara had come along this morning, obviously interested to hear the young gossip, particularly as her nephew was involved, but equally keen not to appear at all concerned with such matters. Betty settled next to her on the bench. They had been enjoying many conversations recently, finding much to chat about and commented on the young love that was obviously blooming.

Betty explained that Sindy was such a thoughtful and kind girl, but she wished she had more friends to go out and about with; 'she just sits in the front room with me most nights, drawing and doodling, which is company for me, but it's not right for a young girl. She doesn't really get on with her mum and dad. Mind you, Pat's only a bit better than Ted used to be and his wife seems more interested in her knitting machine than her daughter. How about those two nephews of yours, what are they up to?'

'Jack is an architect and he seems to enjoy his job, he's very professional with his camera, as you probably saw the other day. Never seems to go steady with anyone, that I hear of anyway, and Paul is very quiet. I find it quite charming that Paul and Sindy seem to be getting on well.' Betty thought it might be a bit more than 'getting on well' but kept her own counsel on that for the meantime.

'So, Betty, what is that very handsome brother of yours doing these days? Peter, I remember, thought he was going to be quite a rival for my affections at one time. Didn't he join the RAF years before the war?'

'Yes, Charlie joined up in 1930. We didn't see very much of him after that. Always abroad, flying here and there. He wrote long letters though, so we did have some contact. Then the letters stopped. It was such an awful time. He was posted missing in action in 1942.'

'I'm so sorry. How very thoughtless of me,' Clara replied. Betty reached for Clara's hand and explained that although she had made lots of enquiries about Charles at the time, nothing had been discovered. Eventually, they had said goodbye to him properly and a memorial service had been conducted, in Scotland where he was last based. Over the years, she continued to try and find out more, but seemed to be blocked at every turn. Time moved on. She had met and married Ted, and changed, almost overnight, from being a carefree Betty Lancaster, to a downtrodden Betty Turner. It was obvious that Clara felt for Betty and she talked about losing her husband, Peter, and went on to say that even now, she hadn't really got over it.

Their conversation ended on a happier note however, both of them recalling how striking Charles was, particularly when out riding his beloved bay mare, Poppy. Clara remembered seeing him galloping along the beach, jumping breakwaters and looking very dashing whilst doing it. This was all before he joined up, and both women remarked on what a catch he would have been, had he lived.

DOT

The Seabourne Dippers, as Dot had nicknamed them, were becoming quite an established swimming group. As the days went on, new swimmers came along now and again, sometimes there were nearly fifteen of them, all ages, and all sizes. Dot was thrilled to have inadvertently started such a positive thing, particularly at a time when fuses were short, with the relentless heat, combined with a serious water shortage. There were water-saving signs everywhere, often the supply was turned off with everyone fetching bucketful's, from a standpipe in the street, which sometimes ended up with tempers running very hot. The relentless summer didn't really feel fun now, just an ordeal to get through day after day. The carefree youngsters, had all taken to wearing 'Save Water-Bath with a Friend' badges. Sea swimming and making new friends, were more important now than ever.

One Sunday morning, Rob decided he'd like to come down with her. Dot was delighted. She'd obviously told Rob all about the growing group, but left it up to him to decide if he wanted to join in. She knew him well enough to know if she pushed something, he'd not be interested so she just waited, and was rewarded by his company.

As it happened, on that day, Isabella brought her dad, Samuel, along as little Lizzie was desperate for her grandpa to meet her new 'grown up' friends. Rob had never really met Samuel although he'd noticed him around. Once Dot had introduced them, they realised that they'd both moved down from the same area in London at around the same time, but for very different reasons. Samuel, because Brixton had begun to feel angry: he had many friends of all nationalities there, but he didn't share or really understand the new tensions that were brewing. However, he could see the way things were heading and decided to take his precious family away from this environment.

Once they started chatting after the swim, Rob and Samuel found out they had a lot more in common. Samuel was a skilled carpenter and could do just about anything with a piece of wood. Rob, being a builder, was glad to meet someone who knew the value of timber and, once they'd sat down on the pebbles, they were clearly in for a long conversation. Dot could see the benefits of this new friendship and smiled. Samuel, it turned out, had recently been made redundant from a building firm; so many companies were feeling the pinch these days with the economy being what it was, with strikes and walk outs. There was doom and gloom in the papers every day now, Dot had given up reading them. By the end of their chat, they were shaking hands, looking like best mates and Rob had offered Samuel a job with him. He could really use a skilled chippie right now as he was working on quite a big contract, this chance meeting had worked well for both of them.

Lizzie wanted some 'grandpa time' and so the two men took her back in the water for more swimming. She often came down at the weekends and was getting really proficient. Watching him with the little girl, Dot couldn't help thinking how much Rob would like a grandchild, although he never said anything. Neither of them did. Isabella wandered over and the two women sat on the shoreline, with their toes just in the gentle waves, and chatted about the benefits of their swimming group. It really felt like a special community. Sunday was generally the best cake day and Benny had not disappointed today. He'd made a luscious lemon cake, it was wholemeal which was new, but it was really moist and tangy. It got the thumbs up from everyone.

BENNY

Benny was just popping some shortbread, flavoured with the aromatic lavender that was so prolific outside his flat, into a Tupperware box, when the phone rang. It was still pretty early and he felt a chill go through his bones, an early or late phone call was rarely good news. As Benny lifted the receiver to his ear, he could hear the painful sound of his mother attempting to hold back her tears on the other end and his heart sank.

'Benny' she whispered. She could barely speak but Benny realised immediately that the end of a generation had come for them both.

Esther Freshwater, Benny's Grandmother, had been as fit as a fiddle and had simply not woken up that morning. This was going to be a huge hole in their small family and Benny tried to console his mother, but felt very inadequate. Grandmother had always been there, whether it had been cooking up a huge bowl of Jewish penicillin (whole chicken soup) or making challah. She had encouraged his love of baking and she had been so pleased for Benny when he'd got his job at the Planning Department but he felt he had let her down on the marriage and children front. He was going to miss her so very much. For a couple of days, he simply couldn't bring himself to swim or do anything, and it wasn't long before Isabella knocked gently on his door to see if he was okay.

Benny, who, up until that moment, had been stoic, keeping all his emotion in check, now broke down with Isabella's kindness and, after talking for some time about his grandmother and his young life at home, moved on to his non-existent romantic life and just how much he longed to build up the courage to be honest with Jack about his feelings towards him.

'Why don't you just ask him to go to the pictures or something casual, like we did last month? If it's not for him, at least you'll know, and you will never know, if you don't ask.'

Benny wasn't sure that he could summon the courage, as they had become friends over the recent weeks and a rejection would blow everything sky high.

'You can do this Benjamin Solomons, you're stronger than you think. Not to mention you look amazing, the swimming is really beginning to show. Also, who wouldn't want to wake up to the smell of your delectable baking every morning?'

'Thank you, Isabella, you say such kind things.' Benny was pleased, he thought no-one had noticed that he'd lost a few pounds. It was the swimming. Yes, he might just be able to do this. He was touched that Isabella accepted him as he was, she was the first friend who had really done that. Perhaps he'd ask Jack next week, after the funeral, when his emotions had calmed down a bit.

Benny had taken on all the arrangements as Matilda, his usually steadfast mother was struggling. He was pleased to do it and had poured all his emotions into making a feast-like spread for afterwards. As he walked out of his flat, wondering why he'd made so many cakes and things, he realised there would not be many people coming back to his home and felt a bit foolish. His mother and grandmother had been non-observant Jews and had led a very quiet life with only a few close friends. So, when he arrived at the cemetery and saw all the dippers there to support him, he was overcome.

Everyone was there, including Jack, who simply walked up to Benny, squeezed his hand and said quietly, 'you know Benny, I've been imagining our first date since the day we met on the beach, and it was going to be very different to this, but never mind, at least I know there will be lots of cake.'

Benny stifled the inappropriate laugh that was bubbling up in his throat, and his teary eyes just smiled with grateful thanks.

DOT

All the lawns had become dusty cracking concrete, gardens were brown with dead or non- existent plants. Even Clara's sharply manicured estate was suffering. The streets of Seabourne smelled of heat, rubbish and dog urine as nothing was being washed away. The town felt like it was about to snap, crackle and burst into flames.

Finally, the dark congregating clouds broke. At first, there were a few heavy, isolated drops out of nowhere, then more and more until it felt like the sky had burst. It was early evening and without any co-ordination, the dippers celebrated the first downpour in a long time, by rushing to the beach and quite literally dancing in the rain and the sea. And they were not alone. People had come from all over, with nightlights, home-made barbeques and lots to drink. In a matter of minutes, the shelter under the pier and thereabouts had turned into one crazy rain party. After months of heat and drought, the instant and almost insane relief of the pouring rain infected one and all.

There were enticing aromas in the air; the earthy smell of rain hitting the sand and the pier, sweet smoke from the barbecues, mixed with hot, sweaty people smoking and drinking. Samuel had brought his treasured 'Yacht-boy' radio down and some local girls had brought a cassette recorder with a dance tape they had made. Soon, people were joining in with "Dancing Queen", "You Should be Dancing" and "Don't go Breaking My Heart", which, when the batteries ran out, Benny, Isabella and Jack performed together. Whilst everyone noticed what a sweet voice Isabella had, Dot, took this thought a bit further. Samuel and Isabella could really sing and dance, and some of the others were pretty talented as well. She had been very involved with amateur dramatics and pantomimes at her children's school, years ago. Dot had sadly accepted that was a happy stage of her life which was behind her now, but seeing this group of clearly talented people, gave her second thoughts.

Clara, who had come along, on Jack's insistence, wasn't sure whether this was her type of thing, but she was grateful when the youngsters gave up their seats for her and Betty. The music was actually rather enjoyable and at one point Dot saw Clara tapping her foot a little bit when she thought no one was watching.

The next day was a stormy morning, black clouds made it look like night time and the rain was sheeting down, stinging the dipper's heads as they swam. Clara sensibly decided to sit this one out at home. Vengeful thunder and lightning began rolling around the skies and Dot suggested they take cover whilst getting dry, under the overhang of the old Mermaid Theatre, which made a great shelter. Everyone agreed, to avoid being struck by the lightening which was heading their way, and together they made the 100-yard dash down to the end of the pier. Jack was busy with his Polaroid as usual, and got some action shots. Water was flooding down the guttering of the theatre, and pouring over the wooden planks of the pier into the sea, looking like out of control waterfalls. He'd name this collection, 'Storm drain.' He left the group first and said goodbye to everyone, as now he had to drive over to Brighton, to spend a couple of days at an architect's convention.

As Dot was drinking her 'Thermos' tea, chatting with Isabella and Sindy, she noticed a poster for a pantomime, just inside a broken window in the foyer of the theatre. Many of the details had faded or been torn away except the date, which was January 1936 and it was *Cinderella*, starring "The Mermaid." Dot briefly wondered who she was, and if she was still alive. The theatre was pretty old, and to her mind, in need of much refurbishment, although it was far from falling down. It was, as they say, a lightbulb moment.

'Does anyone know who this theatre belongs to?' Dot said to no-one in particular. Her mind was suddenly whirring with ideas. There was only Isabella, Benny and Samuel left who'd braved the weather and Samuel replied, 'no idea Dot, but it's a fine structure and might not need too much work to bring it right back to its former glory.'

Benny scratched his head, he should know who it belonged to, perhaps he'd ask at work tomorrow.

'What's going through your mind Dot?' Isabella asked, as she could see the light in her friend's eyes.

'I'm just thinking, how it would feel to restore it; it's such an iconic building, and then who knows? A pantomime perhaps?' Dot had slipped right back into 'Director' mode and was already casting her dipping friends in her mind. *Cinderella* 40 years on. It could be magnificent. She'd have a chat with Rob. It was probably too much to take on, but if you didn't try, you didn't get anywhere.

'You have seriously lost your mind this time love,' Rob exclaimed as she explained her idea to him over tea that evening. Rob was only half listening as *The Sweeney*, Rob's favourite, was on the telly, with Inspector Regan and Sergeant Carter racing about in their trademark Ford Granada. This may, possibly, have been a forewarning.

'No, really honey, you should come along as well and have a look. Samuel says the structure looks pretty sound. Anyway, Benny, Isabella, Samuel, Betty and me are going to the pub tomorrow evening to have a chat about it.'

'Are you going to The Neptune?' Rob's eyes lit up.

'Oh, I see, you're interested now of course,' Dot laughed. 'I need you to come along and cast your professional eye over the place. I was really hoping we might get permission from the owner, when we find out who he is, to tart it up a bit to start with, whilst I write a pantomime for the dippers to perform at Christmas. We have so much personality and talent in our group.'

Rob realised it was pointless to resist Dot's plans Once she got an idea in her head, she was akin to a terrier down a rabbit hole. There would be no stopping her, they'd been married long enough for him to know this.

BENNY

Jack couldn't make dipping the following morning as he was still away in Brighton and so he'd not heard about the seemingly brilliant plan for the theatre. In fact, no-one dipped that day as the weather was atrocious and they were planning to see each other in the evening. It had been an unusually busy day at work for Benny and he had completely forgotten to ask about the theatre's owner. *Never mind, he could do it tomorrow.* There was going to be a full moon that night and Benny had borrowed the Polaroid camera to take some photos for Jack, as he was missing him rather a lot and was looking forward to showing them to him on his return.

It felt cosy and friendly in The Neptune that evening. Everyone seemed to be in the mood for a good time and Benny drank a fair bit more than he was used to. Samuel and Rob both bought a lot of rounds and he felt he needed to keep up with them, but there was only so much beer he could consume so he decided to go on to whiskey, although he didn't even like it very much. Even Dot, Isabella and Betty seemed to be drinking their Bacardi and Cokes fairly quickly. They chatted about Dot's idea for most of the evening and by the end of the night, the plan was invincible.

Once outside the pub, everyone was a little worse for wear, but unfortunately, still at that giddy stage, when they could do anything in the world! They were meandering towards the pier when they bumped into Sindy, walking home from a babysitting job. A stroll down the pier, to finish off the evening, sounded like a brilliant idea. Sindy joined in and pushed Betty, with Benny taking lots of photos as they went. The moon was catching the tiny waves as they broke onto the shore, creating a magical silver effect in the surf; Jack was going to love these. The rain had passed over during the evening and as the full moon rose it became incredibly bright in the sky, occasionally peeping through the dramatic clouds.

When they reached the theatre, Dot and Benny noticed the front door was swinging open, having probably been blown about by all the wind and rain of the day. This was clearly a sign to go in and have a little look around.

No-one actually felt they were doing anything wrong as they only had the best intensions for the place. Unfortunately, the multiple flashes that the camera was producing, attracted the attention of The Mermaid Theatre's owner, who, seeing that there was something untoward going on, telephoned 9 9 9 and spoke to Police Constable Will Johnson.

The Seabourne Six were having a whale of a time. Benny taking more photos, Sindy and Betty just being nosey, Dot, getting more excited with every step and Samuel and Isabella both noting what a springy floor the stage had, which would be brilliant for dancing. Even Rob was quite enjoying looking at the fine structure of the place, the original builder had obviously known what he was about. The only works needed were pretty much decorative, as far as he could see. He had just started to tap a few timbers when all hell broke loose.

PC WILL JOHNSON

PC Johnson had had a long day. He was due to go home at ten-thirty but now he'd have to go down to the pier, see what was occurring and then do all the paperwork before getting off duty. The phone line was rather crackly but the person on the phone had said there were at least five of them, so he'd need backup. *Damn.* He radioed the nearest station and luckily there was a patrol car in the area. He said he'd join them asap.

PC Johnson in his Ford Cortina and his colleagues, who were lucky enough to have a new Granada, came speeding down the pier, sirens blaring and lights flashing, screeching to a stop at the theatre doors. Officers rushed in with their torches and the first criminal they handcuffed was Benny, who was still, merrily, taking photos.

The initial recce and fun came abruptly to an end with all six of them, including Betty, being taken to Seabourne police station. The camera and all the photos were taken as evidence. There were many apologies and explanations and eventually PC Johnson said it would be down to the owner as to whether they wanted to press charges. Dot couldn't even look at Rob since he'd not been particularly happy with the idea from the start. He was making his 'I told you so face,' but with the addition of a smirk that was infuriating. She'd never hear the last of this. Sindy looked as though she might start crying at the thought of what her Mum and Dad would say, and it was Betty who decided to take the initiative.

'Will Johnson, isn't it? I remember you coming into Turners with your naughty friends and stealing some cans of spray paint. Do you recall that I was very lenient? I didn't tell your parents and I don't think too much should be made of this either. Wouldn't you agree young man?'

'I do recall that incident Mrs Turner and I am ashamed of myself. I would have to add, however that was well over twenty years ago.'

Betty felt like she needed to have the last word. 'And take those handcuffs off Benny. The only thing he's guilty of is baking too many fancy cakes.'

Samuel burst out laughing and even PC Johnson cracked a smile. It was at that moment Isabella noticed he was rather dishy. *Hmm, probably the uniform.*

At this point at the stroke of midnight, the owner of The Mermaid Theatre made a rather theatrical entrance.

JACK

Jack hadn't been enjoying the conference much, he had been looking forward to hearing about exciting innovations and new projects, but it seemed the focus of this week was to stick with old ideas and familiar styles. A pity, he loved Brighton, in his mind there was so much potential for a fresh outlook. There were some great buildings here, both modern and very old, with the Pavilion being his favourite. The Lanes, which were a tangle of tiny alleyways, were full of really quirky little boutiques and jewellery shops. It was all so lively and cosmopolitan, and he felt much more accepted here than most places he visited. Whilst looking round the town in his free time, he was pleased to see lots of shops and bars, clearly designed for people like him and Benny. He felt at home here and decided to book a surprise weekend at a smart hotel for them both, perhaps in the autumn. He missed Benny and his room was uncomfortable. He'd rather fancied staying at The Grand, but unfortunately the company budget had not run to that. So, when a message came through to his hotel late that night to say that he must return home immediately, he'd welcomed the opportunity to leave early. He enjoyed driving his Escort Mk 2, it was showroom new, pretty fast and very flashy. A pleasure to drive back from Brighton at top speed, listening to Radio Luxembourg at top volume.

The message had said he should return to Seabourne and go straight to the police station. He wondered what was up, and hoped no-one had been hurt. He parked quickly and rushed into the brightly lit police station, closely followed by the Granada driving police constable and his aunt Clara, still dressed for dinner in a stunning, if rather old fashioned, moss-green velvet, floor length gown.

'Oh, good heavens, it's you lot,' Clara exclaimed as she entered the interview room. 'What in the Devil's name did you think you were up to?'

'What are *you* doing here Lady Harrington? You weren't involved, so you can't possibly be charged by the theatre's owner' exclaimed Dot, wondering why on earth Clara was there at this time of night and how much worse this was all going to get, at the same time, noticing how incredibly well dressed and stylish Clara was, even at this hour of the evening.

CLARA

'No Dot, I am not in trouble, because I am the owner of both The Mermaid Theatre and the Pier and I am seriously wondering what possessed you six to break the law.' Clara looked over at Betty, 'I have to say Betty, I am surprised to see you mixed up in this debacle.'

'I can explain' cut in Dot. 'This is all my fault. I had an idea of refurbishing the theatre and possibly staging a Seabourne Dippers' pantomime, perhaps *Cinderella*, there for Christmas. I just wanted to have a look round to see the condition of the place, I am sorry. I had no idea it belonged to you. We didn't actually break-in, the door was open so we just walked in.'

'Without having permission from the owner? That sounds very much like breaking and entering to me.' Clara had decided to draw this out as long as possible, now that it had such a surprising and slightly amusing conclusion.

Jack had seen the glint in her eye and decided to try to put an end to the torture. She was like a playful feline with several baby mice. 'If we're not careful, Aunt Clara, we will all be charged with wasting police time, and we really don't want that, do we now? PC Johnson, can we put something in your Policeman's Ball Fund tin over there and consider the whole incident forgotten? It's very late after all.'

PC Johnson had had enough today, 'Bugger off, the lot of you. Oh, sorry I didn't mean you, Lady Harrington.'

'No offence taken Officer. Please thank your colleague for the lift to the station. I quite fancy a new, Ford Granada motor-car, it was both very fast and rather comfortable.'

This amused Rob no end. He conjured up an image of Lady Clara Harrington featuring in an episode of his favourite crime show, driving a Granny.

They all left in a hurry, being keen to get out of the building, with Clara chattering about the charms of her old Rover, and Benny unfortunately leaving the camera and photos on the police station counter.

PC WILL JOHNSON

Later that morning, the first person to arrive at Seabourne police station was not a member of the constabulary, but Anna, the cleaner, who was also working part time for the local paper, hoping to get a reporter's job someday. She was always on the lookout for a 'scoop.' Probably due to the lateness of the hour, the previous night, Will Johnson had left the report on the desk and Anna couldn't stop herself reading it. She immediately connected it with some brilliant photos of the miscreants, also left on the side. *Would it be worth it?* She wondered to herself. Even if she got the sack from this job, the Editor of *Seabourne Matters* would absolutely love this piece and she might even secure herself a full-time post there. *What the hell?* She sprayed a bit of polish around, emptied the bins and went home with the gist of what had happened, some brilliant ideas to jazz it up a bit, plus the three best photos.

Will Johnson came in later and got busy with his paperwork. There was a lot to do today after last night, but his mind kept wandering to Isabella Williams' curly hair, her shining eyes, which had looked guilty and amused at the same time. She had such a softness about her. He'd not seen her in Seabourne before and wondered about her situation. Her dad seemed an agreeable man. Surely a woman like that would be happily married, they usually were. Will was not the luckiest man when it came to love. If not for his younger brother, George, he would probably have been celebrating his wedding anniversary this month. They'd been so happy together and then his brother had left the Army, come back to Seabourne, and made off with Carol, his sweetheart and she hadn't put up much of a fight. Will had been devastated, he hadn't seen this, or anything like it, coming in a million years. He'd effectively lost his brother and his girl in a few short weeks. The two of them lived somewhere in France now and good riddance to them. The bell on the counter pinged and brought Will back to the present.

'Hello again Officer,' Jack was bright and breezy. 'I believe my friend left my camera and some photos here last night. Would it be possible to have them back, now that there are no actual charges?'

'Indeed. No problem with that Jack'. Will remembered Jack from school, as being one of Seabourne's decent guys. He gave Jack the camera along with the remainder of the snaps. 'Actually mate, could I ask you a few questions, off the record, as it were?'

Jack stiffened a little bit, wondering what this was going to be about. Always dreading that outright question.

'Isabella Williams, you know her from the swimming group, right? What's her situation? I mean, is she married, or perhaps you two are more than friends? If not, I'd be really keen to ask her out. What do you think?'

Jack relaxed and laughed. 'Sure Will, we're just mates and no, she doesn't seem to have a boyfriend or a husband, just her little daughter, Lizzie. I can ask my friend Benny to give me a bit more info as he knows her much better than me.'

'I'd really appreciate that, she's so pretty. Probably out of my league.'

'From what I do understand, she'd be looking for a guy to do right by her. I'll get back to you then,' and with that Jack left, pleased to have got his precious camera back and interested to see Benny's photos.

DOT

After a morning off, the dippers were back in business. Dot felt she had to go down and apologise once again to anyone who would listen. She'd no idea how Clara had taken all this and which way things were going to go. On the one hand, it was great that Clara owned the theatre, but after what she'd done without telling her, would she ever speak to any of them again?

It was another incredibly hot morning; the previous storms hadn't really cleared the air. Even the holiday makers were complaining, especially about the water shortage. As Dot walked down to the front, she recalled last nights' evening news: Dennis Howell, the new Drought Minister, told everyone to use your washing up water to flush the toilet, which she had actually been doing for some weeks now, and they paid him for that advice! Dot hoped that James Callaghan would do a better job than Harold Wilson. The country seemed to be falling apart.

She caught up with Samuel and Isabella and together they laughed off the previous night's brush with the police. None of them had ever been in trouble before, and now that it was over, Dot couldn't help seeing the funny side of it; even Rob had chuckled about the whole thing when they had returned home that night. Dot considered what Margaret would have said, and how outraged she would have been that her parents had apparently taken leave of their senses, and it made her smile quite a few times throughout the next few days.

'At least Dad was there, and involved in the deed, and I didn't have to explain it all, like I was 15,' Isabella joked.

Betty and Sindy, who had just arrived, were both pleased that her mum and dad would not get to hear about it; they weren't the most understanding of people and there was also a definite lack of a sense of humour in that house.

'I did rather enjoy all the excitement of the police station though, not something I was expecting at my age. Goodness me, how young and handsome the policemen are these days. Aren't they Isabella?' Betty said with a wink. Sindy and Betty then burst out laughing together, as they often did. Remembering the rather attractive PC Johnson, Isabella blushed slightly.

Unfortunately, there was no sign of Clara this morning. Dot had wanted her to show up so that she could apologise again and also see where they stood. They had a lively swim, however, with the waves dancing around with a delightful unpredictability and an incredible view of the full moon disappearing as the brilliant sunshine rose into the bluest of skies.

BENNY

The day of Esther's Will reading had arrived. It was just Benny and his mother at the tiny solicitors in Seabourne. It was only a formality as they had always lived in his mother's cosy house with just enough to get by. Jack had suggested they meet after, at the new Wimpy Bar in Cliffbourne, the slightly bigger town along the coast, and try one of these hamburgers and chips. So, food was all that Benny was actually thinking about when the bombshell was dropped by the rather petite man with a huge moustache, sitting behind a desk that also swamped him. The solicitor had been talking for quite some time and Benny had zoned out entirely when his mother touched his elbow.

'And, as I said Mr Solomons, if you can just sign this form to confirm that you have understood the conditions of the Will, the cheque will be in the post to you in a couple of days.'

'I'm sorry, I must have missed a bit. What am I signing for?' Benny felt a bit embarrassed.

'Well, Mr Solomons, you're going to be quite a wealthy young man, the cheque will be for £20,000, and Mrs Solomons will be receiving the same amount. The condition of your inheritance as I said, however, is that you invest it in a business.

Once Benny had fully caught up and his mother had recovered from the news of their unexpected fortune, they both decided to celebrate, just a little, at the new Wimpy Bar, with Jack. Benny couldn't wait to tell him the exciting, if somewhat bewildering, news.

Mrs Solomons made her decision surprisingly quickly. She

would pay off her mortgage and put the rest into savings, and also splash out on some little treats and a trip for herself. She wanted to visit Germany, having not been back since the war; there were a lot of people she would like to see again, if they were still alive. She had many memories that she wished to try and make some sense of. Benny, also had much to think about and wanted to take time to talk it all through with Jack. He knew nothing about investing in a business, in fact he knew very little about business in general, with the exception of the planning side of property. It was a life changing amount of money, what on earth was he going to do with it?

CLARA

Seabourne Matters came out every Saturday. It was the only local paper and pretty much everyone read it cover to cover. Most people had it delivered but Pat Turner, of Turners Hardware Shop, liked to pop into the newsagent, have a chinwag and a moan to John, who worked there, and pick up his crisp copy, first thing in the morning.

'What the?' Pat stormed home and showed it to his wife, the pair of them gawked at the front cover which read:

**'LOCAL SWIMMING VANDALS BREAK
INTO OUR MUCH LOVED,**

MERMAID THEATRE'

Underneath this headline were three photos of the six vandals, larking about and unfortunately caught red handed, in The Mermaid Theatre.

Pat's whole face was growing more scarlet with each line. Doreen, his wife, thought he was going to explode.

"Our Reporter has it on the highest authority that the ringleader, Mrs Dorothy Baker (49) together with her husband, local builder, Robert Baker, (65) forced their way into the old theatre, breaking several panes of glass in their endeavour to vandalise the building and probably steal whatever they could get away with!!! The gang also included Local Council employee, Benjamin Solomons (40), Samuel Williams (53), together with his daughter Miss Isabella Williams (26), who, our sources tell us, teaches, YES TEACHES, part time at OUR local infant school!!! Do we, the respectable, law-abiding people of Seabourne, want our children to be taught how to vandalise and steal? Also, long standing resident of Seabourne, Mrs Betty Turner (previously Lancaster) (82) featured in the main photo with her granddaughter, Sindy Turner, were also in league with these unpleasant criminals. Many of you will remember her husband, the charming Edward Turner who owned Turners Hardware Store. He must be turning in his grave at this sort of behaviour! What is the world coming to, Readers, when we cannot trust our neighbours?"

This was sensationalistic journalism at its best, the newspapers sold out in about an hour and 'Our Reporter' got herself an immediate place on the payroll.

Meanwhile, at Rutland Manor, Mrs Jackson had read the article with a smirk. Although her employer was a hard taskmaster, she couldn't help being secretly fond of her and was glad that she seemed to have forgiven Jack and Paul. These days Clara came back from her morning walks looking happier than she had done in thirty years. She folded the paper carefully, put it on the silver tray and brought it up with the usual pot of tea.

'Good morning, Lady Harrington. Bit of a do in the paper today,' and she left the tray on the side table.

Clara hadn't been in a hurry to meet up with the dippers. Let them sweat it out a bit, she thought with a wry smile. More importantly, she had asked Green, the gardener, to bring down the trunks with the silver mermaid symbol stamped on the side, from the attic, and put them in the conservatory, for her perusal. Poor chap, she hadn't realised how old he had become. He was really struggling with things now. *Should I let him go with a decent pension? Goodness, what has got into me lately?*

Clara had spent over a day sorting through all the old costumes. Many of them, *her* old costumes. They were in a fair condition, considering their age. Peter had built the theatre for the love of his life and Clara had starred in any number of plays, pantomimes and musicals before war broke out. It had been her life and her passion, and now she had a decision to make. Did she back this rather hairbrained scheme to refurbish the theatre and allow Dot to put on a production, or did she put her foot down on all these silly ideas once and for all?

BETTY

Betty and Sindy made their way down to the beach, both looking forward to a swim. The dippers met an hour later on a Saturday to allow for a lay-in. By the time they were all on the seafront, news had got around, people were staring and pointing and shaking their heads. No-one could understand it, until eventually Jack and Benny turned up, with the newspaper in their hands. They had been talking all night about Benny's decisions and had only just seen the front page.

Betty could see that Dot was dreadfully embarrassed and Rob was obviously cross as he said the paper was printing lies these days. He wasn't 65! It was a misprint and he would demand an apology. People would think he was an O.A.P. for goodness-sake! He was only 56. This amused Betty; he was such a kind and helpful man, but apparently a little bit vain. It was only when Sindy read the article and saw her photo that Betty's smile disappeared. Sindy started to look very upset. Benny told them he had thought there were a few photos missing but hadn't given it much thought until he opened the paper and realised where they had gone. Betty and Isabella were fuming and decided to go straight to the police station to find out how and why this story had been leaked.

As it was such a hot day, Isabella was wearing the tiniest pair of shorts, plimsoles and a light green blouse; she was dressed for the beach, rather than a full-blown argument at the police station. She marched in, pushing Betty in her chair and rang the bell with quite a bit of force. Slapping the paper on the counter, she asked, 'Who authorised this? Why on earth have they printed such lies. You know we were only having a look round. Lady Harrington didn't press charges so what's all this about and how did they get those photos? Those were Benny's property.' Isabella was getting so cross, she couldn't stop. 'Now you've exposed where I live and spoiled everything.' She started crying and Betty realised there was much more to this than simply some bad press.

Will Johnson was aghast; mostly by the fact that it had been printed at all, but also because it had affected Isabella so deeply. He knew this wouldn't have been leaked by his colleague and so there was only one conclusion; the young woman who cleaned occasionally had begged him for this job. He hadn't liked her very much at first sight but felt sorry for her. There had been rumours that she also worked for the local newspaper, but he would never have thought she would be capable of this sort of thing. This was going to upset a lot of people, but he cared mostly about the cross and very unhappy vision standing next to Betty Turner, who was not looking happy either. Betty also explained that Sindy, her granddaughter, was such a hard-working girl, and received little credit from her parents who would not take this news well.

'I'm very sorry Miss Williams, Mrs Turner. I am pretty sure I know who did this, and they didn't have my permission at all. I will sort this out today. In the meantime, is there any help that I can give you?'

Betty thought this would be more of a family matter and decided to go and see her son before Sindy got a dressing-down that she didn't deserve. Isabella didn't want to tell Will about Neil, the obnoxious, absent, father of her child and how, even though she had not been running away, she was comforted that he didn't know their whereabouts. Isabella acknowledged that it wasn't Will's fault and they left, but without feeling much better.

Betty decided to face this head on, she knew her son's daily habits and that he must, by now, have seen the headline.

'Come on Isabella, if you don't mind, can we go round to Turners now? I really want to calm Pat down before he makes a twit of himself, and it would be helpful to have your support my dear.'

'Just try and stop me, Betty love.' Isabella was ready for an argument with someone, it didn't really matter who. As they left the Station, Betty spotted Pat storming toward the dippers, where Sindy was now being comforted by the rest of them. They all looked up as he started shouting. Betty sighed. *A bit late then.*

Will was already locking up, enroute to the newspaper offices, when he, too, saw what was in the offing, judging by the raised voice and aggressive stance of one man in particular. This was his fault and he was damn sure he wasn't going to let it get any worse, so grabbing his helmet, he jumped in his patrol car and sped off towards the front.

Unfortunately, taking after his father a bit, Pat Turner tended towards bullying behaviour. He was a rather ignorant, unfulfilled man who, full of self-righteousness, had decided to put the dippers and Sindy, in particular, back on the right path in no uncertain terms.

Pat was in full flow when Betty and Isabella reached him. Samuel was trying to calm him down and tell him the facts of the matter which unfortunately only made Pat more aggressive. As Will walked quietly up behind Pat, he was starting to throw his fists about and unluckily for him, one of them collided with that most sacred of objects: a policeman's helmet. Everyone gasped as it fell to the ground, and Will moved up a gear into professional mode. The handcuffs were out in a jiffy and Pat was locked to the very convenient bench. He quietened down pretty quickly after that.

Will explained what had happened and that he was on his way to speak with the Editor to get the facts put right. Pat was cautioned by Will, but much worse was on the way.

'Don't turn into your father, Pat.' It was all Betty needed to say.

Dot was next, 'yes, Mr Turner, we were a bit silly, but it was well meaning. Surely you don't believe everything you read in the newspaper?'

'If I ever hear of you throwing your weight about like that again with any of my friends, I'll be really unhappy. Do you understand what I am saying, Mr Turner?' Benny wanted to say a lot more but settled on that. Jack was very proud of him.

Samuel and Rob just stared at Pat. They were both tall chaps and didn't really need to add anything.

'I'm sorry.' No one was expecting this. 'I acted before I knew the full facts. I apologise Mum, Sindy. I've made a fool of myself and I don't ever want to turn into him. If you'll unlock me, Officer, I'll make my way home and will certainly not be causing any further trouble.'

Sindy couldn't help herself, she gave him a hug, which was something she hadn't done in a long time. 'Thanks Dad.'

Whilst Betty was chatting with Sindy and Pat, Rob suggested that Samuel join Dot and himself for a bite to eat tonight, as they seemed to be getting on so well. There was a new Berni Inn just opened in Cliffbourne, and this was clearly the 'in' place to go. The three of them went off, the men discussing who would drive, which pleased Dot immensely and meant she could have a couple of drinks.

This left Benny and Jack, together with Isabella and PC Johnson. Will knew he should be getting to the newspaper offices, but couldn't tear himself away. The conversation was so easy with her and she was relaxing a lot and laughing now.

Heavens, she was beautiful. The guys were good company too. Will was just deciding whether this might be the right time to perhaps ask her out when Jack came to his rescue. 'Benny and I are popping out for a drink tonight to celebrate his fortune.' Benny looked enquiringly at Jack. *They hadn't planned this at all.* Then he realised what Jack was planning. *What a brilliant idea, why hadn't he thought of this?*

'Oh yes, we really are. Why don't you two join us? I bet Sindy and Paul will be very pleased to have some quiet babysitting time.' Benny added, to secure the deal.

Betty was pleased to hear all these arrangements being made. *What a delightful bunch of people.* Pat pushed Betty in her chair back home whilst actually listening, for the first time in a long while, to his daughter talking about the possible theatre and pantomime plans. Diesel was overjoyed to see them all back home, but suspected that he had missed out on something.

SINDY AND PAUL

The following morning, Paul and Sindy were swimming, chatting, laughing and looking very comfortable with each other. School tomorrow for the last day of term, which neither of them were dreading, as they now had three brilliant changes in their lives: someone to talk to at breaktime, a boy/girlfriend, which gave them both a lot of credibility, and a mate to walk home with, which stopped the shouts of 'oi loner' and 'what you up to tonight? Oh, yeah, nothing, saddo,' which they had got a bit fed up with lately. In September they were both going up to 5th grade. Although they were sixteen and in the same class, Paul was nearly a year older than Sindy. He was creative, enjoying science and he wanted to do cooking although school had decided this was not for boys. Sindy was much more interested in art and design. Neither had the slightest notion of what they wanted to do on leaving school, although there were decisions to be made as 'work experience' would be looming and they had to choose where they might like to work for a week in the spring of 1977.

However, school and work were far from their minds this morning. The babysitting evening had been uniquely special for them. Neither had any previous sexual experience and, as Lizzie was completely out-for-the count in her pretty little pink bedroom, they had both decided that this was an opportunity to confirm their feelings for one-another. It had started rather awkwardly with a lot of fumbling about, which had caused quite a bit of laughter. This immediately broke the tension and an unforgettable evening had unfolded. They hadn't, however, prepared for this and with their combined limited knowledge on the subject, the practical side of these things had completely escaped them.

CLARA

By the following day, Clara had sorted through five crates of costumes, and there were still more to go. There were also many tea chests filled with props; this occupation had bought back so many happy memories and Clara had made her decision. The weather was still fair and the occasion demanded some dramatic dressing, more stylish than usual. She selected a peacock blue suit with a suggestion of a bustle. For full effect, now that she was back in a theatrical frame of mind, she dressed her hair with a small peacock feather. Nothing vulgar, of course, and made her way towards the congregating dippers.

Dot noticed Clara first and felt apprehensive. She wanted to apologise, but before she could say anything, Clara had an announcement:

'Good morning, one and all. Ah, I see we have a new swimmer.' Clara noticed Will, who had accompanied Isabella this morning. 'Well done PC Johnson, how very pleasing to see you again and so soon. It was all a little unfortunate the other evening and I cannot help but think that if you, Dot, had shared your ideas with me and if I had been a little more open, we could have avoided meeting PC Johnson here, but perhaps that was meant to be,' and she smiled at Isabella.

Dot was about to speak but Clara raised her gloved hand, quite regally. 'I am more than happy for this group to go ahead and refurbish my theatre, but I will be signing off on every detail. Dot, you may perform *Cinderella* on my stage and I would like to help, since I have a fair bit of experience in this area. I think I am right in saying that you don't know who played Cinderella in that 1936 production. I can tell you that I was indeed, The Mermaid, and I might add that whoever takes this role may have a hard act to follow.'

Clapping just seemed appropriate, followed by cheers and whoops for Clara's soliloquy.

'Let's meet later today if everyone is free and make some plans. There will be a lot of work to do if we are to get the place shipshape and ready for a panto at the end of December. There followed much exchanging of ideas and they arranged to meet at the theatre at three o'clock.

Clara was pleased to see Rob, Samuel, Will and also Jack, taking more photos, making rough drawings and starting to weigh up the costs involved. Benny didn't think there would be any planning issues, and so kept himself busy with supplying rations for the troops.

Clara pointed out the stage entrances and exits to Dot, adding that these were important when planning and writing a pantomime. Dressing rooms were useful too and, no surprise, The Mermaid Theatre had the very best. Clara was like a different person, happy and so very involved. She and Peter had designed the theatre together, with careful thought and professional knowledge. Dot was more than excited; she couldn't have wished for better. It even had a trap door for magical entrances and an ariel rope for anyone wishing to fly.

The hours flew past with plans and ideas bouncing around the theatre, it had got dark and little Lizzie had fallen asleep on an old sofa in one of the dressing rooms. Benny, who always brought the snacks, had actually run out of food for everyone! The moon was rising, the evening was still and balmy and Benny carried Lizzie home, whilst Isabella and Will chatted about all that had happened over the last few days. Jack walked behind, camera flashing occasionally. These would be named 'Togetherness.' Paul and Sindy walked Clara home and then Paul walked Sindy back to Betty's. Hand in hand, they talked about everything. In his quiet way, Paul was so excited about the theatre plans and so grateful to be involved.

WILL

The first thing on Will's agenda the next morning was the newspaper office. He was a gentle, even- tempered man, but betrayal of trust, for him, was just about the worst thing you could do. He walked calmly into the offices and asked to see the Editor, a man with whom he'd had previous dealings, not all of them enjoyable. There was quite a racket going on, a few offices down the corridor and, being a copper, his ears pricked up.

'And I could have you reinstated in a heartbeat.' The voice was getting more familiar.

'To think, Peter and I launched this newspaper nearly fifty years ago, and you have reduced it to a load of foul smelling, libellous, bilge water. You should be ashamed of yourself. What does go on at these offices?'

PC Johnson realised who was in the driving seat and grinned to himself and continued to listen. An unattractive male voice seemed to be mumbling ...

'No, don't get clever with me, Mr Davison. There will be a retraction in the next edition. Edward Turner was an adulterous wife beater and should never have been glorified by your silly little sub-reporter. I have prepared a full apology for you to print, exactly as it is. Isabella Williams is a personal friend, and a more talented music and dance instructor, you would have to go a long way to find. The school and the parents are lucky to have her. Again, you will see I have prepared apologies from both yourself and your reporter. You will be fully covering all the theatre refurbishment works as they occur, promoting the pantomime on a weekly basis and generally doing your utmost to make amends to all concerned. Have I made myself quite clear? I will leave it to PC Johnson as to whether he wishes to charge your associate with stealing. Good day.' And she marched out of the offices, silver mermaid cane in hand, winking to Will as she went.

Wow, she could teach me a thing or two, and I've been in the force very nearly five years. Will thought to himself. He firmly marked Davison's card, and spoke to Anna, the probably soon to be ex-cleaner of the Police Station.

'Stealing, lying and abusing my good nature is not the way to keep your position. I know things are difficult for you but taking items from a police station? Really Anna?' He was about to suggest some better things she could do, as, after all, it was because of these events that he was getting to know Isabella, when she stuck two fingers up at him and walked out. Oh well, you couldn't help everyone.

LOST IN FRANCE

A couple of hundred miles away, across the murky English Channel, the latest edition of *Seabourne Matters* was being studied, as it had been, every week, for many years. His breakfast table was littered with books and papers, sprinkled with delicious buttery croissant flakes, numerous empty espresso cups and the butt of a rather indulgent 'breakfast' cigar, still wearing the band, as if it had been enjoyed by quite the cad.

It was late morning and the streets were bustling with life. Rays of sunshine were moving past chimney pots and the quirky roofs and spires of the old buildings opposite, throwing shafts of light across the room. The exotic aromas of *Gauloises* and fresh coffee drifted up to his small balcony. Impatient car horns and people conversing rapidly in the elegant French language reached his ears. Paris felt like home now, but it would never actually *be* home. He studied the photos carefully and smiled.

He had found her, which was so encouraging. It seemed to be a bizarre set of circumstances however; there must be more to it than the article he was reading in the newspaper. The photos were interesting and he casually wondered who the photographer was, and also who some of the others were who had been involved in this seemingly juvenile jaunt. He would look forward to next week's edition with interest to see if this story was going any further, and then start to make some plans. Now though, he must take his late-morning constitutional. Always starting at Notre Dame, he generally walked down by The Seine, criss-crossing the river until he was tired, then, sometimes getting a ride home. Today, however, he had quite the spring in his step and walked for miles, contemplating his next move.

DOT

Swimming numbers were down the next morning as of course, the newspaper had not done them any favours at all and a retraction wouldn't be read until Saturday. However, the usual crowd were there as they now had much to organise and plan. Rob and Samuel had taken to swimming out a long way together, whilst discussing the pros and cons of using oak, rather than the cheaper pine, for various jobs at the theatre. Rob was working on a large project at the moment, but it was nearly finished, and he would soon be paid. He could then afford to devote a few weeks to the theatre. He hadn't seen Dot this happy and engaged in anything for a long while and he couldn't be more pleased for her. Missing their two kids, who had remained in London with their busy lives, together with all the women's stuff had really dragged her down this last year. Rob felt bad because although she had helped him immeasurably get over the loss of John, he really didn't know what to do or say to help her now. Who would have thought, some swimming with a chance collection of Seabourne folk, plus an old theatre could have been the key to all this? She really was shining again these days.

Dot was pleased to see Betty and Clara watching the fun together, whilst sitting on the bench, soaking up some early morning sunshine and talking about the refurbishments. Betty had told Dot that she had started to ache a bit after swimming the last few times. Dot wasn't sure what to say, after all Betty was getting on a bit. She suggested that Betty speak to the Doctor but Betty said she had done and he had told her to go home, take an aspirin and stop that silly swimming.

That seemed bad advice to Dot, who decided to chat it through with Sindy when she saw her next. Dot noticed that Benny and Jack were not around this morning which was unusual, but after a brief dip, she sat on the bench by the sea and continued to write her version of Cinderella, almost feverishly, in her notepad.

The script was coming on well and Dot looked forward to the day when everyone was assigned their roles. It was a classic tale, easy to write and not too much to change, as who didn't love the original story. She had written it around the dippers and their personalities, including lots of local references and things that were going on in the country generally. Her characters were, she felt, going to be brilliant. Just the last few scenes now, which she was going to finish soon. She had decided on the following:

Cinderella – Isabella Williams, it was her voice that clinched it.

Buttons – Jack Harrington, he just seemed right for this role.

Wicked Stepmother – Samuel Williams, he was so flamboyant in his usual style of dressing and Dot could clearly see him in a dame costume.

Ugly Sisters – Benny and Will. Benny was so outgoing now and everyone in the audience would enjoy seeing their local bobby in a voluminous skirt, towering wig and false eyelashes.

Prince Charming – This would be Sindy. She was tall for her age and elegant, the fishnets and boots would suit her.

Fairy Godmother – she wanted Clara but would have to see her reaction.

Ghost (there always has to be a ghost) – Rob said he didn't mind as long as he was covered in a sheet and no-one recognised him.

Prompt – Betty. She was very keen to be involved, and this would be just the ticket.

Lighting – Paul, as he was young and up to date with the

gadgets.

BENNY

Mornings were always busy in Seabourne High Street, especially with the children going back to school soon. It seemed that everyone had come out to get organised. Plimsoles, blazers, stationery, you name it, (and you did have to name it) was all being purchased from the High Street. Benny and Jack negotiated past busy mums, toddlers, school kids (wishing they were anywhere else but here) and pushchairs. They were due at the estate agents soon and Benny had asked Jack to come along, both for support and his professional opinion. Although Benny could drive, he didn't have a car and Jack was happy to help out, as well as feeling pleased that Benny was sharing this with him. Goddard and Smith, the incredibly old-fashioned firm of estate agents couldn't have been more helpful. The reception smelled of leather, beeswax and very old files. There were a surprising number of businesses for sale locally, and even more in the bigger towns. They had decided on Seabourne, however, and it would probably take them all morning.

Benny and Jack looked at five businesses, only two were interesting, and one of those was an absolute match. It was at the end of the High Street, not too far from Seabourne Spa Railway Station. Jack had arranged to go back the next day and run a closer, technical eye over the building, leaving Benny to look into the planning side of things with some work colleagues. There was a lot to be done with this new and slightly scary idea, but now the sun was setting in glorious technicolour, and they had a panto to get excited about. They were thoroughly looking forward to finding out what roles they would be playing, and reading their parts around Clara's huge, dark oak dining table. Benny had agreed with Jack that they wouldn't talk about their day or what was on their minds, mainly as he did not want to intrude on Dot's evening and Benny also needed to finalise his plans before telling everyone.

At Rutland Manor that evening, the scripts were ready, crisply photocopied and stapled. The roles were just waiting for their voices and the first reading was this evening. Dot was that excellent mixture of nervous and excited, about the whole thing. Benny had organised some food and Jack had brought a case of Champagne; Benny felt very proud to be friends with this stylish man. Jack said it was a momentous occasion and that they should celebrate accordingly and no-one was arguing with that. Sindy hadn't tried Champagne before and everyone laughed as she exclaimed there were a lot more bubbles than the cider she sometimes drank at Christmas.

Dot gave each person their script with their role. The room was buzzing with anticipation and the reading began. It was hilarious, with Samuel trying out different accents and Benny and Will bouncing off each other effortlessly. One and all thought the jokes were funny, and that it would be a brilliant show. Betty said she'd not had so much fun in ages, and that if this was just the start, role on panto season. Will was so very glad to have become involved in all this, particularly getting to know Isabella, who, with her father involved as well, was obviously having a wonderful time. As the end of the story approached, Dot glanced over at Clara to see what she thought.

PART II – THE FAIRY GODMOTHER

Isabella

Samuel was clearly delighted to be part of all this theatrical fun, particularly as his precious daughter was clearly enjoying herself and letting her hair down for once. Isabella deserved some attention and pleasure. She was a talented and hard-working girl who, some years ago, had unfortunately got involved with the wrong man. Isabella had been working at a nursery school in South London; she was quite an introverted young woman and kept herself to herself. She always said she didn't really like grown up people that much, although she adored children. Neil, ten years her senior, had marked her at the school gates, when picking up Jane, his daughter. Little Jane was one of Isabella's favourites; she always looked in need of a nice cuddle. When Neil started talking to Isabella, he claimed Jane's mother, who he said was a much younger woman, had run off with a foreign man and Isabella felt sorry for him. This story was completely untrue. Neil was aggressive and controlling and had not allowed Jane's mother to venture out very much, she was basically trapped in his dingy, damp flat. Neil was calculating and clever, as well as being handsome in a pinched, rat-like way. He watched, bided his time and, one evening when it was raining hard, offered Isabella a lift home in his old Datsun. He played it just right, not coming on too quickly, but allowing Isabella to develop more than feelings of pity for him.

They had a couple of dates in the West End, but it soon

became clear to Isabella that there was nothing more to him than a veneer, which she was beginning to see through. On their last evening out together, she tried to explain that their relationship was not for her. He appeared incredibly distressed and suggested they have a couple more drinks. She was just drinking tonic water but he had a plan in mind and had bought a half bottle of vodka, for slipping into her glass and soon, being unused to a lot of alcohol, she realised she was quite drunk. He took her to a friends' empty flat, appearing to care about her being safe. Once inside the front door, he took advantage of her situation, and then pushed her out the door, saying that she had 'asked for it'.

Isabella was much too upset and ashamed to say anything to anyone at the time and nine months later, Lizzie was born. When she eventually told Samuel what had happened, he said she should have reported it to the police. However, they found out that Neil had got into a lot more trouble and had left the country, according to one of the other nursery teachers. She never saw or heard of him, or his little daughter again. She had always planned to find out where Jane had ended up and what her mother was actually like, but time had moved on. Isabella happily spent all her time with Lizzie and it was such a horrible memory that she just left it in the past. Even now, however, Samuel vowed if he ever showed up again, he would kill him. Isabella never doubted this.

Back in Clara's drawing room, Isabella was thrilled to have been given the lead role. Although she was shy, she knew she could make a decent job of this part. Her voice was strong and clear and any dancing she would enjoy, but would this be a further promotion of where she was living and cause both Samuel and Lizzie pain and problems? She needed to think this through in the cold light of day as she knew her first responsibility was to keep her daughter as safe as possible. She was just going to talk about it with Samuel, when Clara decided to make another of her, now quite frequent, speeches.

'Dot, your version of *Cinderella* is perfectly charming, if you'll pardon the pun. All credit to you for your ideas, your hard work and vision for the Mermaid Theatre, and, yes, I would be delighted to accept the role of the Fairy Godmother, how fitting my dear.'

By the end of the evening, everyone was giddy on laughter and champagne. Benny and Jack escorted Isabella home as Will had left early for a night shift. Dot and Rob went shortly after and Samuel took Betty, leaving Paul to walk Sindy home, now that these two seemed inseparable. Once at her flat, Isabella gave Benny and Jack a hug and together they went back to Jack's house, across town.

BENNY

There was no moon tonight and a menacing darkness seemed to be swirling around the whole town. The wind had got up whilst they were at Clara's and some squally rain was coming in straight off the sea. The lights running down the pier were waving about wildly in the wind and the waves were crashing on the shore. Benny and Jack turned their collars up against the salty rain, held hands against the wind and were laughing and chatting on their way back home from the script reading. Despite the weather, they felt light-hearted; they had so many plans for the future, the pantomime being just one of the things they were looking forward to. Jack had really opened up to Benny lately, particularly about his feelings for him and he'd also spoken about previous relationships which sounded very negative, bordering on poisonous. Benny wondered to himself how anyone in the world could hurt such a kind soul as Jack.

Benny had confessed that he had found his sexuality confusing and had tried to date women for years before finally accepting the obvious. His grandmother had died without knowing the truth and he doubted his mother had any idea either. When Benny said he'd had more of a 'thing' with his oven and his cake tins over the last ten years, than any man, Jack had burst out laughing, but in a sweet and concerned way that made Benny just stop in the street and kiss him. In the distance, coming out of the other, not so friendly pub in the town, The Ragged Cat, a bunch of youths who were shouting and swearing, turned around and noticed this moment of affection. Benny felt immediately worried. He was gay, fat and Jewish, and had been picked on and bullied by just such gangs of boys all his life. He could feel their ignorant, pent up aggression a mile away.

For a split second they looked at each other, not sure whether to cross the road, run or what to do. More of the gang were still pouring out of the pub and they had started marching towards Benny and Jack. Someone threw a beer bottle at them with the rest jeering and running now. After hearing about some of Jack's previous relationships, Benny decided that Jack would not be struck by anyone else, if he could prevent it, and quickly told him to run to the phone box, it wasn't that far, and call the police. Benny would deal with these lads. Jack was not happy, but it was about the best plan under the circumstances and there was no time to delay. He sprinted round the corner, almost fell into the phone box and dialled 9 9 9.

'Oh dear, yer bleedin' poofter! What yer goin' to do now yer boyfriend's run away?' One of them shouted. Benny's blood went cold, as now that they were nearly upon him, he saw that they were all wearing Dr Martens' boots with rolled up jeans and it was clear they were here for only one thing. *Shit.* Benny tried to apologise, reason with them, offer them a drink, beg them not to start trouble, when the first punch winded him and knocked him to the ground. Jack came racing back, screaming for them to stop but it was not for several minutes, when the blue light of Will's police car came racing round the corner, that they looked up and ran. Will radioed immediately for an ambulance. Benny was unconscious and almost unrecognisable. Jack was crying, shivering, beside himself with worry, guilt, shame. *Why did I leave Benny on his own? Christ, I am such a coward.* He would never forgive himself but his thoughts were broken by Will saying:

'You did the right thing mate. I know that lot. They're a national front gang, come down from London with exactly this sort of thing on their minds and they wouldn't have stopped. You'd both be half dead by now.'

Benny was carefully placed on a stretcher and safely inside the vehicle when the ambulance driver backed Will up, 'I think it probably looks a lot worse than it is although he's going to take a while to recover, but I agree with PC Johnson here, you definitely did the right thing, getting help. Meet us at the memorial hospital.

JACK

Will gave Jack a lift to the Memorial, whilst radioing to all available cars to be on the look-out for the London gang, the ringleader was very well known to the police and Will was going to get the bastards this time. There was a lot more he needed to do regarding this vicious attack and so he left Jack at the door and sped off to the station.

Jack sat with Benny who had gained consciousness and was heavily dosed up with morphine. He was going for X-rays to make sure there were no broken bones as the doctor suspected a possible fractured rib or two. Jack just couldn't get the picture of Benny, on the floor being kicked and punched, out of his mind. Jack had also taken a couple of thumps but nothing compared to Benny. *If only I had stayed with him,* but then what Will had said crept back into his mind. Also, he had to be strong for Benny, this was no time for self-pity. What would Benny do in his situation now? He knew immediately, and decided tomorrow he would get on with it.

After an hour or so, Benny returned from X-ray. It was good news, although he was severely bruised, there were no breaks. He was covered in bandages and said he thought he looked like an extra from *M.A.S.H.* Jack laughed, although tears were streaming down his face. The nurse said they would keep him in for a couple of days to manage the pain. Once she had finished all her checks, they could finally talk. Before Jack could even start apologising, Benny raised his best hand a couple of inches, indicating that he was going to be doing the talking: 'one single word of apology from you, young man, and I'll call the doctor and have you sent away. We were in the wrong place at the wrong time and they wouldn't even have noticed us if it wasn't for me. Your quick action lessened the outcome immensely. Let's remember all the things that we were planning just minutes before this happened and focus on that. I need you to go to the estate agents and the solicitors tomorrow morning to get things rolling for me.' *He needs to be kept busy or he's going to fall apart,* Benny realised. 'Oh, and by the way, I know this is probably not the best time, but that seems to be the way of our romance, I love you, Jack Harrington and it's me, not the drugs talking.'

'Benny, I ....' Jack started. Benny raised his eyebrows to show that he was not having apologies in any form.

'Love you too, you perfect human being.' Jack finished off.

The formidable nurse came in then and said Benny needed to rest and that Jack, also needed to go home and get some sleep.

The following morning was grey and muggy, which echoed Jacks mood, he hadn't slept and was feeling angry, guilty, vulnerable and just plain sad. Exhausted, he went down to the beach and spoke to Dot, Isabella, Samuel, Sindy, Paul and Betty. They needed to hear what had happened from him first, as word was surely going to spread fast in this gossipy town. They were all furious, shocked and upset at Jack's story, but what was so heart-warming was that everyone there, had accepted their relationship weeks ago and were just pleased that they had found each other. It was the 1970's after all. Jack's next stop was possibly not going to be so straightforward.

Before he got to Rutland Manor he saw Clara with the rising sun behind her, resembling a biblical figure, immaculately adorned as usual, managing the steps with a new-found lightness. Her eyes widened at the considerable cuts and bruises to his face. There was a stone bench half way along her gardens and they sat down together, brushing against the vigorous rosemary which was flourishing in the heat and drought. Jack wasn't sure where to start. He gave her the facts of the attack; she was never one for beating about the bush.

'I assume this was a homophobic assault on Benny and yourself?'

Jack had thought he'd kept his feelings private, but clearly not. 'I'm sorry Aunt Clara,' was all he could think to say.

'For what exactly Jack? I've known for years about your 'persuasion', shall we call it? Benny is a delightful man and I hope you will enjoy many years together. I think, however, with prejudices and feelings running high with certain types of people, that it may be best to keep shows of affection in private. Perhaps one day, things will be different, but how would I know? I'm simply an old lady. I shall visit him later on today, but please give him my best wishes.'

Jack thanked her. *What an incredible lady she was, there was nothing remotely old about her.* He continued on into town, feeling a lot better than when he had got up this morning. His business completed; he went home to bake Benny the very best cake that he could.

BETTY AND SINDY

Although Sindy had enjoyed the sea today, Betty thought she looked a little pale and was hoping that she wasn't coming down with a bug. *She had spent quite a long time in the bathroom this morning,* Betty thought. Then she put two and two together. *Oh, blimey, this is going to put the cat amongst the pigeons!* Luckily Sindy wasn't working today and so Betty said she'd put the kettle on and they could chat. There was so much to talk about, particularly the nasty business with Benny and Jack and they had decided to make a cake to take to the hospital, that afternoon during visiting time. It seemed the right thing to do and Betty could turn out a tasty Dorset apple cake, if the occasion warranted it, and this certainly did.

Betty thought she would make it as easy as possible for Sindy. 'So, my love, how's things?'

'Nan, I've really messed up.'

'Well, presumably it still takes two, even these days? It's not just your problem Sindy love.'

'I don't know what to do. I've known for a couple of days but how can I tell him? We're both at school for God's sake. Everyone's going to call me a slut. I haven't even thought of what Dad's going to do.'

'Well, Sindy, he can't throw you out, as you live with me now and you will always have a home here, baby as well, if necessary. I think the first thing you need to do is to go to the doctors, and get this confirmed. Go to the surgery in Cliffbourne, the doctor in Seabourne doesn't know his arse from his elbow, if you'll pardon my French.'

'Thank you, nan. What would I do without you?' Sindy asked, giving her nan a long hug.

'You'll get through this, whatever the outcome. I'll always be here for you and you have a lot of friends in Seabourne now. I don't know Paul that well, but if his aunt is anything to go by, he'll do the right thing by you. Now, let's get ready and catch the bus into Cliffbourne.

On their return home, the plumpest apple cake was produced and taken to the hospital whilst still slightly warm. They bought some clotted cream to go with it, and some paper plates and plastic spoons from Woolies. This was going to be a feast, although the thought of rich clotted cream wasn't doing Sindy any favours at all.

DOT

On the way home from the beach, still reeling from Jack's news, Dot decided to pop by the yard and let Rob know what had happened, he would be so sad for the boys. She needed to get a few more Xerox copies of the script done anyway. The estate agents had been very helpful, even if they had charged quite a lot; 8½p each page! You could buy a pint of milk for that. Rob had kindly said he would pay for this and put it through his books as 'printing costs'. As she walked up to the iron railings of his builders' yard, she watched him for a while, unnoticed. He was still a handsome man, his eyes always shone with kindness and his full lips were gentle and sensual. Standing there, watching him work, she felt a huge rush of love for the man who had been her best friend for so long. She suddenly realised that time was getting on. *She really needed to think about the business of the day, and not peep at her husband of thirty years, unseen, like a weirdo. Too late!*

Rob turned and waved, looking slightly amused. He made Dot a 'workshop' black coffee and added a generous amount of condensed milk. She told him today's sad news and Rob decided to take an hour off at visiting time. They would go in together and show their support. Dot decided to bake a Victoria sponge, you couldn't go wrong with that, although it might not be quite as light as Benny's.

She picked up her scripts, which the young lady had very kindly stapled together, and went home, hoping she had enough self-raising flour in the cupboard. There was plenty of home-made raspberry jam and everything else she needed. It came out of the oven looking rather good, and Dot hoped the comforting, homely smell of vanilla would cheer them up.

CLARA

Clara had a million and one things to do today, starting with learning her lines. Once she had read the script a couple of times, she realised that the words just did not stay in her mind as they used to do. She had a meeting at the theatre today, with a local lady who made curtains, and could possibly re-upholster the seating, this was a huge job but Clara was keen to give the business to a local person. She was also seeing Jack to organise some photographs of the refurbishment. *Seabourne Matters* were going to do a double page spread, promoting the pantomime, combined with lots of pictures of the progress being made at The Mermaid, and a very fulsome apology to one and all. She wanted to have these on Mr Davison's desk today, as printing would be tomorrow.

Mrs Jackson had the day off and Clara was not particularly *aw fait* with kitchen matters. However, she had decided to make Benny a ginger cake as she recalled making one during the war. The aga seemed hot enough and so following her Mrs Beeton recipe, she got on with the task. Seemed fairly easy, *what on earth do people make such a fuss about?* After around half an hour, the warm aroma of ginger seemed to be seeping through the whole house and Clara judged that it must be 'done'.

She put it on a cooling tray, feeling very pleased with herself. It was, possibly a little flat but as she had followed the recipe to the word, that was obviously how it was supposed to be. *Was there no end to her talents?* Visiting time approached and she packed it into her wicker basket and set off.

BENNY

On the dot of two o clock, Jack burst into the ward with a large Tupperware box. He'd made a coffee and walnut cake, using Benny's recipe and it looked nothing short of luscious. A couple of hungry looking nurses eyed it up and said that although it wasn't strictly regulations, Sister, was off this afternoon and as long as they could have a piece, they'd see what they could do about some plates. By the time the nurses came back, there was also Betty's apple cake, Dot's Victoria sponge and then Clara walked in and announced her ginger cake. The nurses cut everything up and it became quite a party in Ward Four, which was also against the rules, but Benny was such a sweetheart, they decided to turn a blind eye. All the other patients felt Christmas had come early. The food wasn't very tempting there and these cakes were the best they had ever tasted. The nurses brought in teas and coffees and more plates.

Benny was overcome. He praised everyone's baking, paying particular mention to Clara's ginger biscuits! At first the room went very quiet, and then Rob couldn't contain his mirth any longer and burst out laughing, quickly followed by everyone else in the ward, including Clara, who said it was the thought that counted, and that perhaps Mrs Jackson's baking wasn't so bad after all. Sindy was really enjoying the gingerbread however and Betty asked if they could take a little home. As the others were leaving, Isabella popped in, very close to tears when she saw how bad Benny looked. She felt guilty, as this wouldn't have happened if the boys had gone straight home. Benny would hear nothing of it, and told her that she and

Lizzie were one of the best things that had happened to him. She'd bought him some flowers and grapes which Benny said would make a change from all the cake. He never thought he'd hear himself saying such a thing. Samuel sent his love but was looking after Lizzie.

ISABELLA

Walking back from the hospital, Isabella bumped into Samuel and Lizzie, walking Diesel, Betty's greyhound. Lizzie loved dogs and Betty said it would do her a favour as she and Sindy had a busy day. Samuel had picked her up from school and he said Lizzie was shrieking with excitement when she saw who was with him. Together they let Diesel have a run on the beach and suddenly they could see what these dogs were made to do. Run. He was simply running for the joy of it, on the warm soft sand, for what looked like miles down the beach. Coming back, they saw Betty and Sindy, which was convenient for all. They briefly discussed how learning their lines was coming along. Betty said she couldn't wait to be the prompt, and would know everyone's lines by the time the show started. Isabella thought Sindy seemed a little quiet, but it had been an emotional day, so that was not surprising. It was time to go their separate ways and Lizzie spent some minutes saying goodbye to Diesel before she was prepared to part with him.

'She's going to be asking me to get a greyhound now, every day, for the next year at least,' Isabella laughed, as she and Samuel followed Lizzie's sorrowful gaze.

As they walked back, through the car park, Isabella thought she recognised the shape of someone from the past, just the walk and the way he held his head. No, surely, she was mistaken. It couldn't be. Samuel had been chatting to Lizzie about fossils and hadn't noticed. Isabella decided it was the shock of Benny's ordeal, bringing back bad memories into her mind.

JACK

Jack was pleased that he had such exciting news to bring Benny at visiting time. Benny's offer had been accepted; the agents had said the current owners were 'over the moon'. It was in solicitors' hands and because it was a cash sale, everything should proceed quickly. Jack had plans drawn up, ready to show Benny when he was home. Benny had also been as busy as was possible, stuck in a hospital bed. He'd made a list of everything he would need for the project, together with costings and approximate delivery times. Things were really progressing now and Benny said as soon as he was out of hospital, they should tell their friends.

Jack also had today's edition of *Seabourne Matters*. The whole thing was splendid. There was a large headline apology, lots of photos of the theatre being refurbished, all the details of the pantomime and players, and a personal note from Mr Davison that he hoped all the good people of Seabourne would lend their support. Tickets were going to be sold from the newspaper offices, at £1 each and 50p for children. This was just what they needed. They chatted whilst eating some of the remaining cake from yesterday. Jack was pleased to see that some of the bandages had been removed already and that Benny was also learning his lines. Apparently, all the nurses had joined in and wanted tickets already which was encouraging, as Jack knew the theatre had a lot of seats to fill.

Dot had said they should do two nights: Friday 31st December and Saturday 1st January, with a matinee on the Saturday afternoon as well. Benny and Jack had quite a lot on their plates right now.

LOST IN FRANCE

The following day, he picked up some wine, bread and cheese for supper and continued on to the *bureaux de post* where he picked up his new copy of *Seabourne Matters* and read it with interest. So, the previous week's article had been total rubbish, he thought as much. He was delighted to see that Betty was still alive, active and obviously knee deep in this new project to get the Mermaid Theatre back into shape. He was so grateful that he had seen the photo, as this was the ignition he needed to go back home, to his only family.

She was still alive too. Of course, she was! Women like that don't give up until they're at least 105. From the photo, she looked just the same. She still had that haughty cut to her jib, irritating but irresistible expression of grandeur, and that smile. He hadn't seen that smile in nearly fifty years and looking at it again, he realised it had haunted him. He had made his mind up, enough time had been wasted in his life and if he wasn't careful, he would be too late. He spent the morning writing letters, paying bills, and preparing to leave his life in France to spend the rest of his days back home, in Seabourne. He had many friends here however and decided to visit them and say goodbye over the next couple of days. A plane ticket was purchased, it was final and he would be in England by next weekend. There was a lot he would miss here; the food, the wine, the coffee, the charming language, but so much more to reclaim back home. His beautiful, shining, laughing sister. Blast that Turner chap, writing back all those years ago and saying she had died, what kind of a person would do that? He wondered what sort of life Betty had lived with the man and hoped that she had had some happiness.

So many of his letters and photographs had been returned from England, back to France. He'd kept them, although they were fading and going yellow with age, and they smelled, somehow, of sadness. He thought he'd lost her. And now, very soon, they would be reunited, an unaccustomed feeling of excitement was rising in his chest. He had only ever rented his apartment in Paris, and so there was no house to sell. Claudette, his wife, had died some years ago and there had been no children, they had spent years hoping, but it was not to be.

BETTY AND SINDY

Betty knew what the letter would say as soon as it hit the doormat. Sindy wasn't downstairs yet, so she made a cup of tea and took it to her room. The bathroom was occupied and Betty didn't need to read it to confirm that Sindy was expecting. The poor lamb was reaching something dreadful. Ginger, that's what Betty remembered would help. She had some ginger ale somewhere in the cupboard, so she poured a glass for Sindy and left the tray outside the bathroom, saying that she was happy to talk when Sindy wanted to.

A little later, and Sindy emerged, looking better but tired, and threw herself on the sofa next to Betty. They opened the letter together, yes, the doctor had confirmed what they already knew. Decisions needed to be made.

'The first thing you need to think about, my love is whether you want to keep this baby. You are very young with your whole life ahead of you. The baby will take all your strength, love, time, money, everything. They can be hard work even when they are planned, more so in your situation Sindy love. Having said that, you are a very caring, thoughtful girl and a child is a joy. You only have to look at poor Clara to realise how different her life might have been if she had been blessed with a little'n before her husband had gone to war.'

Sindy sat quietly listening to all her nan had to say, before she said, 'I'm definitely keeping it nan. It's part of me and part of him and I'm not going to kill it. I've been thinking about it all night and this is the right decision. Even if Paul doesn't want anything more to do with us, I'm not going to change my mind.'

'You've got an old head on those young shoulders, my love. I will support you for as long as I've got, but remember, I'm an old girl now, I won't be around forever.'

'Don't say that, nan. I won't let you go, ever,' and Sindy jumped up, flinging her arms around Betty's shoulders.

Oh, that unshakeable optimism that was youth, Betty thought and smiled. This was going to be a lot for her to help with, but she'd do all she could.

They both thought that Sindy should tell Paul next, and that there was no time like the present. Paul lived with Jack in the family home. Sindy dialled his number and, luckily, he was in. They agreed to meet at Betty's because Sindy needed some privacy and also the comfort of her surroundings. He was delighted that she had called, and, after showering, splashing on way too much Brut, and finding his clean jeans, he was off, on his new Chopper bike, which had been a birthday gift from Jack.

Within ten minutes, the doorbell chimed and they both went into the lounge to talk, Paul completely unaware of what was on Sindy's mind. Although heavily tempted to eavesdrop, Betty went into the kitchen and tried very hard to listen to the radio. It was Diddy David Hamilton, who was on Radio One and Radio Two apparently because of cut backs. Betty wasn't really enjoying "Blinded by the Light" and couldn't make out what the song was even about, or indeed "The Killing of Georgie", which she thought was an odd thing to make a song about, but then Acker Bilk came on the radio, which was much more up her street.

It was about half an hour before they both came out of the lounge. They were holding hands and Sindy had obviously been crying.

Paul spoke first, 'Mrs Turner, I am sorry. I should have been much more responsible; I am seventeen now after all.'

Sindy went to interrupt, but Paul continued: 'Sindy and I

have talked about this, and we are both going to be the best Mum and Dad this little baby could have. I know we won't have much money, but I can get a job, and we might have to take up your offer of a home for a while until we can get on our feet.' This was the longest sentence that Betty had heard Paul utter.

'Then congratulations are in order for the both of you,' Betty replied and drew the pair of them in for a hug.

'I'd like to tell Jack and Aunt Clara before we tell anyone else. Sindy is okay with this, aren't you angel?' Paul continued, 'Benny comes out of hospital tomorrow so let's wait until then.' Betty agreed, as Jack had been through quite a bit recently.

Betty thought the next step after this would probably be going to see Pat and Doreen, his wife. *Blimey, that was going to be more painful than childbirth,* Betty thought, and wondered if there was any way she could soften the blow.

DOT

Now that people had been reading through their lines for a while, it was time to organise rehearsals. Dot had checked with Clara who was happy for them to rehearse at least once a week in the theatre. Dot thought Monday evenings would work and this appeared to suit most people, when she asked the following morning whilst swimming. They all remarked that dipping, without Benny being there, was not the same and everyone was looking forward to his return. Rehearsals would start next Monday when Benny had been home for a few days and could manage to get out and about.

There were many props to be made, Dot was quite handy and had made a start with a huge *papier-mâché* pumpkin, and a plywood cut out of a coach and horses, which Samuel had made for her and which she was rather enjoying painting and decorating with glitter and tinsel. There were also costumes to be altered, scenery to be painted and make up to be purchased. This might involve a trip to London to the stage make up shop, they had everything, she recalled. Whilst thinking about a trip to London, Dot realised, that with all that had been going on recently, she had completely forgotten it was her birthday next week.

That evening, she mentioned it to Rob, who had also forgotten. He suggested a trip to London to see the new Andrew Lloyd Webber musical, as he knew Dot was keen. Then he added that why not see if any of the cast wanted to come along and they could make an evening of it, perhaps a bite to eat as well. Dot's eyes welled up, as this was so thoughtful and a little unexpected. She would check with the gang tomorrow and then they could book some tickets and think about a restaurant. Rob said he would treat them all to the tickets; he'd been paid for his big project, with a bonus for doing it within budget, so he was feeling a little flush. Also, and more importantly, he said, this was Dots' fiftieth birthday. Quite a landmark and he wanted her to remember it as a special night.

Dot was so very pleased to see Benny and Jack down at the beach the next morning. Benny wasn't ready to swim yet, and so he sat on the bench with Betty and Clara and seemed to be just enjoying being outside, with his friends, in the sunshine. Everyone enthusiastically welcomed him back. Clara had brought down another cake, but said not to worry as Mrs Jackson had made it this time.

Dot mentioned her birthday idea to go and see 'Jesus Christ, Superstar' and Clara said that she had also been thinking about booking tickets. Indeed, they all thought it would be a fitting way for their 'Director' to celebrate such an occasion. It was settled, they would go next Thursday which was her birthday, as long as Rob could book enough tickets. It would be ten of them and they agreed the train would be best. Dot felt really warm inside and grateful that her new friends wanted to celebrate with her.

CLARA

Clara was very pleased with the way the refurbishments and also the pantomime plans were going. Everyone was really pulling together, it reminded her of the happier times during the war. She was just having an afternoon cup of tea when the telephone rang. Goodness, it was like Piccadilly Circus these days at Rutland Manor, and she rather liked it. It was Betty, and she wondered if Clara could possibly pop over sometime. Betty couldn't manage Clara's steps and even the sloping driveway would be too much without someone to push her. Clara sensed that Betty wanted to talk privately and said she would be over in about an hour. She very much hoped Betty wasn't unwell as she had been complaining of a general aching feeling lately.

Clara knocked and thought Betty must have been almost standing behind the door, she opened it so quickly, *this must be exciting, or serious, or both,* she thought.

'Come in dear, I've just put the kettle on and got some fresh Earl Grey from the posh supermarket in Cliffbourne. That is the one you like, isn't it?'

'Betty, that is really kind of you to go to so much trouble. I'm thinking that what you want to talk about is quite serious, so let's get down to business.'

'I wish we had been friends twenty years ago, because I am so very fond of you,' Betty said, patting Clara's hand. The two sat down, leaving the tea to brew in the pot. 'I am betraying a confidence now, and I hope you will understand why I'm doing this,' Betty began.

'Because Sindy is pregnant, with young Paul being the

father?' Clara replied. 'I'm assuming that you wouldn't have told me yourself if there wasn't a very good reason, so go on...'

'Yes, of course. They are both adamant that they want to keep the baby and settle down together, and I am going to do all I can to support them. Paul says he's going to find work now and I have said they can live with me until they find something better, I have a nice big back bedroom.' Betty started to fill Clara in. 'It's not ideal but I wouldn't seek to change their minds. The big fly in the ointment is my son, Patrick.'

Clara interrupted, 'Betty, please don't say any more, I am well aware of the shortcomings of your son, sorry dear, but he is a bit of a pompous twit, isn't he?' Both women tried hard to stifle their laughter and then it burst out. Clara reached for her lace handkerchief, as if that was going to help. Neither woman had had a fit of the giggles in about forty years and it was so cathartic. They needed to do this more often. It was Betty who pulled herself together first:

So, Clara, I'm trying to think of a pre-plan, if you like, to help smooth things out. I have had an idea and I wanted to see what you thought, another cup my dear?'

I think this is definitely a two-cup afternoon, Betty, thank you. No, you sit back, let me be mother, oh, good heavens, what am I saying?' More laughter followed.

The afternoon continued in a surprisingly light hearted way, with both of them wanting the best outcome for the youngsters. The plan they had come up with was clever and sounded like it could work. Marriage had not been mentioned by either Sindy or Paul, most probably because they didn't have the money, were feeling embarrassed about the situation and wanted to play things down, however Clara had an idea.

'I don't want to overplay my hand here, but from what I have seen of Patrick and Doreen, they are keen *to keep up with the Joneses* and often worried about *what the neighbours will say*, would that be about right?'

Betty nodded, feeling slightly ashamed of her prig of a son and his wife.

'So then,' continued Clara, 'nothing would be lost, and a lot gained, if we encouraged Paul to propose to Sindy. I can cover the cost of the whole thing, actually it would be my pleasure, and we can turn an accident into a very fortuitous marriage for their daughter, as Paul and Jack will jointly inherit my estate upon my death. Yes, of course they are too young, but Patrick is not daft; he might even guess about the baby, but it won't matter when they're married and settled.'

'That is a very clever idea, and along the same lines as I was thinking. It is also exceptionally generous of you,' Betty replied, smiling now. A lot of people would have said *are you sure?* but one just didn't ask Clara that sort of question.

Betty continued, 'goodness you should be in politics with your ability to manipulate a situation.' They both laughed again and said that the two newly-weds could decide to live with Betty or Clara as they chose, until they got themselves sorted out. Betty also confessed to feeling in a fair bit of discomfort these days and confided in Clara that she had an appointment in about a week to see the doctor in Cliffbourne. Clara was pleased to hear that Betty was going to see someone.

They both agreed to *keeping mum* over the next few days, which almost caused another fit of giggles. Clara would wait to hear their news and then suggest the marriage idea to Paul. Betty understood that Sindy would be cross if she knew how this had all come about, but also knew she would prefer to have her mum and dad see the whole thing in a positive light.

BENNY

It was Benny's first day back at work after the attack, and he was a little nervous. Some of his colleagues greeted him kindly but many, having heard on the grape-vine what it was all about, were cool and distant, clearly uncomfortable with their newly acquired knowledge about him. These were mostly men that he'd been working with for years; they had enjoyed a productive, professional relationship and plenty of the homemade cakes that he'd taken into the office, but things had changed. It brought it home to Benny that he would encounter a lot of this type of behaviour now. He wasn't sorry that he wouldn't be there much longer and it confirmed that he had made the right decision to hand in his notice the following day.

It was wonderful to get home and see Jack, who had made dinner, candles and everything, at his place. Paul was out with Sindy, they seemed to have something on their minds, leaving Jack and Benny to themselves. Benny's plans were surging ahead now, and he felt it was time to tell their friends. They decided to tell them tomorrow morning after swimming, so Benny made some flapjacks, flavoured with cinnamon and nutmeg; Jack was always happy to test new recipes and he thought these tasted of autumn. Jack had been tasting a lot of new biscuits, cakes and pastry recently and had no complaints whatsoever. He knew Benny's bold new venture was going to be a roaring success.

The new premises couldn't have been better; there had been an old-fashioned pie shop there for as long as Benny could remember, the kitchen and ovens were clean and functional. The current owners were retiring and so there would be some trade straight away. In fact, there wasn't too much work to be done at all. Benny had ideas to change it in the future, when he'd got into the swing of things and started making some money. He had plans for the next six months all organised, for everything he needed to purchase, and exactly what he would bake each week. He would change it seasonally and have a special cake on each day. He was going to do lunches for train journeys, as the sandwiches from the station left a lot to be desired. Christmas, which Benny adored, was an exciting project. Cakes, puddings and mince pies for which he had some brilliant recipes, would be loaded into the window, and he would dress it with huge bunches of greenery to set the scene. Picnics for the beach next summer, would also be on his menu. He was bursting with ideas. Initially he would bake late evening and early morning and then work at the counter throughout the day, but if things took off, then he might employ some help to serve. It was all moving quickly now and the one thing he couldn't decide on was the name.

'It should be *Benjamin's,*' Jack said, he thought it sounded up-market and Benny deserved the credit which he would inevitably get, once word got round about his delicious food.

Benny thought it should be *Esther's,* after his grandmother, after all, he wouldn't have been able to do this without her encouragement throughout his life and the money she had left him.

Jack won in the end, as they thought *Benjamin's Bakery* rolled off the tongue a little easier. The painting of the shop sign, bags, price lists and lots more had to be organised. He needed a logo. They had both seen the impressive artwork that Sindy just doodled when she wasn't doing anything else, and Benny decided to ask if she would help.

As if on cue, Sindy and Paul walked in. Benny offered them coffee and flapjacks and asked if they could sit down and have a chat. Paul glanced at Sindy and replied 'that's funny, we were just going to ask you guys the same thing.'

Paul and Sindy told them their news. Jack wasn't exactly surprised although he was cross with Paul for not taking precautions. A little late for that now. Benny was delighted for them and couldn't wait to do some babysitting when the time came. Jack said that they could obviously live there as well if they wanted to, although the house was a little damp and really needed updating. It was Paul's home and they also had enough room.

Both Jack and Benny congratulated them and wished them luck in their life together, which unbeknown to them, made an easy lead-in for what Paul had been preparing to say. He had been thinking about it all day and knew this was the right thing to do. He produced a Christmas cracker ring from his pocket and got down on one knee.

'Sindy, I know this is all a bit of a shock, but I love you. Will you marry me?'

ISABELLA

Isabella had a brilliant idea; the panto needed some children. Everyone loved to see little kids doing a fairy dance and she was in a perfect position to organise this, with her classes. A bonus would be that all the mums and dads, grans and granddads would definitely want tickets. She decided to pop round and chat this through with Dot and see if there was an appropriate point in the panto for her idea.

Dot was delighted to see her and they both realised there was a brilliant spot, in front of main curtains when the scenery was being changed for 'The Ball,' and so a song and some tap dancing would help to mask the noise. Isabella had a class of fifteen, a perfect number for a simple song and dance routine, the children would love it and it would be confidence building. They enjoyed a coffee together and then Isabella realised time was getting on and she needed to get back.

This time, she was not mistaken. She *had* seen Neil. Today he had been lurking in a passageway in the High Street on the other side of the road. When she saw him, he had quickly ducked into another alley and was gone. She should have realised that the articles in the paper would not go unnoticed by him, if he was in the country. Things had been going so very well for her lately. Lizzie was happy at school, the flat was just right, her new friends, everything. And she knew there was only one reason Neil had turned up here; to spoil it all for her and Lizzie in some way.

She wasn't sure who to turn to at first; Samuel was hot tempered and she needed to think this through before she told him. Her relationship with Will was developing slowly and she didn't want to do or say anything to mess it up, as although it was early days, she felt he was the one. Benny, of course. She knew Benny had been through an awful lot lately but he had an inner calm; she felt she could tell him anything without being judged. The next day, a couple of hours before swimming, she could hear him clattering about in his kitchen so she gave him a knock and asked if he would pop into hers for a chat.

Isabella told her difficult story. Many tears, cups of tea, and flapjacks later, Benny gave her a very gentle hug as he was still quite sore in lots of places. Benny, being Benny, reminded her that the silver lining was Lizzie and that she had a lot of friends and support. He joked that now that he'd handled a gang of twenty plus, he could easily take on a loser like Neil, which did make her laugh. He understood how she felt about everything, however, he was adamant, that she should confide in Will and that if his feelings for her were genuine, this would not make any difference. He hoped he was right. This chap was clearly watching her and Benny felt that the less she was on her own at the moment, the better. Benny gave Jack a call to say that he would be missing swimming today and would fill him in later, then they got Lizzie ready together and Benny walked them both to school and then straight on to the police station.

Will was delighted, if a bit surprised, to see them both and they all went into an interview room to talk privately. Benny just sat quietly for moral support, whilst Isabella, for the second time that morning, told her story. Somehow, sitting in the police station, telling Will all the sordid details, it felt even worse and took her right back to when it happened. She noticed the pain in Will's face as she spoke, and mistook it for disgust until he got up, apologised to Benny for not being very professional, and just took her in his arms and held her, whilst tears poured down both of their cheeks. Benny was also quietly sobbing, and realised this was his exit signal. He wandered outside and noticed that *his* bakery was just a couple of doors down, there was nowhere to get a coffee around here, and so he added this to his list of services.

After hearing everything, Will said he couldn't believe how strong she had been and that he was more in love with her than ever. It slipped out, just like that, and they both looked at each other. He then apologised and said that although he hadn't planned to say this yet, as he was worried it would frighten her off, he was not going to retract it and that was how things were for him, at least. It was Isabella's turn to reassure Will and she told him exactly how she felt.

Once Isabella had left, safely with Benny, Will did a police background check on Neil Cartwright. He'd had a variety of names, but from the detailed description that she'd given him, this was their man. He was wanted for a string of really nasty offences, mostly against women, but also burglary and many forms of assault. Will smiled to himself as this type of man would be easy enough to find now and bring to justice for the many lives he had fractured. They had caught the London thugs last week and they were on trial at The Old Bailey for even more serious crimes, Benny's ordeal would be added to the list. They wouldn't be seeing daylight for a long time; he knew the judge that was sitting and their luck had run out. Will called in some favours from various friends in the force and put out an APB on Neil. Will hoped so very much that he would be the one to catch this piece of shit.

DOT

The theatre tickets were in Rob's wallet, the restaurant booked. It was all organised and tomorrow was the big day. *Where had fifty years gone?* Dot had bought a new suit in *Richard Shops* and felt like the cat's whiskers. She went to bed that evening feeling happy and grateful for her husband, their friends and life in general. This felt wonderful, especially after being so low for such a long time. She woke up to breakfast in bed, a pretty card and some flowers from Rob. They had decided no other gifts as Rob had spent quite a bit on the tickets.

They both went down to have a quick dip and Rob was pleased to see such a turnout at the beach. All the cast were there, plus lots of the occasional dippers. Jack had brought Champagne, and Benny had outdone himself on the cake front. It was like a wedding cake, with several layers, all with seaside icing decorations on it. Everyone was amazed. They'd not seen anything like it before. It turned out that Sindy had designed it and Benny had turned those designs into icing. The cake was cut, 'happy birthday' sung, and then the champagne flowed, which felt rather bohemian as it was only actually 9am by that time. Jack took lots of pictures, thinking he might call these 'Early morning Fizz'.

The show was everything Dot had hoped it would be, they would be singing those songs for a long time to come, she felt. It had been really moving, and so up to the minute. It was helpful to be in a big theatre environment just now, as it gave her lots of ideas for their, rather more modest, performance. Dinner afterwards had been at an incredible Chinese restaurant with rather a scary owner who actually threw a meat cleaver at someone who queried the bill; thankfully not one of their party. They wandered through China Town on their way back to the station, enjoying the lanterns, and the sweet spicy smells, wafting from doorways. It had been a magical evening and had gone by too quickly. As they were just turning the corner into Gerrard Street, laughing and joking as they went, they almost bumped into her daughter, Margaret, out with a group of people. At first Dot thought that perhaps Rob had organised this, *how thoughtful of him,* but on looking at Margaret's face, she quickly realised that this was an accidental meeting and not a particularly happy one. Rob had probably drunk a little too much rice wine and was just about to say a rather loud hello, when Dot realised that Margaret intended to ignore them and was walking straight past. There had been no card in the post and she clearly didn't remember it was her mum's birthday at all. Worse than that, she obviously didn't even want to acknowledge her parents and their friends, in front of the people she was with. Dot just squeezed his hand and said quietly, 'Rob, she wants to ignore us, don't say anything,' which just put another crack in her heart, that Margaret had already broken quite a few times.

This sobered Rob up rather quickly. He stopped and put his arm around Dot. 'You are the loveliest, most intelligent, kindest woman and mother in the world. I would have given my eye teeth to have a mum like you, don't forget that my darling.' He gave her a quick peck on the cheek and they hurried to catch up with their friends.

NOT LOST IN FRANCE ANYMORE

Charles arrived at London Airport on time. He hadn't been back for over forty years and was astonished to see how much everywhere had changed. It was so built up compared to parts of France. On his taxi journey to Seabourne, he considered his options. He had booked in to a local hotel, and he could stay there for some time before venturing into Seabourne. One thing he did know, this was going to be a huge shock for Betty, perhaps he should write to her first? *He didn't think so.* What would her reaction be? Initially he felt she would be cross until she knew the full details and then she would be even more angry with her late husband.

Perhaps he should contact Clara first? She was a bit younger and possibly more able to help him blend back into Betty's life. They clearly knew each other these days, he could see that from the articles in the paper. From what he had read, Clara had lost her husband years and years ago. He wondered if she had married again, she was still Lady Clara Harrington, so possibly not.

There were so many question-marks for him at the moment, and he was starting to wonder if he had done the right thing at this stage of his life. *What life?* He had spent years in a POW camp, lost most of his memory until fairly recently, married the woman who was nursing him in the French hospital and then spent many years in an unhappy, childless relationship until her recent death. If he wasn't man-enough to make a go of the last few years left to him, he might as well end it all now. He was only 70 for goodness-sake, roughly the same age as Clara, he recalled.

Charles arrived at the well-kept up 1930s' Art Deco hotel, relieved to find the staff friendly, the room airy and bright and the bed rather comfortable. Looking out to the English Channel, he knew he had made the right decision. He settled himself on a squashy old leather sofa, with the latest edition of *Seabourne Matters*, and lit the cigar that he had been keeping for a while now. Browsing through the room service menu, he realised it had been a very long time since he'd had a 'full English' and was rather looking forward to that tomorrow.

CLARA

Betty, Sindy and Paul would be arriving shortly. Mrs Jackson thought Clara was unusually jittery today and wondered about the cause, even Clara herself realised she needed to regain her composure. She rearranged the lilies in their vase, adjusted the blinds in the drawing room so that the low, bright sunshine which reflected off the sea, didn't blind everyone. Eventually, Mrs Jackson brought them in and followed up with a tea tray.

Clara was pleased that Paul took the initiative and started speaking first. 'Aunt Clara, Sindy and I have some news for you. Sindy is expecting a baby and I am the father, and so, although we are young, I have asked Sindy to marry me and she has said yes. We wanted you to be one of the first to know.' Paul looked relieved to have got it all out in one go.

'Well, Paul, Sindy, this is a surprise but what a very happy piece of news, Congratulations on both fronts,' and Clara went up to Sindy, held her hand and welcomed her to the 'Harrington' family. There were further visitors at the door, and Mrs Jackson brought Jack and Benny in. Betty laughed as she and Clara realised that their plan had come together without them doing a single thing. Conversation then flowed easily amongst everyone and Clara beckoned Paul into the hallway, asking if she could borrow him for a moment.

'You have done the right thing young man, I'm proud of you,' Clara said whilst reaching in a drawer for a small '1837' blue box. She opened it to reveal a stunning diamond engagement ring. 'Your uncle bought this for me in New York in 1923, and I would very much like you to give it to Sindy as her engagement ring, I trust you have not purchased one yet?'

'This is incredible, Aunt Clara, thank you so very much. You're right, I proposed to her with a plastic ring out of a cracker.'

'Young man, I'm surprised she accepted you at all. Go and do it again, this time with a bit of style.' Clara replied, smiling and feeling so happy to be involved in all this. Peter would have loved it and poor Dennis, had he been well enough, would have enjoyed the celebrations.

Paul walked back into the drawing room, feeling ten feet tall. He got down on one knee and began, 'I know we have had a practice at this but, Aunt Clara has given us her treasured engagement ring and I would now like to do it properly. So, Sindy Turner, will you marry me?'

Jack turned his camera on quickly and started taking photos, he wasn't going to miss this.

'Yes, it's still yes, Paul Harrington.'

Paul slipped the ring on her finger; it could have been made for her. Clara couldn't help but think this was quite a *Cinderella* moment. Betty's eyes were filling up with happy tears which prompted Sindy to give her a kiss. They sat together for some time just holding hands and chatting about the baby, with Sindy glancing at her beautiful Tiffany engagement ring, every few seconds. Mrs Jackson popped in with some more tea and Clara asked her, as an old friend, to sit down and have a cup with them, telling her about the wedding news.

Clara announced that she would be very pleased to cover the cost of the wedding and that perhaps, under the circumstances, that should be sooner, rather than later. They decided that a reception at Rutland Manor would be the icing on the cake. Jack approached Clara, quietly thanked her, and gave her an unusually sensible hug.

'Now Jack, I know you are the oldest Harrington boy but I'm not sure my ring would have suited Benny anyway,' Clara said, perhaps a little louder than she meant to. Everyone looked over at Benny to see what his reaction to this would be.

'Quite honestly Clara, I'm much more of a sapphire man, myself,' and the whole room shook with happy, silly, laughter. 'Please give me the honour of making the cake,' Benny said to Paul and Sindy.

'That goes without saying, mate,' was Paul's response.

Sindy realised, amidst all this joy, that there was still a big hurdle to overcome. They hadn't asked her mum and dad yet. She would need their consent to get married. Clara came over to her, seeing her looking a bit concerned, and assured her that they would take this better than she thought. It was decided that they should go together to tell them, so that Clara could put a stop to any unpleasantness if necessary. She was more than a match for Pat Turner, Sindy realised, and as the gathering was finishing up anyway, Jack drove them round to Turners.

Pat was just closing up when the car arrived and he looked rather cross and surprised, thinking them to be late customers. Paul parked the car and opened the door for Clara, who got out in her usual finishing school style. Pat looked up and smiled.

'Lady Harrington, this is an unexpected pleasure. I was just closing up, but there's always time for you, of course. What can I find for you?'

This man was ingratiating. 'A cup of tea, if you happen to have the kettle on and half an hour of you and your good wife's time, if you can spare it.'

Sindy and Paul were getting out of the car and they all walked in together, through the dreary shop and into their brown and beige front room. Doreen, did have the kettle on and the best China was on a tray in pretty short order.

'Hello Sindy, Paul. So, what can we do for you Lady Harrington?' Doreen asked, she was a lot more relaxed than her husband and Clara hoped that after the wedding and baby's arrival, her relationship with her daughter might improve.

'Thank you for your kind hospitality, its Doreen, isn't it?' Clara was on a charm offensive. 'Dainty crockery, if you don't mind me saying, now, Sindy and Paul have some news for you, which they have already shared with me, as a close relative.'

Clara looked over to Paul and he began. 'Mr and Mrs Turner, I have proposed to Sindy and she has accepted. We know we are rather young, but I love her very much and we have come to ask for your blessing. If we have that, my aunt, Lady Harrington, is going to cover the cost of the wedding, and has kindly offered Rutland Manor for the reception. I am going to leave school and find a job, so that we can save up for our own home, but in the meantime, we will continue to live with Betty, as she is finding life a bit more difficult these days, as I am sure you already know, plus Sindy wants to continue caring for her.' Paul gained momentum as the speech went on.

Well said, that man, Clara thought.

Whilst Paul was speaking, Clara could see the cogs going round in Patrick's brain. Was this going to cost him anything? Apparently not. How could he benefit from this situation? Social standing in Seabourne was going to rocket, now that his daughter would be a 'Harrington'. How should he reply? Look attentive, suck up to the old girl, who knew, he might make money out of this eventually, and also continued free care for his mother was a bonus.

However, it was Doreen, who replied, much to Patrick's annoyance, but even *he* realised it would look rude to interrupt her.

'Congratulations, Sindy my dear. That's exciting news and of course you have our blessing. Don't forget I have my new knitting machine if there is any need for baby clothes at some time in the future.'

Sindy blushed slightly, Clara smiled and Patrick realised that he'd been hoodwinked somehow but wasn't exactly sure how it had been done.

BETTY AND SINDY

Betty could almost feel Sindy's excitement for the future, popping in the air, and she was so very happy for her. Many plans were being made now, both for the wedding, and, more privately, the baby. They had decided against an engagement party, but would have a get-together after the wedding ceremony. The date was fixed; 23rd October. This gave Sindy a few weeks to get everything ready but she wouldn't be showing very much by that date. She had agreed with Betty and Clara that they wouldn't tell her dad about the baby just yet. Her mum had obviously guessed, and that was okay. Sindy also wanted to have the first doctor's appointment done before telling anyone else or buying anything for the baby, and Betty thought that was very wise.

Benny was going to provide the wedding breakfast, as well as the cake, and that would be his gift to them. Everyone who had attended the funeral for his grandmother, said it was the best buffet they'd ever had. Benny made a note to add 'outside catering' to his list of services. Jack loved buying Champagne, and so that was also ticked off the list. It wasn't going to be a big 'do' as they both had small families, and not too many friends, with the exception of the dippers.

Doreen had telephoned Sindy and said that she would like to pay for a proper wedding car. She had a little money put by and it would really please her if Sindy and Paul would accept this. Sindy was touched, she had spoken more to her mum in the last couple of days than in the last year. Her mum also offered Sindy her old wedding dress, saying it wasn't very fashionable now, but Sindy could alter it or do whatever she liked with it.

Sindy remembered looking at their wedding photos from time to time. Her mum had an elegant figure and the 1950s dress showed it off brilliantly. It was very much like the one Audrey Hepburn wore in *Funny Face*. Sindy loved it. She was really excited and told Betty all about the call. Chatting over a cup of tea, they both wondered whether, if at first this news had been a bit of a shock, it might bring the family a little closer. *Funny how things turn out,* Betty thought. She was beginning to get a bit nervous about her forthcoming appointment with Dr Skudder, in Cliffbourne. Her general aches and pains seemed to be getting a bit worse and she was more tired these days, still there had been a lot on her mind lately, it was probably that. The doorbell rang and it was Jack.

'Afternoon girls, I was just passing and wondered if you'd like me to take the wedding photographs? Paul is ok with it but said you had the final say.' Sindy was thrilled as she'd seen Jack's work, it was modern and edgy and was exactly what she wanted.

'Thank you, Jack, I'd love that.' *Another thing off the list.*

Sindy had designed and drawn all the wedding stationery herself. The invitations were exquisite, with tiny images of mermaids, seahorses and fish, forming the border. When Benny saw his, he knew he'd made the right decision for the bakery, although they still hadn't had the opportunity to tell anyone about it yet.

BENNY

All those years, working for the Planning Department, and when Benny handed his notice in, Brian, his boss had been very cold. Strange really, because they had always got on well together at work and Benny suspected that Brian might actually be gay as well. Perhaps that was *why* he appeared so cross and said that Benny might as well clear his desk and leave straight away. That suited Benny as he had a hell of a lot of things to do at the moment.

That afternoon, being unexpectedly free, he put on his new Hot Chocolate tape, got the oven up to temperature and made a large assortment of little pies, cakes and biscuits. He decided to take them down tomorrow morning to get people's opinions for the wedding buffet. The lemon meringue pies looked like they had come out of a magazine, and he'd experimented with coffee Viennese whirls, and some rose petal shortbread, which really did melt in the mouth. When Jack came over that evening, he'd had to stop him eating the whole lot.

The following morning, the sky was ablaze with colour, the sun was rising and the oranges, purples and pinks were changing minute by minute. Jack did his best with the Polaroid, but couldn't really capture the intensity of it and he decided to treat himself to a new camera for the wedding. He fancied a Pentax, which was what David Bailey was using at the moment. He really admired that man's work.

The colourful skyline had brought nearly all the dippers out, even Betty and Clara had come down for the sunrise and Benny felt it was time to share his excitement.

He banged a cake tin to get everyone's attention. 'So, guys, now you've all heard about Sindy and Paul's wedding plans, I wanted to tell you that I also have some exciting news. I have left my job and am starting a new business, in just a couple of weeks.'

Samuel called out, whilst devouring his third piece of shortbread, 'well if it isn't a bakery, you've made the wrong decision, Benny-boy.'

'Funny you should say that Samuel, as that's exactly what it is.' Benny went on to tell everyone all the details, and as Sindy was there, asked if she would do some artwork for him. Sindy beamed and got her notebook out there and then and started sketching. Isabella was overjoyed for him once she'd heard the story. Everyone was. Clara said she would be putting an order in each week, so he'd better get busy. Betty was delighted for him; he was such a kind lad. Even Diesel seemed to be extra happy and jumped about wildly, trying to procure himself one of the fine smelling things that were just out of his reach, up on the sea wall. Dot said Benny should definitely add birthday and wedding cakes to his menus. Jack thought it wouldn't be long before Benny would need some help and Paul volunteered straight away. The thought of working alongside Benny, with food, would be his dream job. This was an excellent bit of news.

'I won't be able to pay you very much to start with, until I get really busy, is that okay?' Benny asked, a bit concerned that it might take a while to get enough trade.

'I'd happily work for nothing, just to get some experience and be around all those things you make,' Paul replied.

CLARA

Clara was impressed with just how much Sindy was organising, and being so thrifty. She was certainly not taking advantage, if anything, Clara wished she would consider spending a little more and had offered to pay for some really special wedding flowers, which Sindy accepted gracefully. They had gone to the church together, with Paul and Jack, and Clara was astonished to see the vicar who had married her and Peter, still working and not looking very much older.

Heavens, he must be at least a hundred, she thought. Perhaps there was something in religion. She turned her attention to what he had to say, it all sounded straight forward. They had just enough time for the banns to be read. Clara thanked the vicar and reminded him of her own wedding. He recalled it immediately and said how smart Peter had looked in his Naval uniform. *Impressive memory,* she thought.

Together, the four of them made their way to the theatre, to see how things were progressing, as the first rehearsal was tonight. They found Rob and Samuel hard at it; well, they were having a tea break, listening to Kid Jensen on the radio, but they had made a huge amount of progress since Clara's last visit. All the windows had been mended or replaced, frames painted and the walls given a new coat of turquoise paint. There was some delicate silver painting work to be done on some of the ornate fixings and Sindy volunteered to do that. Whilst looking around, Sindy noticed the original poster for *Cinderella* still hanging in the foyer. It was far too precious to be thrown away and Sindy decided to carefully pop it in her bag, and bring it back, as much as she could, to its' original state, thinking it would be a lovely surprise for Clara. The auditorium was looking fit for purpose again and Clara was delighted, they would be ready to hang all the curtains in a week or two. There was still a lot of work to be done backstage though, and Clara asked Rob if he needed more help.

'I'll help,' volunteered Paul, he was so eager to do his bit. That was two more on the team and would aid the progress considerably. Clara also thought perhaps a working weekend, where they all pitched up and did whatever Rob needed, would speed progress. They decided the coming weekend would be just right, before Benny's opening. Clara was happy with the way things were going inside. Outside, however The Mermaid Theatre looked more than a little shabby and she and Rob chatted about it, whilst walking around the pier. The original copper roof was in good order, but the walls and window frames badly needed a coat of paint. Rob said this would be quite a job, especially with autumn and winter approaching. He did know of a company, though, and would give the chap a ring tonight. There was also the matter of a ten-foot silver mermaid, on the front elevation above the entrance, that Rob said looked like it needed attention. Clara corrected him, '*she* needs attention, she's not as young as she was.' Rob smiled. It was time to get home and have some food, before the rehearsals began this evening and they left, looking forward to coming back later.

ISABELLA

She hadn't seen Neil again. This was probably due to the fact that Will had hardly left her side, and when he wasn't with her, Benny was. Will had suggested that he move-in with Isabella if she would like that for a few weeks. Although it had seemed rather early in their relationship, she felt safe with him there and Lizzie loved his company. They played silly games together, which Isabella sometimes lacked the energy for. Samuel had to be told about Neil's presence in Seabourne and he was, as predicted by Isabella, enraged. Will had to tell him in no uncertain terms that he shouldn't go looking for Neil. This wouldn't help anyone and might end up making things worse. Will assured Samuel that Neil would 'get what was coming to him' but that he must leave it to the police. However, Samuel was on the alert now, constantly looking to keep his precious Isabella and Lizzie safe. Isabella had alerted the school, as she had no idea of exactly why he was back, only that she felt they were both in possible danger. She didn't want Lizzie to feel scared though, and so life carried on as normal. As Neil had found her anyway, there was no point in missing all the pantomime fun and so Isabella threw herself into learning her lines with a vengeance and was feeling quite confident already.

Dot had given her a list of the songs she would like to include and Isabella had chatted about them at school with the music teacher, Miss Abbot. They agreed it was a fair selection and Miss Abbot, said it all sounded so promising and she wished she was involved. Isabella felt sure Dot would be happy with her inviting Miss Abbot, to come along to the rehearsal this evening and see what she thought then.

Lizzie was also coming along and when she got tired, she could doze on 'her' sofa which it had become, covered with some colourful old shawls and rugs that Clara had rediscovered, backstage. The scene with the children had been agreed; they would be dressing up as magic fairies and dancing along to Bibbidi bobbidi boo, whilst the pumpkin was changed into a shining coach and horses, for Cinderella. The first rehearsal at school had been chaotic to say the least, but Isabella could see that it didn't really matter how professional the dance was, the kids were so cute, although she was going to do her best to get them in time with the music.

DOT

Dot thought she was early, but most of the cast were already there at six forty-five, excited to get started. They were all pleased to meet Miss Abbot, who said they could call her Joyce, but in fact she remained Miss Abbot because she was a teacher through and through and somehow calling her by her first name just seemed wrong. There was a really old *Bechstein* piano just to the side of the stage and Samuel pulled up a stool for her to see what she thought. Although it desperately needed tuning, Miss Abbot astonished everyone. She was a gentle, diminutive lady, with a soft grey bun and slightly milky-blue eyes but once behind the ivories, things changed. They were all expecting a variation of "All Things Bright and Beautiful" but instead, she started playing some *Oscar Peterson, Duke Ellington* and *Miles Davis* with the most incredible flourish and without any piano music whatsoever. Samuel grabbed Isabella and they started dancing on the stage, Benny and Jack just clapped to the music and Dot stood there for quite some time with her mouth slightly open. She needed to change some of her suggested songs to something a lot more upbeat. This lady could really play.

Just as Miss Abbot had moved on to "Now you has Jazz" from High Society, Clara walked in, actually singing along. She had been listening for a few minutes outside and realised immediately who was behind the piano. Once Miss Abbot had finished playing, Isabella was about to introduce Clara but there was no need. The two ladies already knew each other and were delighted to meet again after, they thought, at least twenty years, probably thirty.

'Well, Joyce,' Clara was happy to use her Christian name, 'that is certainly the way to start our first evening of rehearsals. Thank you. Glad to have you on board.'

'We're going to rock this place,' was Miss Abbot's quiet response.

The evening went from strength to strength. Everyone had made a huge effort to learn their lines and they all agreed that rehearsing on the actual stage really brought home what they would be doing, for real, in a couple of months' time. Dot was in her element, they ran through the whole thing, with her making changes, giving the thumbs up to some ideas, and down to others. Everyone had suggestions to enhance their parts, and it worked really well. Miss Abbot added musical sound effects or the occasional bar of popular music when she felt it added to the story. She was incredible, and Isabella remarked to Dot that she must be rather uninspired in her school job.

The following morning, the sun seemed enormous as it rose over the headland. The feeling of being in the sea, watching the pale apricot ball shining over the pewter rippling waves was enveloping. There was no need to talk as they all faced the sun's rays, and Dot offered up a silent prayer of thanks to whoever was up there. The sea was cooling down now and getting out and dry was important, before you started shivering too much. Hot drinks were shared with those who had forgotten them and everyone felt their day was already rejuvenated before it had even started.

JACK AND BENNY

There were just a few days to go now before the grand opening of 'Benjamin's Bakery' and Benny could not have been more excited. He had worked hard and planned everything, right down to the last fairy cake. Samuel and Rob had taken a break from the theatre work and painted the whole interior in, what would be, Benny's trademark colours; shell pink and a very light blue. It was unusual and a bit daring, but he had carried on the whole seaside theme right through to the napkins. Sindy had been busy with his logo, using the same colours, including shells, sand castles, buckets and spades, waves and seahorses. The bakery looked like something out of a seaside fairy-tale which was exactly the look Benny was aiming for.

Everything was ready, he just needed to fill those glass shelves with tempting products. Behind the counter, Jack had found a large mirror which Sindy had decorated with drift wood, sea glass and shells. Next to that, they had decided to hang a blackboard to show what was available that day and the price. A very old and rather ornate metal till had been discovered right at the back of one of the cupboards and they all agreed it would be just the job.

Unbeknown to Benny, Clara had had a further word in Mr Davison's shell-like, suggesting he send a reporter round to take lots of photos of the bakery, do an 'exclusive' interview with Benny and promote all the services he was going to be offering. Benny had just finished polishing the shelves and windows when he heard the old-fashioned bell go and he was surprised to see a young man, equipped with a huge camera, asking if Benny could spare half an hour. What luck! This would really boost opening day which was to be Friday 1st October.

Jack was so pleased for Benny, after the horrible attack, things were really looking up. Jack was thinking how he could help on 'opening day' and this was very much in his mind as he went in for a meeting with his boss, he had no idea what this was about but was hoping it might be a new project as he was coming to the end of his current one. Steve offered him a seat and said he a had a date that Jack needed to keep free. Steve had a 'once in a lifetime' opportunity for Jack in London, it would be working long hours, and he would be 'on call almost twenty-four hours a day. It would probably take about two weeks, initially. Steve felt this job would really put Jack's name about in the architectural world as he was going to get the chance to work with a very famous architect on an already, impressive building. It was partly built, but there was a lot of detailed work still to be done.

'So, are you up for it, Jack?' Steve didn't really need to ask as this was a real step up on the ladder and Steve had called in a few favours to get Jack on the team.

'Consider me in, when do I start?'

'They're having the initial meeting on Friday 1st October, so I'll need you to be up there the day before. Your hotel and all expenses will be paid for the next two weeks.'

'Thanks Steve, I really appreciate you trusting me with this.' *Oh God, how do I tell Benny?* he thought as he went out through the door.

BETTY AND SINDY

As they went through the door into the surgery, the familiar, strong smell of ether hit Sindy's nostrils and she had to go straight to the ladies. Betty's appointment had come round quite quickly, with everything else that was going on. The doctor gave her a very full examination and said he would like to have some tests done at the hospital. Blood and urine first then a possible scan. Sindy came in with Betty and asked what he was looking for. Dr Skudder said it was too early to say but these tests would give him more idea as to what was wrong and that it was difficult with general aches and pains. However, he thought Betty looked a bit pale and was probably anaemic and so he prescribed some iron tablets. Sindy was relieved that he was getting things checked and hadn't dismissed it as old age. They went to the chemists and a few other shops and felt that as it was such a warm afternoon, they should perhaps have a walk along the front and make a bit of a day of it.

Cliffbourne was a pretty seaside town and the two decided to have a cup of coffee and a slice of cake there, partly because they fancied one but also to see what sort of competition Benny had in the general area. The cakes were very 'shop bought' and nowhere near Benny's high standards. Whilst chatting about the bakery opening, a tall, oldish gentleman walked in and beckoned the waitress. He was very well turned out and when asking for a table near the window, he was clearly well spoken, with a slight accent. Sindy didn't really take much notice, but Betty hadn't taken her eyes off him from the moment he had appeared. It was almost like she'd seen a ghost.

'You okay nan? You've gone a bit pale.'

'I'm alright Sindy love, it's just that man, you see him there, on the other table, reminds me so much of my brother, Charles, it's something about his voice and the way he walked in. Silly me, just an old lady going doodle-alley. What were we talking about love?'

CHARLES

As Sindy was about to reply, the man got up, walked over slowly and asked if he could possibly join them. Betty was speechless and so Sindy nodded her consent and he pulled up a chair. The waitress came over and moved his things across and he ordered a tea, no milk but a …

'slice of lemon on the side,' Betty interrupted, and she looked up into his face.

'It can't be. I thought you were dead. Where have you been all this time? Why didn't you write, Charlie? Have you any idea of just how much I've missed you? Where the hell have you been?' Her questions just kept coming, until Sindy put her hand lightly on her arm.

'Nan, is this your brother, the one from the war? Sindy couldn't quite believe it either.

Charles spoke then, 'Betty, I don't know where to start. There is so much I have to tell you, but the first thing is that I have been writing to you these past twenty years and your husband has been returning all the letters and photos, telling me that you didn't want anything to do with me and more recently, that you had died. I stopped writing then. I have all my returned letters at the hotel with me so I can show you them if you don't believe me. I'm so very sorry to have to tell you this. I have just returned from living in France, having seen your photo in Seabourne Matters.'

'Why were you reading that paper?' was the only question that had formed in Betty's shocked mind.

'Because, deep down, I never really wanted to believe him

and reading the paper each week made me feel closer to you, somehow, I know it's awfully silly.' Charles went on to tell Betty all that had happened in his life, the capture in France, the memory loss, the POW camp, from which he left out a lot of unpleasant details.

'So, you settled in France eventually?' Betty asked, slowly coming to terms with things.

'I was in hospital for a very long time and fell in love with Claudette, the nurse who was caring for me. Eventually I was able to leave the hospital and we got married. We were happy for a while but when it became clear that we could not have children together, we both got very bitter, and life was just something to get through.'

'So, when did your memory come back, Uncle Charles?' Sindy was interested to know.

'Oh, my word, I am so sorry, I haven't even introduced Sindy. This is your grand-niece, Charlie, and I can tell you that she is the most impressive person in the world.' Betty added, feeling embarrassed about her manners. Sindy just squeezed her hand.

Charles was very pleased to meet Sindy and he told her how his memory had come back in dribs and drabs. He said it was very strange as one moment there was nothing and then he recalled whole weeks, sometimes months and even years of his previous life. Eventually it all came back and Betty was never far from his mind. It was then that he had started writing letters. He asked Betty how life had been for her, although he was beginning to get an idea.

Betty's eyes filled with tears and Sindy spoke. 'I'm afraid Edward Turner was a pig of a man. He made nan's life a misery at every turn. They had a son, my dad, who can be a bit of an arse as well, sometimes. Nan and I live together now and it suits us down to the ground, doesn't it nan?'

'And tell me, Sindy what are you doing with your life?'

Charles asked, he had noticed her drawing things on a napkin with a small piece of pencil that the waitress had left behind on the table, and he was impressed. She certainly had a skill. He had spent a lot of time painting in France, earning quite a few francs for some of his work and could clearly see the talent in this young woman, his grand-niece, his family.

'It seems you have turned up at just the right moment, Uncle Charles, as I'm getting married next month.'

Charles was surprised as she looked very young but it was none of his business.

'Congratulations,' was all he decided to say.

They ordered more tea, and chatted for some time about their lives, both the big things that had happened and every-day stuff that seemed both completely irrelevant and so important at the same time. They enjoyed cottage pie for lunch, which was a lot better than the cake, Betty thought.

Sindy told him all about the dippers, and they realised that if it hadn't been for the whole theatre adventure, they may never have found each other. Charles was very interested to hear about the artwork that Sindy was doing both for the bakery and the theatre. Sindy told him a little about her fiancé, Paul. She felt very grown up, just saying the word. Charles replied that he would be delighted if he could come along, meet everyone and join in with the dipping and the theatre work.

'I'm sorry,' he said suddenly. 'In my excitement to see you both, I have appeared much too eager to get involved. I do apologise. Who wants some seventy-year-old, homeless man turning up without notice and burrowing his way into their lives?'

'We both do,' was Betty and Sindy's response. They ordered treacle pudding and custard and talked some more. Eventually Charles tentatively asked about Clara, and Sindy picked up immediately on his feelings for her and thought, *crikey, she could eat him for breakfast.*

'Come to our next rehearsal or even down to the beach tomorrow morning and you'll see her again,' Sindy said kindly.

BENNY AND JACK

Jack's mind was a muddle of guilt and excitement. Benny was everything to him and he loved, admired and cared for him beyond measure. The bakery looked like a dream, all due to Benny's hard work and vision. He would have given anything to be there on his opening day. But! He had been working up to a project like this for the past five years at least, and he would never get an opportunity like this again if he turned it down. From reading the brief, it sounded challenging, interesting and something he could really get his teeth into, just his sort of thing. *Bloody hell!* Why couldn't it have been just one week later?

He left work early, went down to the shoreline and tried to think it all through and get his brain into some sort of order. Getting out his sketchpad, he made a list of pros and cons for doing the project and letting Benny down versus telling Steve no thank you, on this occasion which would be professional suicide, and he knew it. Also, he realised Benny would be furious with him if he turned it down. After an hour or so, he realised that he always mulled over any difficult decisions with his best friend, and so he decided to do just that.

As he walked through the High Street, he noticed a large bunch of really delicate pink and blue flowers with wispy little white ones in between, in the trendy flower shop that had recently opened up. He wasn't sure what they were, but felt they would look excellent in the bakery on opening day. Armed with these, he walked in. Benny beamed as he saw the flowers and then his smile turned slightly sad.

'Those look incredible Jack, but a man with flowers only

means one thing. Who are you apologising to and what for?'

Jack put the flowers carefully on the side and sat down rather too heavily in an old bamboo hanging chair that Benny had found in a junk shop. Benny had filled it with cushions and things to amuse little children, whilst their parents were buying lots of cakes. As soon as Jack sat in it, he realised he looked ridiculous; teddys and cushions went flying and Benny tried his best not to laugh. Flustered now, and desperate to get out of the chair without knocking the whole lot down, Jack asked if they could talk out the back.

Once they had closed the door, Jack threw his arms around Benny and started apologising. Benny's eyes filled with tears, immediately assuming the worst and that Jack had been unfaithful or wanted to split up. After all, how could he ever have actually kept hold of this young, gorgeous man? He'd always known, deep down that Jack was much too good for him. This day was going to arrive, he just wished it had lasted for longer. After a minute of two of these thoughts, Benny broke away suddenly, realising that if Jack had someone else, the last thing he wanted to be doing would be cuddling up to Benny's, still slightly rounded, body.

Jack was slightly shocked at this and said 'Please let me explain,' which only confirmed Benny's suspicions further.

'I love you Jack, and that's why I am going to let you go without a fuss. It's been the best couple of months of my life and I wish you well with whoever you have found. Perhaps one day I can meet him, but I don't think I'm ready to do that just yet. Benny's face had gone very red with the effort of holding back an inevitable flood of tears. He started to usher Jack towards the door so that he could retain a shred of dignity.

Jack started laughing, almost maniacally and whirled round to Benny. 'You, silly sausage, you've totally got the wrong end of the stick. I love you and always will, you are the only one for me. Yes, I have got a huge apology to make to you but I wanted to talk something over with my best mate, and you're him, buddy.

They talked it over, munching on the remains of the delicate seashell iced biscuits. Benny was thrilled for Jack. 'Your work is part of who you are and nobody is going to limit that while I'm around. We can chat on the 'phone and I can pop up to London, once the bakery has got established. We can possibly get together on Sundays, as the shop will be closed, obviously. Your career is going to take off in London and I don't mind how long it takes you. To think that you had even considered turning it down. Jack Harrington, what am I going to do with you?'

ISABELLA

It had been some days since she had seen Neil, and with so many other things happening, thoughts of him were slipping to the back of her mind, at least occasionally. Will was sleeping at home today after a long night shift. Benny was busy at the bakery, there were only a couple of days now until he opened up and Isabella assured him that she could pop to the shops for ten minutes on her own. It was rather refreshing to have a minute to herself. Although everyone had been so kind, things had felt a bit claustrophobic, always having someone with her, as she had been on her own with Lizzie for a long time now.

Just as she was queuing up at the butchers, someone tapped her on the shoulder. She jumped and spun round, very much surprising Mr Jenkins, one of her colleagues from school. He was just buying some liver and bacon for his tea. *She needed to get a grip of herself.* She finished her shopping and bumped into Samuel, buying a couple of things they needed from Turners, for the theatre. Again, she said she would be fine, just walking to school to pick up Lizzie and then they were going to pop into the bakery to see how things were coming along. Lizzie had said she wanted to work there when she grew up. Walking through a leafy lane, Isabella heard heavy footsteps quickening behind her. She started walking much faster and it was only when she turned a corner and looked back that she saw one of her own student's granddads, rushing to get to school for pick up time. *Enough! She needed to calm down.* This was beginning to take over her whole life.

Lizzie had been painting at school, and had made a picture of Benjamin's Bakery. They walked in to find him practising his lines and cleaning the oven at the same time. Lizzie rushed up and gave Benny the picture, which he said he would frame and put on the counter as it had been painted by an artist which made Lizzie beam with pride. Isabella always had her script with her and they ran through quite a few scenes together with Lizzie sitting in the hanging chair and making a game with the teddys. *He has thought of everything,* Isabella hoped the opening would be a brilliant day.

They all walked home together, with Lizzie nibbling an iced shell biscuit, that she said she didn't want to eat because it was too beautiful making Benny smile. It was busy as they crossed the High Street, but Isabella thought she saw him again, this time driving an old red car. She couldn't be sure, as he'd been wearing sunglasses. Should she mention it to Benny? She'd had two false alarms today and was feeling slightly foolish, so she kept it to herself.

Jack and Benny joined her and Will for the evening. Isabella had made steak sandwiches on garlic bread, which apparently were all the rage, according to the copy of *Woman*, that she had been reading in the dentist the other day. Benny had made a creamy bread and butter pudding; Jack bought some wine and they settled down to watch *The Six Million Dollar Man* together. Jack told them all about his London project and they could not have been more pleased for him. Isabella thought Benny was being very brave about it though, as she knew he would have wanted Jack to have been there on his first day. *That's love for you*, she thought. Anyway, all the dippers would be popping in throughout the day and Paul had said he was happy to work as many hours as was needed.

The evening had been delightful, *her and Will were a real couple now*, she thought and smiled as they wished Jack the best of luck and waved goodbye to them both.

CLARA

Clara and Dot had arranged a short musical rehearsal on Thursday evening. It worked well for everyone as Jack was not needed, and Benny who was up to his eyes in cakes, didn't really have to be there either. They had a new list of much more up-tempo songs for the pantomime and she had agreed with Dot, that a music focussed rehearsal would be useful.

Betty had telephoned Clara the very next day after meeting up with Charles as she felt it would be kind to forewarn her. For once, Clara was lost for words and, after listening to the whole story, said how pleased she was for Betty, and her whole family. In a way, Clara felt a little envious, wishing Peter had just come walking back into *her* life and then she felt guilty for thinking that. Well, she would certainly be interested in meeting up with him at some time. Yes, forty years ago, they had both found each other rather attractive, in an annoying, challenging sort of way. She recalled that he would gently poke fun at her and her lifestyle, saying she reminded him of the Queen of Sheba. She wondered if he still had that cheeky sense of humour or if life had knocked it out of him, she hoped not.

As Clara walked down the pier, she was charmed to see the warm lights shining from the theatre windows, and to hear Joyce Abbot, thumping out some lively stuff on the piano. If she shut her eyes, she could almost be transported back to her hey-days, as Joyce, her old friend, used to play in the pantomimes and musical nights before the war.

Much work had been completed over the weekend in the theatre, and again she was taken back in time. All the seats had now been re-upholstered in a heavy-weight patterned material in blues and greens. Everyone was on stage, and Dot was ready to start a musical run through. Clara had been struggling with remembering her lines, but she was getting there, strangely she had no problems remembering song words. The first half went well and they were just sitting down for an interval break and a 'well earned' drink when Charles walked in.

He looked handsome in a very smart corduroy suit, expensive shoes (Clara liked that in a man), and a cravat. Clara couldn't help smiling to herself, he had obviously made quite an effort. She had also worked hard to make herself look wonderful without apparently even trying. She had a feeling he would pop in tonight and couldn't help herself saying, 'Welcome to my theatre' in the most high-handed way possible, and held out her hand. At first, he smiled, then laughed out loud and told her she hadn't changed a bit and that he was so glad. *They were clearly going to annoy the hell out of each other*, he thought, but how agreeable that was going to be. He introduced himself to everyone and then settled down on one of the comfy fresh seats, to watch the second half of the rehearsals.

BENNY

He was up with the lark and by eight o'clock, the Bakery was brimming with cakes, pastries and biscuits of all sorts. Jack had left the car which was really useful, although it didn't make up for how much Benny was missing him this morning. Paul joined him shortly after and they got busy preparing the last-minute ingredients for sandwiches and rolls. The time flew by and just before nine, Isabella turned up with Jack's Polaroid, taking photos as Benny flipped the 'open sign' and unlocked the door, ready for trade. Most of the dippers popped in really early and bought something. It was a bright and breezy day and Benny felt this was a good omen.

Clara swept in, exclaiming how divine the shop was. She bought a cucumber sandwich for her lunch (asking Paul to please cut the crusts off) and also a chocolate cake. Then things got a little quiet.

Benny was concerned because so far, all his customers had been dippers, keen to support him, which was great, but they needed more people. Paul said he reckoned trade would pick up at lunch time. It was only ten o'clock. Lots of people looked in the window, smiled and then walked by. Lunchtime came and went with only one person wanting a sandwich, he looked a bit seedy and requested something that Benny had to go and look for. By the time he came back, both the sandwich and the man had disappeared, without paying. Benny consoled himself with the fact that at least he hadn't stolen the till, which was too heavy, but unfortunately not with his proceeds.

Paul felt for Benny, he'd made such an incredible effort and Paul had an idea. 'How about cutting one of the cakes up and giving small pieces to passers-by to try?' He said, and Benny got straight to it. They decided on the lemon cake and Paul put it on an old -fashioned tea tray with doilies and went out into the street. He chose his people carefully, ones who looked like they would come back and spend some money, he even went into a couple of shops and offices. Everyone said it was delicious, the best cake they had tasted, but no extra customers came into the shop.

Five-thirty rolled around and they agreed to shut up for the day, both of them feeling pretty downhearted. There were so many unsold cakes. They wrapped and stored them carefully and then Benny thanked and paid Paul and said he was sure it would be better tomorrow. He cashed up and after paying Paul's wages, he'd made a total of £1.50. The next day, Saturday was bound to be better. In fact, it was slightly worse and Benny said that perhaps Paul had better not come in on Monday.

Benny got home, and sat with his head in his hands for a while, feeling sorry for himself. *What more could he do?* The bakery was enticing, the food was delicious but he couldn't make people come in and spend money. He picked up Jack's jumper from the chair and sat hugging it. He was rather glad Jack had not been there to see his failure, and yet what wouldn't he give to feel his arms around him? He'd just made a cup of tea, cut a piece of raspberry and rose layer cake, and was wracking his brain for ideas when the doorbell went. It would probably be Isabella, popping in to see how things had gone. He really didn't want to see anyone right now, but she was a good friend and so he got up wearily and answered the door.

BETTY AND SINDY

Following their reunion, Betty and Sindy had taken Charles round to Turners, to meet Patrick and Doreen. It was the second bombshell they'd had in little more than a week. After the initial shock and surprise, there was much to talk about and Charles invited them all to dinner on Friday night at his hotel. He included Paul as well, which pleased Sindy and it actually turned out to be a very convivial evening. Charles had the ability to put people at their ease and immediately brought out the best in Patrick. Doreen secretly thought he was rather dashing. Charles told them how his life had been, and that he now wanted to buy a house and possibly invest in a local business. Patrick said he thought that made perfect sense and the two of them enjoyed a couple of brandies and found they both had a weakness for Cuban cigars. Betty was overjoyed to see this more relaxed and confident side of her son; he had clearly needed a male role model all these years. It was just so reassuring to watch, they were chatting, laughing about things, swapping ideas on this and that, they even had the same political views!

Towards the end of the evening, Paul spoke about his day and how bad he had felt for Benny. He explained how hard Benny had worked and that he thought he just needed more advertising and a lucky break. Charles and Patrick put their heads together with Paul and Sindy and came up with a leaflet drop plan. Betty was so proud of her little brother, and her son, she could have burst. By Saturday afternoon, the leaflet had been designed and photocopied and was ready to go. Betty called Dot, to rope her in and Dot called everyone she could think of, to help. She divided the town into sections, and organised maps for at least twenty people, feeling that she was probably being a bit optimistic.

Everyone Dot called agreed to come, it would be fun, many of them said they'd bring a few friends along as well. Clara suggested perhaps a 'cake party' on Sunday at the bakery, firstly to say thank you for everyone's help and also to get people coming into the shop. She'd seen how many cakes and biscuits Benny had made, ready for the opening day; they wouldn't last forever and they would be brilliant tasters for whoever turned up.

BENNY

It was everyone! Clara marched into his lounge and was the first to speak. 'Now Benny, we've heard that your first days have not been spectacular and as your friends, we're here to help. Put that cake away and let's get busy. We have a plan, young man, and we need all hands-on deck.' Benny looked down the hallway and saw Isabella with Lizzie and Samuel, Dot and Rob, Paul and Sindy and even Betty, Charles and Diesel, and a few others he didn't immediately recognise, all standing there with bags full of leaflets.

Clara continued, 'we all have maps and our plan is to deliver one of these to every house in Seabourne, Dot and Rob are going to make a start on those bigger houses in Cliffbourne. Benny didn't know what to say. Clara handed him a leaflet, which had Sindy's trademark shells, seahorses and waves all over it. All coloured in the bakery's pink and blue, she had designed a brilliant flyer; advertising all Benny's products and services, and stating that if customers brought this leaflet with them, they could have 10% off, and that the first fifty people through the door on Monday would receive 20% off. On the back of the leaflet, there was an invitation to a free 'Tea and Cake' party, to be held at Benjamin's Bakery on Sunday at ten o'clock.

'Your ideas are sound Benny, your products are first rate, you just need to get the word about. People are always resistant to change and slow to try new things; they generally need a well-meaning kick up the backside. Come along then, crack on.' Clara was in fifth gear by now.

'Thank you so very much everyone,' Benny just about

managed to say before he was marched out of his flat, given 500 leaflets and a map of his delivery area. I must pay for all this printing, who do I owe?' he asked and amidst the confusion of chattering people, a bouncing greyhound, a very excited little girl and Betty, who couldn't quite turn her wheelchair around in the hall way, Pat Turner stepped forward and said 'nothing for you to worry about lad, I've put it down to expenses.' You could have knocked Benny down with a feather.

By the time they left Benny's flat, weighed down with leaflets, there must have been nearly thirty people. The drop was completed in a couple of hours and they finished, as these things so often do, just opposite the pub, where, after more than a few thirst-quenching drinks, they left some leaflets on the bar. Dot was thoroughly pleased with their work, Clara admired her organisational skills and Benny just went around in a bit of a daze, thanking people again and again.

DOT

Dot suggested she help Benny with coffees and teas on Sunday, just in case it was really busy. They arrived together with supplies at around nine and were surprised to see a fair few people milling about outside. Dot worked well in any sort of crisis and quickly had Benny open up and organise the cakes, whilst Paul cut up the samples, and she started making hot drinks. People were streaming in, and spilling out of the Bakery onto the High Street. It was a very mild morning and she guessed folk just liked the sound of a party. Samuel brought music; his *Joan Armatrading* tape just seemed to compliment the relaxed vibe of the day. There were people she'd never clapped eyes on before, even though she'd lived there a while now. Benny, she could see was overjoyed and overwhelmed at the same time. People were placing orders for cakes, and, more importantly, paying for them. Isabella pointed out a couple of mums from the school, who had booked catering for birthday parties coming up, and a lot of people asked about Christmas cakes and puddings, already!

Once things had got underway, Dot took a step back. This was Benny's show and she settled in the hanging chair with a piece of blackberry and apple crumble cake which tasted like heaven, although it was very crumbly and she was making quite a mess. Out of the corner of her eye, she noticed Rob, watching her, smiling to himself as she picked up all the bits and popped them into her mouth. She wasn't being very elegant, but his eyes were shining with love and she felt the years melt away for a few minutes.

BENNY AND JACK

Jack's first meeting went really well, it was in a huge board room on a very high floor; Jack could see London from almost every angle. And, when the meeting began, he had to pinch himself that it was him, sitting amongst these big players, who were really interested to hear his input, and he immediately felt he was 'on the team'.

The work proved to be really demanding; did these people not sleep at all? However, so far, it was everything he'd hoped for and he couldn't believe his luck. He phoned Steve on Monday morning to thank him again and Steve mentioned the brilliant cake party he'd popped into the previous day, at Benjamin's. Jack was a little surprised, although he'd not been able to get through on the phone and realised that Benny wouldn't have been able to reach him easily either. He would try again later and give Benny the number of the hotel. After the initial high, he was starting to feel lonely; the hotel was quite swanky but, when he did finally get back to his room at night, there was no-one to talk to about everything, no-one to share a meal with and no fabulous smells coming from the non-existent oven.

Jack's days went by in a whirlwind of drawings, meetings, planning, and site visits and he was exhausted by the time he got back most evenings. The contrast of being so busy and involved in the day, really hit him with his solitary nights.

Benny's week exploded on Monday morning. The shop had been cleared of every edible thing on Sunday and he had spent the afternoon baking like a person possessed. Paul came in at eight-thirty sharp to find a queue down the street and Benny grinning like an albeit, pretty stressed; Cheshire cat. Benny was impressed to see Paul thinking on his feet, apologising to the people waiting, giving them tiny shortbread biscuits to get them thinking, and then darting behind the counter to help serve. *Paul was going to be quite an asset,* Benny thought as they finally had five minutes to make themselves a cup of tea. They literally didn't stop all day. Sindy popped by just after lunch with some drawings for different seaside biscuits; some of which Benny thought would look incredible, but some looked so intricate, he wasn't sure he could turn her designs into sweet reality, but he'd jolly well give it a try.

Benny left Paul to the counter work whilst he cooked more cakes, releasing a heavenly mixed aroma of chocolate, ginger and vanilla, which travelled out of the door and snaked down the High Street, like magic smoke from a genie's lamp, enticing even more customers into the bakery. Luckily, he'd made enough, to last round until tomorrow, and now the time was coming when he must turn his mind to rehearsals. Benny gave Paul a bonus and even after that, they had made a decent profit. They cleaned up together, shut up shop and walked home, chatting about the wonderful day. The exertion of the last couple of days had helped Benny with missing Jack, and it was a pleasure to have Paul to talk to, he was really coming out of himself lately.

As he walked into the flat, the phone had just stopped ringing. He dialled 1 4 7 1 but the number didn't seem to be available. *Damn and blast.* It had probably been Jack and he would have loved to have told him all about his day. He now had just under an hour to eat some food, shower and get down to the theatre for rehearsals. Benny enjoyed Monday nights, but it would be strange without Jack, everything was strange without him.

ISABELLA AND WILL

They were both looking forward to rehearsals. Will realised he enjoyed acting, it made such a change to his day job, and he got to spend even more time with Isabella and Lizzie, who he was becoming very fond of. He realised that he was letting his guard down completely, Isabella could tire of him at any time; and he would be heartbroken, but the risk was worth it. He thought he had been in love with Carol, but now he was head over heels in love with Isabella, he realised that his previous relationship had been just an infatuation and he actually hoped that she and his brother had made a go of it together in France.

They knocked on Benny's door and all four of them went to the theatre. On the way down, Isabella stared at an old car, making its way along the front. Will noticed it as well and realised who was driving it. So, he was still here. He considered giving chase on foot, but that would have been hopeless and just frighten everyone. He would bide his time, but he realised that this had unsettled Isabella and decided to ask her if she and Lizzie would like a short holiday, after Sindy's wedding, during half term. He felt a break away from Seabourne was becoming essential.

The run through went really well this week. Dot had been busy making props, including an endless woollen stripey stocking that one of the ugly sisters was to take off, prior to trying on the shoe that wasn't going to fit, anyway. There were yards of it, and everyone laughed as it went on and on as they tried to remove it from Benny's leg. Both Isabella and Will knew their lines for the first half of the panto. It was interesting how much more you could put into your part when you weren't holding the script, and Betty was the best prompt; she was so focussed, and seemed to know when you were going to forget a line or word, before *you* did.

Lizzie was asleep on her sofa by the interval and Will suggested they go somewhere different, just for a couple of nights. He had weeks of holiday due to him and Isabella wouldn't be working during half term, so he thought it would fit in nicely. Isabella was delighted, saying she hadn't had a holiday for years and could they please go to the New Forest, as she loved the ponies and Lizzie would enjoy all the trees, streams and open spaces. Will said he would look for a hotel in the Yellow Pages, and book it as soon as he could. He was so happy, imagining their first holiday as a little family.

CLARA

Mostly due to Dot's enthusiasm, good production and direction, rehearsals were going extremely well; they were on track for after Christmas. Clara had been watching Dot closely lately with a particular purpose in mind. *No need to mention this until a bit later on however,* she thought. Tickets were going like hot cakes and she had to concede that Davison at *Seabourne Matters* was keeping to his word regarding the pantomime publicity and advertising. There was a small article in the paper each week and it felt, somehow, as if the whole town was behind them. Clara was enjoying the role of Fairy Godmother, she had picked an aquamarine and silver costume from decades ago, which she had worn for a pantomime, she couldn't quite remember which one, but it still fitted beautifully and made her feel just right for the part.

Charles had been back a whole week now, and he turned up again, this time at the start of rehearsals, offering his help in whatever capacity was needed. Annoyingly, Clara couldn't disguise the fact that she was pleased to see him, which appeared to flatter and amuse him equally, by the look on his face. *Irritating man,* she thought. He had telephoned earlier in the week and asked if he might walk her home from rehearsals tonight and she had accepted with as much condescension as she could possibly get into her voice. *Why did he bring out this side of her nature?* Every time she saw him, they seemed to be playing power games just under the surface. Clara thought back to before the war and remembered it was similar then, before Peter had walked in, swept her off her feet and proposed to her without any dilly-dallying on the way. Charles was not

Peter and never would be, but he was a wonderful distraction.

CHARLES

Watching the rehearsal last night had been a lot of fun, the show was spot on, there would be rave reviews. Clara had been on top form as he had walked her home, it was rather windy however and they could barely hear what the other was saying. He waited around a bit, feeling like he was eighteen, as opening her front door, she laughingly said, 'well I suppose I had better offer you a drink for your trouble,' and he walked into Rutland Manor for the first time in over forty years. He was not particularly surprised to see it hadn't changed a bit, dark oak panelling, heavy curtains and huge sofas, the smell of lavender and roses, just as he remembered. He followed Clara through to her drawing room, and they bumped into an old lady, just preparing to leave for the day.

Astonished to see her, Charles burst out, 'Ruth Jackson, as I live and breathe, how on earth has she managed to hang on to you all these years?'

'Good evening, Mr Lancaster, how are you these days?' Mrs Jackson casually replied as if she'd seen him just a couple of months ago. Clara rolled her eyes at his behaviour and invited Mrs Jackson to join them for a night cap. The three of them talked for hours, recalling the old days, war time recipes, songs, people who they had lost, and people who had survived. They finished Clara's very old Remy Martin XO in very short order and then went on to some single malts. The clock chimed one, and they all realised that time had flown. Mrs Jackson was in no state to drive her Mini home and Charles had drunk far too much to even negotiate the steps, let alone drive back to his hotel.

Rutland Manor had more bedrooms than Clara knew what to do with; Mrs Jackson always kept a couple of them aired with fresh bed linen just in case, and so Clara, feeling that she had little choice in the matter, invited Charles to stay. Mrs Jackson occasionally stayed over anyway during the winter, and so said goodnight, and made her slightly wobbly way upstairs. As Clara performed her evening routine, she thought what a relaxing night it had been and snuggled up in her fourposter bed, feeling both light-hearted and a bit light headed.

Coffee and Alka-Seltzers all round, seemed to be the order of the day the following morning, sitting in the kitchen with the gentle heat of the Aga. Charles and Mrs Jackson agreed that they were not as young as they used to be, but Clara would hear none of that kind of talk. They chatted about the wedding plans, with only ten days to go, things were pretty much all in hand now. Charles mentioned that he would like to contribute and suggested perhaps a surprise honeymoon for them, one of these Freddie Laker holidays in Spain, perhaps? Clara agreed, this would be a memorable start to their married life. They all doubted whether Sindy or Paul had a passport and Clara suggested that Charles tell them to get these sorted out and prepare to be away for a week. Clara decided to invite Betty to stay for the duration of the wedding and honeymoon. She had a bright, sea-facing, downstairs room with ensuite, which would be just the job for Betty and also put Sindy's mind at rest, and Diesel could, perhaps have a holiday with Isabella and Will. Everyone had noticed how much Lizzie loved his company. Charles thought it would be only right to tell Betty, Doreen and Pat what they had arranged, out of courtesy and also because Sindy would need a week off work. Charles said he would fill in for both Sindy and Paul, perhaps spending mornings at the bakery and afternoons at Turners.

DOT

It was a mild October morning and Dot was swimming on her own for the first time in ages. The sea was a fair bit colder now, but okay once you got in and started moving about. The waves were gentle, taking a long time to roll in and Dot imagined she was on a dream-like fairground ride. The dolphins were back today, and for a few brief moments, she felt like it was just her and them in the whole world. Clara and Charles came along to sit on the bench, chatting and appearing to Dot, to be gently bickering like an old married couple, which she thought was rather sweet.

Benny and Paul were knee deep in customers, Jack still away, and she knew Betty wasn't feeling so well lately. Dot was glad to hear she was going for some tests this week. It didn't do to ignore what your body was telling you. Sindy was very busy with last minute wedding arrangements and also painting silver mermaids at the theatre and so she hadn't been down in a while. Dot considered asking if the group just wanted to dip every Sunday, now the weather was getting colder and people were so busy.

She changed quickly, teeth chattering a bit, and said goodbye to Clara and Charles who were on their way to get a hot chocolate, which Benny was selling now, and a piece of something sticky and sweet. He had started making individual pecan and pumpkin pies as an autumn special; Dot had tried one yesterday and recommended buying at least one of each. There were a couple of things to be checked out on stage, and, as she made her way down the pier and approached the theatre door, she couldn't help noticing a rather fancily dressed middle aged man, looking around the outside of the theatre. He called out to her as she turned the key.

'Oh, I say, are you the Theatre Manager, by any chance?'

Dot laughed and explained that they were doing a pantomime at Christmas. He seemed very interested and asked if he might have a look around. Dot couldn't really see why not, he seemed a decent, if a bit eccentric, sort of a chap and he followed her in, asking lots of questions. He was clearly taken aback at how impressive the inside was, and asked who owned it. Dot thought she ought to be a bit cautious about giving out too much information, whereupon the man gave her his card. He was a London Stage Director and Producer, and he was looking for a new, South coast, venue for his productions. He was clearly, very interested in The Mermaid. Dot promised to give Clara his card and couldn't get round to Benjamin's quickly enough to tell her the news.

BENNY AND JACK

Benjamin's Bakery had been open now for nearly two weeks. As if in his food mixer, the time had whizzed by, in a frenzy of planning, baking, ordering and serving his customers, although thankfully, Paul had taken over the counter work completely this last week. He was an astute salesman, suggesting an extra this or that, when customers already thought they had enough. Sales had rocketed and of course, the effect of this was cumulative as the more he sold, the more word got round and then more customers arrived. He could scarcely keep up but was as happy as a sand boy. Benny barely had time to miss Jack; they had caught up just once on the 'phone and Jack sounded as if he was enjoying London, but had to rush off to a meeting a few minutes into the conversation.

He had decided to dedicate this afternoon to the wedding breakfast buffet. He'd agreed the menu a couple of weeks ago but he wanted to order his ingredients, and check he had enough crockery. He had purchased a load from a café in Cliffbourne that was closing down, it was very cheap and Benny had offered them more money. The old couple laughed and said that was not the way to run a business, then threw a few other things in the box as well, and wished him good luck. It was a bit mismatched but that just added to the charm. He was also going to marzipan the wedding cakes today. When talking it over with Sindy she had mentioned that Princess Anne had five layers on her cake a couple of years ago, and how impressive it had looked on the television. Sindy never seemed to ask for anything and so Benny was determined to impress her. It needed a lot of marzipan, and the bakery had smelled like Christmas for some days whilst he was baking all the fruit cakes.

As he was scribbling in his notepad, the bell went and he looked up to see Jack, standing in the doorway, smiling. He was overjoyed to see him, but he looked different. He was wearing clothes Benny had not seen before, they were really modern and looked expensive and he'd changed his hair style. Benny was delighted that he was here, but he was not his old Jack, somehow. That fleeting feeling disappeared as Jack walked in, asked Paul to keep shop for a minute or two and rushed out the back to say a proper hello to Benny. It felt unbelievable to hold him in his arms, even if it was for just a few moments. Jack explained that he'd got the afternoon off and had decided to spend it with Benny.

Somehow, although he should have been blown away by this spontaneous and romantic gesture, Benny felt strangely annoyed. He had already planned his afternoon and it appeared as if Jack thought he was doing him a favour. He immediately felt guilty then and seeing Jack's ever-so-slightly crestfallen face, Benny snapped out of it, asked Paul if he would mind taking over for a couple of hours, and suggested they start with a walk along the beach together. They grabbed a couple of filled rolls that were left and set off. Sitting on the pier, chatting just like old times, Jack said the roll was delicious; Benny had made tarragon chicken mayonnaise filling and was pleased with the result. Jack asked about how the bakery was going, however just as Benny started to tell him all his news, Jack interrupted and began talking about his job and London life.

It all sounded very glamourous and high powered to Benny, he was so very pleased that things were going well for Jack and he commented on his new look.

'Everyone is so much more stylish in the city, than here. I just had to alter my look. The shops are incredible and *we* seem to fit in much easier. It's so cosmopolitan. The delis are brilliant with salads, and really healthy food. Mind you, I've been out to lunch and dinner so many times in the last week, I've hardly needed to buy my own.'

'I'm so glad for you Jack,' Benny was just saying when a bit of moist, buttery, chicken fell out of Jack's roll onto his new jacket, and a casual bystander might have thought the world was going to end. Jack jumped up, threw down the rest of the roll which was swiftly picked up by a lucky seagull. He brushed at the stain with his handkerchief, making it worse and swearing; saying it was completely ruined. He said he had bought it from Carnaby Street and was now asking anyone in general if they knew how much designer clothes cost. Benny didn't know.

They had barely spent an hour together but the vibe wasn't the same, and after a bit more jacket fuss, Jack looked at his watch, and said he'd probably head off now, catch an earlier train and meet some friends for drinks in the West End. He marched off down the pier in his fancy kit, and Benny just watched him go, vaguely wondering if he ought to offer to pay for the dry-cleaning.

When Benny got back, Paul was snowed under and they quickly worked together to get things organised again. Paul thought that his brother had looked a bit of a prat, in all his finery and he didn't like the new hairdo one bit. That made Benny laugh, but he felt genuinely sad when Paul told him that Jack hadn't asked after Sindy, Clara or said anything about the wedding. Benny apologised in advance for the cliché but said, 'he's just not the Jack I know and love anymore.'

BETTY AND SINDY

They didn't have to wait too long at the hospital to get Betty's tests done and Sindy suggested they pop in to Benjamin's, say hello to the boys and buy a piece of ginger cake at the same time. Sindy's morning-sickness hadn't eased yet, but she had already developed a really strong craving for anything flavoured with ginger, that, and mashed potato for some reason. When they reached the bakery, the boys were both working flat out and Sindy could see, now, why Paul had been so incredibly tired each evening these last two weeks. Benny had been paying him almost double what they had originally agreed and he was saving quite a bit in an old jam jar. They had been thinking about a day out after the wedding, a sort of honeymoon day, but Uncle Charles had popped by yesterday evening and told them both to get some passports organised as soon as they could, as he had planned a little something for them. Sindy was beyond excited as she'd never been abroad, and wondered where they might be going. She had very few clothes, she didn't need many really, but wondered what she might need to pack, warm jumpers or a bikini and flip flops? She hoped it was the latter, and thought she might be able to get some hints from her mum, or possibly Clara. Betty also knew what was going on but so far, she had refused to spill the beans.

Sindy was going to show Uncle Charles the ropes at Turners tomorrow. Everyone seemed to get along with him; he had an easy, likeable confidence that seemed to infect everybody he spoke to. Even her dad was gentler these days and her mum seemed to be blossoming. Sindy was so glad he had returned to them, and it wasn't just for a fancy honeymoon.

Benny gave them a whole ginger cake and sent them off, saying he was doing important secret work and that Sindy would have to wait until she was 'Mrs Harrington', to see the final result. She smiled because she loved hearing her married name, and practiced her signature in private as often as she could. She thought that Benny looked a bit strained today; she'd heard about yesterday from Paul and felt for him. Jack was a good-looking guy, but if he carried on like this, he would lose him, and Benny was one in a million.

Betty said she'd like to pop in on Pat and Doreen and so they took the cake, hoping the kettle was on. Sindy was surprised to see her mum behind the counter, but happy to see her dad and uncle Charles chatting through the back. They were planning an old boys club or something, according to her mum, who thought it was an interesting idea, and actually she was quite enjoying working on her own, serving the customers. All three women chuckled at that, shut the connecting door and got talking. Of course, Doreen had guessed about the baby, as soon as she saw Sindy, but they all felt there was no need to share this information until after the wedding. Doreen was thrilled for all of it, saying that she felt so much closer to Sindy. They hugged, shed a couple of tears, and said they wouldn't drift away from each other again. Betty was overjoyed to see everyone brought together by both the forthcoming birth and the return of her long-lost brother. She was struggling these days and they talked about what could be done to help, until the tests were back, when hopefully they would know a bit more. Sindy was doing all she could, and they thought a little break at Clara's would be just what the doctor ordered. Doreen said she would do more in the shop, freeing Sindy up to care for Betty.

Sindy went on to explain about her clothes, or lack of them, and both Doreen and Betty realised that Sindy would enjoy the honeymoon much more if she had a few new things to wear. They told her it would be warm where they were headed, and Doreen suggested they pop to Brighton for the day, where there was a big department store, and she could treat her to a few things. Although she was trying to keep it a secret, Doreen couldn't help showing them a new knitting pattern for a complete baby layette, she was planning to make on her knitting machine and Betty realised that Sindy had many safe hands now, in which she could be left, when the time came.

ISABELLA

She had decided to have a lay-in this morning as it was Saturday. Lizzie was still asleep and Will had gone in early for a morning shift. They would have the afternoon together. This morning, she had planned to make a start on cutting out a bridesmaid dress for Lizzie, as Sindy had kindly asked if she would do them that honour, as if Lizzie didn't idolise Sindy anyway! Isabella was happy as she didn't have a lot of extra cash to indulge her daughter and this was a good excuse to make her something really pretty and princess-like. She'd picked up a lovely pattern, there was no debating the colour, of course the dress had to be pink and Isabella had got hold of an inexpensive piece of shiny fabric in the market in Cliffbourne, plus some lace and ribbons, so it wouldn't cost the earth.

The doorbell went and Isabella lazily got out of bed, wearing Wills pyjamas, and opened the door; it was bound to be Benny, with cake or something. But, as she unlatched the door, she realised Benny would be at the bakery by now and before she could shut the door again, Neil Cartwright burst through, and slammed the door behind him. He was drunk, smelt disgusting and looked crazily frightening. Time stood still and she froze.

'Put the kettle on love, I could murder a brew' he said, and he threw himself on the sofa, continuing, 'I've got all the time in the world now, see, cause your arsehole of a copper has gone off, for the day, I'm guessing, as I saw he had a flask and stuff, as he left.' He smiled and Isabella's stomach turned, remembering the last time she had seen that smile. His boots were muddy and the only thing she seemed to be able to focus on was the mud that he had kicked across her sofa. Shaking herself into action, she filled the kettle slowly, trying to think what she should do, got a mug out, and asked him if he took sugar. All she could think about was keeping quiet so that Lizzie didn't wake up, it was early and she might sleep another couple of hours. Her instinct was to keep checking the bedroom door, but if she did that, he would soon wonder why, and so she kept her eyes on the floor. Her mind was frantic but paralysed at the same time. Her head was beginning to throb and she jumped a foot into the air, when he crept up behind her and touched her hair.

'First thing I noticed about you, what's it now, seven years ago? Thought you were too good for me then and I see you still do.' The stench of alcohol on his breath as he spoke was sickening and she bit her lip to stop herself reaching.

'Well, first, I think I'll help myself to some of these expensive looking things you've got around the place, and then we'll see' he continued.

Tears started dropping from her eyes, despite herself. *Concentrate on what you're doing, you've got to hold it together,* and Isabella blew her nose and finished making the tea. She noticed that he'd brought a big rucksack with him and was now walking around the lounge, picking up some of her ornaments, and her radio, and other things, and stuffing them in the bag. For a split second, she considered throwing the boiling kettle at him, but that wasn't really going to help and she didn't think she had the courage anyway. She would miss and just make him angry. *No, play his game, until things get worse,* she told herself and put the mug of tea on the coffee table. He was looking at a silver photo frame, which held a picture of her mother. He followed her gaze, smiled, and put that in as well. She let out a further sob, as she had very few photos of her mother. The phone went, his eyes darted to it and he pulled it from the wall with such force that some of the plaster cracked. Unfortunately, that seemed to launch him into action and he started rummaging in drawers, and throwing things about. Isabella asked him to please stop, and he turned around and pushed her out of the way. She fell to the floor and he advised her to stay there. He kept on trying to put more and more into his bag, which was getting heavy and things were falling out as quickly as he was trying to stuff them in, so he started moving towards the door.

BENNY

Benny was opening up, thinking about Jack and what had happened on the pier, when he made a decision. It was going to be a busy day, but Paul could cope for an hour or so. They finished putting all the cakes in the window, the spicy pumpkin pies looked and smelled wonderful as he got them out of the oven, ready for later in the day. He was walking out the door when a lady came in with an order for half a dozen Christmas cakes and so he went back, offered her a cup of coffee and chatted it all through. *Fantastic,* he thought. Anything that was pre-ordered and paid for was such a bonus; he could get organised and work around it. He considered staying and simply getting on with his day, but something told him to telephone Jack this morning and talk things through. The phone had gone wrong in the bakery and so he told Paul he'd be half an hour and headed back to the flat.

Thinking about his conversation and walking quietly up the stairs, he noticed a really unpleasant smell in the corridor, he had a nose like a bloodhound. This was revolting, a horrible mixture of beer, cigarette smoke and stale sweat, and as he went further, he realised it was coming from Isabella's. Unconsciously, he knew who was in there. Isabella's spare key was on his keyring and so silently he unlocked her door and burst in. He took in the scene for a split second, Isabella was sitting on the carpet, weeping silently, and the vile smelling man was in a heap on the floor. Luckily, the force with which Benny had opened the door had knocked him straight down, he started to get up but Benny punched him once, apparently in the right place, because it knocked him clean out.

WILL

Will felt slightly uncomfortable about going to work this morning, however once he got there, he ploughed through a mound of paperwork and made a cup of coffee; looking forward to the afternoon with his girl, he decided to give her a call. That was odd. The phone rang and then nothing. Number unobtainable. *He had known, this morning, deep down he'd known.*

He jumped in his car, siren and lights on. It took him just a couple of minutes to get to her flat, climb the stairs, and see the door open, with Benny standing, in shock, his hand bleeding, and an unconscious Neil Cartwright on the floor.

After he had comforted Isabella, he radioed for an ambulance for Benny and considered what to do with Cartwright. He had never wanted to kill anyone as much as right at this moment, but that wasn't who he was; Cartwright would be coming round soon and so Will had to act quickly. He dragged him out of the flat and cuffed him to the hand rail on the stairs. His thoughts turned back to Isabella, who was very pale. He got a bottle of whiskey from the cupboard that he'd been keeping for the right occasion. This was not it, but what the hell? Pouring some out for Benny and Isabella, he heard what had happened and he put his arms around Benny, saying that he could never thank him enough.

When the ambulance men arrived, they dressed Benny's hand and said he'd probably need an X-ray, also pointing out that whenever trouble was around, Benny was usually not too far away. They needed a dry sense of humour in their game, they said. Cartwright was taken away under police guard and

Isabella was assured he wouldn't be troubling her or anyone else, ever again. Lizzie wandered in, holding her teddy, saying she had heard the sirens, why was Will making so much noise and what was for breakfast?

CHARLES AND CLARA

On his first morning at the hotel, Charles had enjoyed his full English, and the second, and the third, but now he was politely declining breakfast as he couldn't face another oval plateful of the stuff. It was well cooked, really crispy bacon, just how he liked it, but as a treat, now and again. More recently he took a long morning coastal walk, over to Benjamin's and grabbed a coffee. Also, the sweet young chamber-maid kept on tidying his things up, each day, he could never find anything! He realised it was time for his own home. He had gone to the estate agents, and got a stack of particulars on houses in the vicinity. None of them really excited him, but he needed to throw himself into this, narrowed it down to about six, and asked Clara if she would view them with him. On the telephone, she was her usual self, 'oh, are we going to play happy families then?' she asked in her teasing tone of voice, 'you realise that they're going to think we're married and keep calling me Mrs Lancaster, don't you. Ah, perhaps that's what you're planning, in a roundabout way.'

'Would you prefer they thought us to be living in sin then, *Lady* Harrington,' was his response. He always emphasised the 'Lady' when he was taunting her. They continued the banter for a few minutes until Clara got bored and finally agreed to meet him at two-thirty that afternoon, he would pick her up, he said, 'oh, and you might want to wear a headscarf, Lady Harrington.'

He had tired of taking the bus on day two, (all the other passengers seemed to be old, with grey hair, and although he was in his seventieth year, since he'd been back home, he felt about forty-five) and this morning he would be picking up a brand new, Triumph Spitfire 1500 in Java Green, which would definitely lower his age further. It was a reckless amount of money to spend, but it touched his soul, and the school boy of a salesman had given him quite a discount.

Clara was up early as usual, and whilst taking her morning walk, considered her outfit for today, a headscarf could only mean one thing. *Good grief, he'd bought himself a sports car*, and although she laughed to herself at the witticisms she could make at his expense, she thought they would make a rather attractive couple, and wondered what colour it would be. *Surely not red, that would be just too vulgar.*

She remembered her vow not to go through the High Street if she didn't need to, but walked that way this morning, as if in defiance of herself. *Her wardrobe.* It was stylish, very 'Lady Harrington' but everything was about thirty or forty years old and she made a snap decision. There was one decent ladies' wear shop in the town, 'Seabourne Stylish Selections', she hoped it would still be open as she marched to the other end of the High Street. The young sales assistant was just opening up and said 'good morning, Madam, I'm Susan, just let me know if there is anything I can help you with.' This was a pleasing start. Clara said what she had in mind and Susan understood immediately. She congratulated Clara on her choices and suggested little touches to complement, plus some very stylish, quite high heeled shoes. Clara spent nearly an hour with her and by the time she left, with bags full of new outfits; more were going to be delivered, Susan had earned six months' worth of commission. They had chatted about the pantomime, and Susan said she would be bringing her family to watch it, and hoped to see Clara again very soon.

Clara had always taken her trim figure for granted, but when she had put the cream trouser suit on in front of her dressing table, together with a beige polo neck, an old jet necklace that she'd had for donkey's years, a new silk black and cream headscarf, (Audrey Hepburn style, obviously) she was quite astonished at the woman who looked back at her and smiled. Should she choose a pair of sunglasses? *Of course, she should, there were no half measures with this look.* It was, indeed, sunny and so she wouldn't receive endless teasing from him.

As Clara walked through the front door, onto the sweeping drive, Mrs Jackson was just pulling up. Ruth was transported back forty-odd years as Clara waved hello, she looked marvellous, and Ruth realised immediately who she would be meeting. She smiled back and thought, *at last, she's waited long enough for a bit of happiness.*

Clara didn't have to wait long for Charles, however, as he came speeding up the drive, sending shingle flying, the very image of Donald Campbell (the land speed record man), from years ago. He came to a flashy stop and did a very loud wolf whistle!

'Well, you're not exactly James Hunt, but you'll do,' Clara said as she hopped in. He looked so very handsome, she was in grave danger of losing her head, and not because of the open top car.

Heavens she was a fine-looking woman, Charles thought and decided there and then, not to make the same mistake twice. He'd left it too late nearly fifty years ago, and that wasn't going to happen again. They enjoyed a most convivial afternoon, although Charles winced a couple of times at her condescension, when viewing the houses. Luckily the owners were not in, the estate agent, sensing there could be a large profit to be made, showed them round himself. They were all very bland, nothing made him want to live in any of them and he told Clara he would have to go back to the drawing board. She had another idea, that surprised him; she never failed to.

'You could move in with me,' she casually mentioned over a cup of Earl Grey, at a local teashop. They had tried Benjamin's but it was packed full of customers. Charles looked up from his toasted teacake, he thought she was joking but her face was completely serious. He couldn't resist, 'what, live over the brush with you and tarnish my otherwise spotless reputation?' He was even more surprised at her response.

'And who would actually care, my dear Charles? We have both been very lonely and I have been foolishly bitter for an awfully long time. My life recently has been moving up and up, like one of those wooden roller-coaster things at the fairground. I honestly thought I couldn't find any more happiness, until you breezed back into my life. I'm not suggesting anything untoward you understand ...'

'Oh, that's a pity'

'Yet! Give a girl time, Charles Lancaster.'

DOT

With the exception of Jack, who was still away, and Betty, who was feeling the cold a bit more these days, everyone was at the beach on Sunday morning. Rob had come along and was talking through some more plans with Samuel. The outside decorator chap wasn't interested and so they were going to hire some ladders and safety equipment and do it themselves. Dot was pleased to see that Isabella and Lizzie had come along, she went up to Isabella and gave her a big long hug, telling her that there were only good things to come in her life now. She'd seen the way that Will worshipped her, and thought it wouldn't be too long before there were more wedding bells. Dot was hugging everyone this morning; she had heard what had happened and how brave Benny had been. He wasn't swimming because of his bandaged hand, but was happily handing out cake to everyone and talking about what a success the bakery was becoming. Sindy and Paul were already in the water, having a fantastic time with Diesel, who kept on running in and out and shaking over everyone.

The sea was gently rippling in the fresh October wind and the dippers got dry and changed quickly. Clara and Charles turned up together, in a very shiny green sports car. Dot couldn't decide whether she was more surprised at that, or at what Clara was wearing, when she stepped elegantly out of the front seat. Fashionably dressed in some smart corduroys and a matching turtle neck sweater under a soft leather jacket, Dot was comforted to see that Clara had now left the past where it should be. Rob and Samuel almost raced each other to see the car, asking all about the engine capacity and top speeds.

Had Charles 'opened it up' yet? Rob wanted to know. Samuel immediately offered to take it up to the new, recently opened section, of the M25 to see what it would do. Charles thanked him and said, he'd planned to do just that, and would take the boys with him, if they'd like that sometime.

Leaving the boys to it, Dot chatted with Clara and complimented her on the new look. Did Clara blush slightly? Or was it Dot's imagination? The years certainly seemed to have dropped away from her face. Clara mentioned that she had been in touch with the London theatre gentleman and they had provisionally agreed to meet after the wedding.

'Are there any dates that you can't make? I want you to be at the meeting.' Clara said. Dot was flattered but didn't really know what she would be adding. Never mind, it would be interesting. As the morning was breaking up, it was agreed that they'd meet just on Sundays now, as it was getting colder and everyone had a lot going on. Dot said she'd see them all at rehearsals tomorrow and got back home just in time to hear the phone ringing. It was Margaret, but she sounded different.

'Hello Mum, how are you?' *This was new*, Dot thought and said that things were going really well.

'I'm pleased for you, Mum, I'm sorry, I ignored you and Dad the other day, in London. I was with some clients and was so keen to impress them, that I forgot who I was. I've got a lot to tell you and talk about with you, can I come and stay for a few days? I can book into a hotel if you'd rather me do that.'

'Yes of course you can, darling, and no, you can stay with us if you'd like to. When were you thinking of? Somehow, Dot knew what Margaret's answer was going to be.

'Can I come at the weekend?'

Be strong, I can't cancel my plans, Dot thought, 'you can come then, but there is a very good friend's wedding on Saturday, which I'm really looking forward to, I'm sure they wouldn't mind you coming along as well.

'That would be nice, thanks Mum, see you then.'

Rob had heard the gist of the conversation, 'well done love, you stood your ground, and dealt with that brilliantly, I wonder what's up?'

BENNY AND JACK

What with all the drama of Saturday morning, and an even busier day than usual afterwards at the bakery, Benny had not yet got round to 'phoning Jack. So, on returning from the beach, where it had been so good to see everyone, he made himself a coffee, sat down by the phone and planned to try and get their relationship back to where it had been less than two weeks ago. Jack answered straight away, his voice sounding raspy and Benny was worried he was ill.

'No mate, just hung over I'm afraid.' *Jack never called him mate.*

'Sorry to hear that Jack, hope it was a good night.'

'To be honest, I can't really remember, anyway how's things at the bakery, all going well?'

Benny sensed Jack wanted a short answer, 'all good this end,' he heard himself saying and tried to steer the conversation around to when they might see each other and if Jack even wanted to. He needed to tell Jack all that had happened on Saturday morning, but, again, he realised this was not the time. His hand was throbbing a bit though and he really needed Jack to say something soothing.

'At Paul's wedding, I guess,' was Jack's reply. 'I've got the day off and I'm looking forward to seeing everyone.'

He didn't say me. He's looking forward to seeing everyone, Benny replayed it in his head and decided to ask the question, 'Jack, do you think our relationship has come to the end of the line, do you want to go our separate ways now? I understand that London has offered you more than I could, so it's ok, if that's what you want.' Benny could feel the heavy sadness rising up from his chest.

'Sure, if that's what *you* want, I'm ok with your decision.'

'No, no, it's not what *I* want, I just felt that ...'

Jack had put the receiver down, and in his heart, Benny knew this was always going to be the outcome. He turned up his music, and got busy, he had a bakery to stock and open up tomorrow, there was no time to wallow in self-pity.

Meanwhile, in a cheap hotel room, Jack turned round and said to his bedfellow, 'well, that was easier than expected,' and they both laughed, drank some more and fell asleep.

Monday morning came round for both, but rather differently. Benny opened up, in a bit of a daze, but surrounded by friends, customers and even his mother popped by. It was a busy day, and whilst he was desperately unhappy, the kindness of everyone he spoke to, softened the blow. He didn't talk about Jack. What was there to say? People would know soon enough.

Jack however, woke up, even more hung over, late for work and found that his friend from last night had left and taken his wallet. *Shit. I deserved that,* he thought. Luckily, he slept wearing his watch, the one that his father had given him years ago, on his wrist and it was still there.

He didn't think Benny would ever forgive him. Why should he? He knew that he didn't deserve forgiveness. What the hell had got into him? His head had been turned by the attention of a younger man; too much alcohol and the cigarettes he was offered had left him completely out of control. But; *he* did all this, no-one forced him. What an absolute arse he had been. He recalled the chicken episode on the pier. Even *he* could see himself turning into a different, and dislikeable person. What must Benny be thinking about him now? Well, he was going to make a damn good try at winning him back, but now he was late for work and he didn't want to lose his job and the love of his life in one weekend.

BETTY AND SINDY

They decided to go to Brighton on a Monday as it would hopefully be less busy than the weekend. Doreen drove her big car, Betty's chair fitted in the back and she was feeling a bit better today, she seemed to have good and bad days at the moment. The blood tests were back and Dr Skudder had said he would like her to have a couple of scans and that he would organise these at the hospital. Betty was grateful that Sindy hadn't seen the letter and so she could keep things to herself, at least until after the wedding, which was nearly upon them.

Brighton was its usual heady mix of slightly naughty fun, shopping and seaside silliness, with Sindy pushing Betty through the Lanes, stopping for coffee, tea and cakes every couple of hours. The shops were bohemian and arty and Sindy loved it there. Doreen treated her to some modern clothes from an outrageously trendy boutique, and Betty bought her a couple of sun dresses, some sandals and a new bikini. The shiny department store had an awfully tempting baby section, making them all feel broody and Clara had given Sindy some money to buy a few special baby things. Doctor Brighton had certainly not disappointed. They finished the day with bags full, and afternoon tea at The Grand Hotel. Three generations had bonded in one day, after all these years of not quite seeing eye to eye. Sindy was finding out things about her mum that she never knew; both funny and downright eye popping. Doreen admitted to being 'quite a strumpet', before she had settled down with Patrick, making both Sindy and Betty cry with laughter at her antics. Doreen was making up for lost time with her daughter, and Betty, who wished she had made the effort to get to know Doreen better, was just happy to be there.

On the journey home, they sang songs together, as Doreen's car didn't have a radio, with Betty suggesting war time ditties, Doreen opting for Elvis and the Beatles numbers and Sindy just wishing they would appreciate some more modern stuff like Deep Purple, Black Sabbath and The Average White Band.

ISABELLA AND WILL

Their Monday morning consisted of a long, cleansing swim, the colder water and vigorous waves helped to wash away the events of Saturday morning. Will took the day off and they cleaned the flat from top to bottom together, washing everything he had touched with lots of soap, water, and finally disinfectant. Will popped out and bought some pumpkin cakes from Benjamin's and a big bunch of roses for Isabella. As they sat, munching their cakes with some tea, they talked about the future, and Will decided that this might be the right time. He had gone out and bought a ring, rather impetuously for him, a couple of weeks after they first met, he was so sure of how he felt. He'd also asked Samuel for his blessing, although he had sworn him to secrecy, for as long as it took for him to be certain of Isabella's feelings.

First though, he wanted to tell her all about the holiday, in the New Forest. He'd been there years ago as a kid, and knew they could walk for miles without seeing any traffic, possibly try some pony trekking if Lizzie fancied that, and have a couple of meals out. He remembered that there were highland cattle, ponies and sometimes deer in the forest, which they would all enjoy spotting. There was a cosy little hotel in Brockenhurst, a quaint village, with a stream running right through the High Street. There was a family room for three, which sounded just right; they all needed this break. The hotel was more than happy to accept Diesel, as they were going to be looking after him for a week, whilst the youngsters were on their honeymoon. Isabella was very excited and said she could take the new dress she'd made for the wedding; a green polka dot, halter neck style, with a circular skirt, complete with a bolero jacket. She loved sewing and had just about finished it. They talked about Lizzie, Will wanted to see what Isabella thought of him adopting her as his daughter, which would then make her situation even safer, but there was one big question to be asked first.

Will realised that being in the flat, although it was clean and very sweet smelling now, perhaps wasn't the best place to propose marriage, and so he suggested a walk back to the beach. The slightly watery sun had broken through the clouds and Isabella thought that would be perfect, after all their hard work. They grabbed some sweaters, he pocketed the ring, and they headed down. Walking along the shoreline, Isabella found an unusual piece of blue sea glass and said it was the sign of a good day; she would save it for Lizzie. As she wandered along the sand, her curly hair blowing all over the place, Will realised, for the hundredth time, that he was hopelessly in love with her; quite what he would do if she said no, he didn't like to think. They rested a while on the usual bench and he got the ring out of his pocket, assumed the traditional position, and asked the question. 'Isabella, I knew from the very first time I saw you, that I was going to fall in love with you, so please, would you do me the honour of becoming my wife,' and he opened the tiny box.

CLARA AND BETTY

Betty's scan appointment had been booked in very quickly, which was concerning. Dr Skudder's nurse had telephoned Betty and it was arranged for today. Betty called Clara and asked if she would mind going with her as she needed some company, and she knew Clara would understand and keep it to herself. Sindy was busy working at the shop and the theatre, and Betty didn't want her worrying about anything. Plenty of time for that, unfortunately, when they came back from Spain. The scan didn't take too long and Clara asked what they were looking for. The nurse told them that the result would be back in about a week and they would then see the specialist who could tell them a lot more.

Clara took Betty back in the Rover, to Rutland Manor; they had some lunch and then went through all the things she would need to pack when she moved in for a week, on Friday. Clara was very pleased that she would be able to keep an eye on Betty, she was clearly quite ill. Charles didn't know anything yet, he would also need a lot of help when the time came, and she hoped he would take her up on her offer, even if it was just for a few months, until he found somewhere he liked.

Clara mentioned her idea to Betty who thought it would be perfect, if only to shock some of the rather prim residents of Seabourne, she said, and they both smiled.

'Just imagine what all the old people will say at bridge club,' Clara added and that caused more amusement.

Betty had noticed that both Clara and Charles had been tremendously boosted by each other, and she loved to hear their delightful arguing. Charles' arrival had lifted Betty's spirits enormously these last couple of weeks, but she was not a fool and realised that she needed to make the very best of the time left to her. They talked about the wedding arrangements; it was going to be a splendid day. Betty had a beautiful head of silvery-white hair, which had been freshly permed for the occasion. She was going to have it set on Friday in Seabourne and had a delicate peach dress and jacket, with matching hat, that she and Sindy had bought at 'Seabourne's Stylish Selections'. Clara laughed and reckoned the sales assistant, Susan, was raking it in. Clara was also wearing something from her new collection, a turquoise patterned suit with high heels and a fascinator, all matching, obviously. They laughed as they said they might just outshine the bride.

'Of course, you will,' Charles was just walking in, having spent the morning with Samuel, Rob, and Patrick. Clara had nicknamed them the famous four. He gave Betty a kiss and winked at Clara. They were planning a boy's club or something, which sounded to Betty and Clara like a good opportunity to have a bit of peace and quiet, they were all for it.

BENNY

After hours of work, the wedding cake was finished. The five layers looked incredible and he would assemble it at Clara's house on Saturday morning; he had designed this one himself and had continued the seaside theme and added a few of his own ideas. The buffet was organised, there were going to be lots of canapes, he'd found a couple of local girls to serve them and help him generally. He didn't want a sandwich in sight, instead, he was planning tiny, savoury pies, little crab and prawn puff pastry tarts, plus a variety of quiches with lots of herbs. For the desserts, he had outdone himself. Chocolate cakes, piled high with chocolates on top, falling down onto the plates, individual burnt creams, lemon meringue pies, panna cottas and a mountain of meringues. It really was a feast and he was going to be exceptionally busy up until Saturday.

Although Jack's response on the phone had made him unbelievably sad, he couldn't afford to take his eye off the ball for a second. The buffet was so important and the bakery was continuing to be busy. He had confided, to a certain extent, in Paul, who thought his brother to be a total twit; he was really cross with Jack. Benny, however, reminded him that Jack was both his brother and his best man, and that everyone wanted the day to be wonderful and go without a hitch, which might mean Paul biting his tongue.

After a couple of busy hours at the bakery on Wednesday morning, the bell went and in walked his old boss, Brian. Benny was surprised and also fairly uncomfortable, as he'd left on a rather sour note. Brian however, looked like he'd had a transformation; flared jeans and a patterned paisley shirt, plain cravat and a jumper artfully slung over his shoulders. He smiled widely at Benny and asked how things were going for him now.

'Thanks for asking Brian, things are going really well, we're very busy. You look amazing by the way.' Benny had to say it, because Brian had been the most boring, conservative dresser in the whole department.

'That's very kind of you to say, I'm sorry about when you left, I guess I was a bit hurt and disappointed. Anyway, I've left too. Set up a menswear business in Cliffbourne, I was inspired by you, actually Benny. Always wanted to branch out, but never had the courage.'

Well, this was a turn up for the books. He went off with a roast beef sandwich, and a couple of slices of chocolate cake, casually saying that perhaps they could meet up for a drink one evening.

'I'd like that, Brian, thank you. Let's do it next week.'

Paul grinned, *that would show his stupid brother, what he could lose, if he wasn't careful.*

DOT

Rehearsals had gone well on Monday and even though she had heard the jokes now many times, it all still made her laugh. Her day had started with brilliant news when she'd popped into the newspaper offices to see how ticket sales were going. The lady behind the desk said they had sold half of the tickets already and there were lots of enquiries every day. This certainly boosted morale, and Miss Abbott joining the group, had really brightened the whole production with her music. Most people didn't need scripts anymore and could concentrate on their acting. They'd jointly decided to cancel the following rehearsal as too many of the cast were away, and a break would do them good. Also, Clara had telephoned to say that Mr Clements, the London theatre man, was coming down late afternoon on that Monday; she had agreed to meet him and Dot there.

The one worry Dot had was Jack. He'd been away for three weeks now and had missed a lot. Reading between the lines, she thought perhaps he had cooled things down with Benny, which was sad, but she would see him on Saturday at the wedding and could chat it through then. If Jack couldn't continue with the role of Buttons, she would ask Paul, who could now take on that character brilliantly, he was so much more outgoing since getting together with Sindy and working with Benny, and as Charles was constantly asking what he could do to help, he could handle lighting, but these changes would need to be implemented soon.

It had been a busy one for Dot, getting everything ready for Margaret coming to stay, she had spring-cleaned the spare bedroom, but when she'd looked at the sheets and blankets on the bed, she realised they were getting old and she decided it was time to get one of these new duvets and covers that seemed to be all the rage now. She'd popped into town and bought one from Tesco's home and wear store, it was brown and cream with big flowers on it, very fashionable she thought, and it would really brighten the room up. She wasn't sure what was up, but Margaret sounded very different, and she did all she could to make everywhere look welcoming, putting some flowers on the dressing table and making a poppyseed cake that she remembered Margaret enjoying as a youngster.

CHARLES AND CLARA

By the time Mrs Jackson arrived on Friday morning, they were both up, Charles making himself a strong pot of coffee and Clara some Earl Grey tea, bickering happily whilst they sat down with their hot drinks. A busy day in prospect, and the hall was bustling with excitement. Charles was picking Betty, and all her things, up later, and Clara was directing the 'wedding effort' as she had started calling it. The florist would be arriving and there would be flowers and garlands to be arranged all around the house, drinks and glasses to be checked and polished, Benny would be here soon with the cake and some of the food. Thankfully she had enough chairs, linens and cutlery to supply an army anyway. Mrs Jackson had been a marvel, and the house was shining with love and care.

There was also going to be a 'hen night' in the drawing room this evening. Clara wasn't too sure at first, but Sindy only wanted family and dippers to come along, so it didn't sound as if it would be too rowdy. Betty was excited as she hadn't been to a hen night before. Clara had ordered a case of Chardonnay, some crisps and nibbles. Jack, who generally ordered wine for these occasions, seemed to have vanished off the face of the earth; Clara was not happy, but that could be dealt with at the appropriate time.

The boys were also having a stag night. Charles was told in no uncertain terms not to let young Paul get too drunk, as there would be hell to pay if things went off course. Again, it was just the dippers, meeting at The Neptune and, Clara hoped, staying there, and not going on to any other pubs. Sindy had worked so hard for her wedding day tomorrow and Clara didn't want a gang of silly, overgrown boys, who couldn't hold their alcohol, to spoil anything.

Charles had moved his things into her guest suite yesterday. He didn't have a lot to show for fifty odd years; she looked around at this treasured, comforting home with all her familiar possessions and felt sorry for him. It was agreed that if this arrangement was going to work, they would both need their space, and he would have the room furthest down the landing from hers, plus his own bathroom and dressing room. There was a small but bright study just under his suite and he could use the back stairs, which of course, he joked about constantly, suggesting that he should wear morning dress and that Clara might like to call him Mr Hudson, from the television series, *Upstairs, Downstairs.*

As he was setting his things out in the wardrobe, dressing table and bookshelf, Charles thought about what a strange circle his life had turned. He had admired her when they were young, spent a few years at the village school together, before he went off to military training and she, to a finishing school, in Switzerland. They were different people when they arrived back in Seabourne, but the attraction they had for one another was still there. As he was about to start wooing her, Peter Harrington had arrived on the scene, and he had found himself totally outgunned. *If only things had been different.* Still, he was back in her life now and it felt amazing.

Charles picked up Betty and thought how enjoyable it would be to spend even more time with her this week. She was looking rather pale lately, and he must remember to ask Clara her thoughts on this, she was never usually slow in putting them forward. Dot and Isabella arrived, shortly followed by Sindy and Doreen. Miss Abbott and Mrs Jackson joined the girls, saying it was about time they were just 'Joyce' and 'Ruth' and everyone agreed. *All these women.* This was clearly Charles' exit cue. Clara had hidden his car keys, probably for the best, and so he wandered down to The Neptune, enjoying a cigar on the way.

As soon as they heard the front door shut, the fun began in earnest. Drinks flowed quickly, Joyce found Clara's piano, and they didn't stop laughing, dancing, singing and gossiping until just before midnight, when Sindy fell asleep on the sofa and Doreen merrily called a local taxi to take them home. It had been the best evening and they all agreed to have a girls' night more often.

BENNY AND JACK

Charles arrived at the pub to find Jack, sitting on his own at the bar, looking very forlornly into a pint of something. They hadn't met, but Charles knew exactly who he was; he was a carbon copy of Peter Harrington, forty years ago. Charles had heard some rumours about his messing things up with Benny, who Charles was becoming very fond of, and this chap's demeanour certainly looked glum.

'Has anyone told you, you are the image of your late uncle?' Charles held out his hand. Jack turned around, *good heavens, it looked as though the man had actually been crying.*

'Man up, old boy, all is not lost yet. You've got the weekend to turn things around, Charles Lancaster, by the way,' and he shook his hand warmly.

'It's good to meet you Charles, I've already heard a lot about you.'

'All bad I hope?'

'Quite the contrary,' Jack replied, 'you sound like you might have mended the Turner family single handed. I wonder if you could work some of your magic with me and Benny, I've messed up completely and probably lost the most wonderful person I've ever met.'

They continued talking, Charles advising Jack to tell the truth, be honest about his feelings for Benny and hope for some good luck. Samuel and Patrick were the next to arrive, joking and laughing about something as they walked in, and conversation turned to lighter topics. They were soon followed by the groom, Benny and Rob. Charles had put some money behind the bar, and soon they were all talking football, the benefits of bitter, as opposed to the more modern lager, and whether they should all go for a curry down the road soon. Benny and Jack nodded but kept their distance. About an hour into the evening, the bar door opened and in walked Brian, looking very dashing in a chocolate velvet suit and pointed shoes with gold tips around the toes. He had a couple of friends with him, but he was clearly more interested to see Benny who he rushed up to, and said a warm hello.

'Looks like you have some competition mate,' Paul helpfully told Jack, as if he wasn't acutely aware of this. Charles quietly advised him to go and introduce himself, keep your enemies close etc.

'Jack Harrington,' Jack held out his hand and Benny reluctantly introduced them.

'So, how do you know *my* Benny then?' Jack gambled. Saying this could go one of two ways.

Brian seemed a little taken aback, but quickly returned fire, 'oh, I've known Benny for years, we used to work together, didn't we?' And Brian touched Benny lightly on the arm.

This carried on for a minute or two, with both men, trying their best to claim Benny, who was tired, and had had enough. 'Lovely to see you both, gentlemen, but I've got a busy day tomorrow, excuse me.' Benny finished his pint in one go, and walked slowly out of the pub.

Damn and blast the pair of them, he thought to himself as he walked across the road and down to the waves. It was pitch black which matched his mood.

Jack walked to where Benny was standing, just a faint shadow against an inky horizon. He had tried to walk quietly, but that was very difficult on a tonne of pebbles. 'I'm sorry' was all he said at first, and he looked into Benny's eyes.

'What are you sorry for Jack?' was Benny's response.

'I've been unfaithful to you Benny, I'm so very sorry,' Jack explained, without going into hurtful details, about his one, stupid night and how much he regretted it. Benny just stood, looking into the dark sea, quietly, tears running down his cheeks.

'Can you forgive me? I know I can't turn the clock back, but is there any way that we can get past this and stay together?' Jack asked, realising that he didn't stand a cat's chance in hell.

PART III – NEARLY EVERYONE LIVES HAPPILY EVER AFTER

Sindy and Paul's Wedding

There were a lot of excited households in Seabourne, on Saturday 23rd October. Doreen had put Sindy's long straight hair in rollers, and was painting her nails, enjoying every minute of it. She was going to do her make up as well, Sindy didn't wear much generally, but Doreen said this was her wedding, she would look back at the photos for years, and said a little, well applied make up would enhance her natural beauty. When her mum had finished with her, she looked like a fairy-tale bride; the dress was demure, understated but alluring and stylish at the same time. She had some of her hair up, with wispy, curled bits falling down from her tiara. Once they put the veil on, Doreen thought she would cry and ruin her own make up.

She had chosen a hot pink dress and pill box hat, which suited her trim figure and dark hair. Patrick walked past, did a double take and said he thought she looked amazing which made her smile, he was a different person lately and they had been getting on so much better as a result. Sindy was glad she had gone back there for the night; it was heart-warming to see her parents more relaxed and enjoying life with each other. It was as though they had both agreed to flush all their grumbles and petty indifferences down the toilet. She'd slept really well and was ready for *her* new life to start. In the luxurious wedding car, Sindy enjoyed chatting with her father for the first time in ages.

Betty was loving the bustle of being in the 'wedding' house, there was such a lot going on and everyone who passed, said what a beautiful dress, and how wonderful she looked; as the morning wore on, she was getting quite blasé about the compliments. Charles, who looked even more dapper than usual, thought Clara looked quite ravishing in her suit and was even brave enough to tell her so. She turned around, held his hand, avoided the customary mocking response, and simply said 'thank you, Charles, and so do you.'

All the men looked very suave in their best suits, but none more so than Samuel. He had really gone to town, with a dark blue corduroy three-piece suit, red shirt and blue bow tie. Doreen thought he was going to waste without a good woman and determined to hook him up with a friend of hers. Dot and Rob had put on their Sunday best, he rarely wore a suit except for weddings and funerals and Dot had worn her birthday outfit; it felt fancy and Dot, being ever practical, enjoyed getting a bit more wear out of it.

Isabella glowed in her home-made green dress and Lizzie was fizzing with excitement at being a bridesmaid. Will was actually fizzing as well, with the secret that he was going to reveal towards the end of the reception, they didn't want to take anything away from Sindy and Paul's day, but it would be a perfect time to tell everyone.

The wild purple and orange sunrise had been followed by a couple of heavy downpours, but now the sun was shining, the sky clear, and the wind had dropped considerably. Everyone had made their way to the church, including Paul, who was shaking with nerves. Jack gave him a steadying hug and told him to enjoy this day and hang on to her, as she had transformed him from an anxious school boy into a confident young man.

'Thanks mate. Now you have to get your own life sorted out. Don't let Benny slip through your fingers, whatever you do, he's the bloody salt of the earth.' And with that, the organ started up and an elegant young bride made her way up the aisle.

Charles held on to Clara's hand tightly as he could guess the memories which must be flooding back and the emotions she would be feeling at this moment; in the church where she had married her first love. She turned to him, her eyes full, and smiled a 'thank you'.

Everyone sighed as Sindy passed them, she looked radiant, and was only slightly outshone by little Lizzie, a confection in pink ribbons and bows, concentrating really hard on walking slowly and throwing a few petals around on the floor. Isabella and Will exchanged looks which said, *this will be us soon,* and Samuel, sitting next to Will, gave him a conspiratorial wink. Dot remarked to Rob that she didn't think she was ever going to wear a 'mother of the bride' outfit.

'That's okay gorgeous,' because you look much too young for that sort of thing anyway' he whispered, and he gave her a secret peck on the cheek.

The service went by smoothly, with everyone saying the right thing at the appropriate time, and soon confetti was whirling in the air. Jack was relieved to finally have something to do; his new camera was out and he was taking hundreds of shots. There were boxes of extra film in his pockets and bag, he was certainly getting through them quickly. The wind had blown up again, and Sindy looked incredible as she tried to keep her veil and dress under control.

He'd secretly taken quite a few of Benny, who looked tremendous in a new, beautifully cut suit. He'd let his already long, dark brown hair grow even longer, mainly because he hadn't had time to get to the barbers. It suited him. He was putting such a brave face on everything, but Jack could see how deeply he was hurting and wished that he hadn't been the cause of it. Benny left the church first as he had things to do, and the wedding cars soon followed amidst happy shouts of congratulations, another cloud of confetti and joyous chatter and laughter.

Benny's girls, under Ruth's watchful eye, had done well; he hardly needed to do anything. His food looked like a fairy-tale banquet, with lots of colourful plates brimming full of flowers, fruits, herbs and his pies, cakes and desserts, however the first knock-out impression at Rutland Manor was the flowers. Clara and her florist had obviously gone to town; there were garlands of lilies, roses and baby's breath everywhere, the smell was sweet, floral and musky and Benny thought it would haunt him forever. He wandered through into the morning room where he had assembled his cake earlier, just to make sure it was still standing. It was surrounded by yet more flowers and he knew Sindy would be overjoyed. He must ask Jack to take a photo before it was cut, even though he didn't feel like talking to him ever again.

Guests were coming into the hall now so he pushed thoughts of Jack to the back of his mind, plastered on a smile and helped the girls serve the canapes. Ruth was busy with copious amounts of Champagne, Jack with more photos; and the wedding breakfast, toasts, and speeches commenced. People didn't really know who to compliment first; Clara's arrangements of flowers, Benny's delicious buffet, the loveliness of the couple or the cuteness of the bridesmaid. The speeches were witty and thankfully short and then Will got up, right at the end and, tapping a glass, asked if he might make an announcement.

'It's about time, son,' he was being heckled by his father-in-law to be and he hadn't even made the announcement. Everyone laughed and Will continued.

'As we're all together, I wanted to tell you that Isabella has made me the second happiest man in the world, after young Paul over there, and agreed to become my wife.

There were cheers of congratulations, more Champagne and many ladies emoting over the ring. Will and Isabella had also bought Lizzie a special pink ring to match which she showed off, just like mummy.

The whole day went by in a dream for Sindy and Paul. Far too soon, a taxi arrived to take them to Gatwick Airport where they would be catching a plane to Spain for a week. There were endless rounds of congratulations, have a great time, and heartfelt thanks, followed by tears, laughter and finally the boot closed with a soft clunk, on two small suitcases, and they were off, starting married life together, looking forward to their first trip in an aeroplane, heading for somewhere they had only dreamed of.

DOT AND MARGARET

Margaret had telephoned early on Saturday morning to let Dot know that she would wait until the late afternoon to come and see them. She realised the wedding was important and didn't want to intrude upon her mum and dad's enjoyment of that, she said. Dot was surprised and relieved in equal amounts, as she felt that whatever Margaret had to tell them was probably not good news and may have put a damper on the celebrations.

They arrived home from the wedding, with Rob slightly tipsy from the Champagne; Dot had wanted to keep a clear head, and so only had one. Margaret was sitting in her shiny foreign car, on the drive. She jumped out when she saw them and almost ran to put her arms out to Dot, who gathered her up, without hesitation. Rob put the kettle on, he really needed a strong black coffee and decided to absent himself. This looked like a woman's thing and he reckoned at least a couple of hours. He picked up his Saint Bruno and his pipe, found some matches and wandered in the direction of his shed.

Dot made a big pot of tea and they sat down together.

'I don't know where to start mum,' Margaret finally said, after a couple of silent minutes, sipping scalding tea.

'At the beginning sweetheart?' Dot replied.

'Okay, well there isn't really a beginning because it's all muddled up together. You know I got the Sales Director job at work a few months ago, do you remember?'

Dot did remember the conversation.

'So, my new boss, David, was a bit 'hands on' if you know

what I mean, and I hoped it would calm down once he got to know me. It didn't though mum, he was all over me at every opportunity, trying to kiss me when we were in the lift together, which seemed to be all the time, putting his hands all over the place. It was really horrible. He's probably nearly sixty, married with kids and grandkids. I couldn't decide the best thing to do, so I went to the Personnel Department, to find his best mate was in charge there and he laughed it off.'

'Oh, my love, that sounds horrible, I'm so sorry for you, we better not tell dad, he'll just go up there and thump him.'

Margaret continued, 'It's too late now mum, I wouldn't play his game, and he got me fired, just like that. No one seemed interested in what I had to say, nobody listened, even some of my colleagues just giggled and said I shouldn't have provoked him.'

Dot gave her a hug and said they would sort something out.

'I've got more to tell you mum. So, I've lost my job, got no references, lost my flat and I'm afraid I've got another bombshell. I'm sorry.'

'You're pregnant?' asked Dot, in a gentle voice, to show she cared.

'I'm gay, mum. I like women. I am sorry to disappoint you, but I've always felt this way, and it's difficult to be a woman with a man's job, but a lesbian woman just seems to be more of a challenge for the bastards.'

Dot smiled, 'thank you for sharing your news, but I think I probably had an inkling my darling. You haven't disappointed me, or your dad, one bit. We love you whatever you say, do, think, eat, drink, enjoy. Do you get it? We just love you, for who you are, sorry if that sounds a bit corny. We already have a couple of close, gay friends, it is 1976 you know.

Margaret burst out laughing, a real belly laugh that Dot hadn't heard in years, which set her off as well, and then the tears followed, long pent-up ones. Rob was just about to walk in through the back door in search of biscuits when he did an abrupt hand-brake turn, back to the shed with haste.

They chatted for hours, both of them sharing problems as well as the high points that were in their lives at the moment. Dot told Margaret all about the pantomime, and Margaret listened. She was so pleased for her mum, and wondered if she could join in for a while. There were some big decisions to be made and she asked if she could stay for a month or two. Dot was overjoyed and didn't even try to hide it. The thought of them having a coffee together in the mornings, perhaps even going out for a drink, Christmas shopping; it all filled her with a mother-daughter happiness, that she had missed for a very long time. Margaret had one more confidence to share; she had a girlfriend, Kate. They had been together for a couple of years, but no-one actually knew, they were just 'flat-mates'. Dot immediately said she could come and stay and Margaret was really grateful but thought Kate would probably stay in London for a while longer.

When there were all out of talking, Margaret was touched when she saw the effort Dot and gone to with her room.

'I'm sorry I've been so hard to love lately. I've got no excuse, and I plan to make it up to you and dad.'

Dot just smiled and said night-night.

ISABELLA AND WILL

Will thought it would be exciting if they went straight from the wedding to the New Forest, honeymoon style. They had savoured every moment of the wedding and Will said how he'd like theirs to be just the same, although they didn't think they could afford a huge venue like Rutland Manor, or the Champagne for that matter. Lizzie was beyond happy and excited; being a bridesmaid and going on holiday on the same day, together with her favourite dog, Diesel, was almost too much. Isabella smiled, she just didn't have the spare money for lots of treats and so today she was making the most of Lizzie's pure joy.

As Will drove through the forest, to Brockenhurst, they spotted tiny ponies and huge cattle with scarily big horns, on the side of the road; it was magical. Will glanced over at Isabella, her eyes were shining and he wondered if time might stand still, as he couldn't imagine a more perfect day. Their room was cosy and they went out for a short walk before bed; they'd eaten so much at the wedding that no-one had any room for supper at all. Just as well because breakfast was fit for a king. The lady at the hotel couldn't seem to do enough for them, and said they were a jolly and beautiful family. The three, dream-like days flew by. Lizzie wasn't sure about pony-trekking as she thought it was too bumpy but Will could see Isabella was rather taken with it, and seemed to be a natural. On their way home, they drove by an enchanting stream, so they stopped, gave Diesel one more forest walk, and ate their picnic. Suddenly the late October heavens opened calling time on their holiday. Will dropped the girls off and thought he should just pop back to his flat, to make sure all was okay.

The door was difficult to open because of all his post, he hadn't been back for a while. Most of it was junk, but there was a handwritten letter at the bottom, and unfortunately, he recognised the writing.

BENNY

Once the happy couple had been driven off, slowly down the drive, with yet more confetti and shouts of congratulations, the clearing up operation began. The leftovers were divided up and everyone went away with a box of something. Benny had to smile to himself seeing Betty, Clara, Charles and Ruth snuggled up, each with a cosy blanket on the sofas, finishing off the Champagne and nibbling a variety of puddings. Jack appeared to be staying over, and so Benny went into the sitting room to say his goodbyes. Charles congratulated him on a fabulous job, well done, and Clara walked him to the back door, where he was parked. *Oh God,* He was still using Jack's car! *He needed to sort this out,* and decided to walk home.

Benny was just walking out, when Clara beckoned him into her morning room and shut the door. She wasn't a hugger, but having watched Benny closely for most of the day, she realised he must feel very deflated, and she put her tiny, graceful arms around him. *Don't cry, don't cry,* but it was too late and he was doing the one thing he had promised himself not to. Clara poured him a large one and suggested they talk. Jack had told her everything; she was furious and ashamed of him; three weeks in London and he'd blown his relationship sky high, and for what?

Clara listened to Benny; it was good to really talk about his feelings for Jack. He felt so stupid for falling in love with him so quickly, and unreservedly. This was probably the worst part, that, and missing Jack so much that he may as well have had an amputation.

Benny didn't know what sort of life Jack really wanted now,

as it had taken him no time at all to go off the rails, and Benny remembered the liaisons that Jack had told him about, from his past. All of this was very different from the calm, trusting, quiet relationship they had formed over the last few months. He couldn't stop himself asking Clara what Jack had said; they'd barely exchanged two words over the course of the day. At that point, there was a gentle knock at the door and Jack walked in.

'Sorry to interrupt you, Aunt Clara, but I *really* need to talk with Benny. Would that be okay with you, Benny?'

Clara was very tempted to tell him to 'bugger off and wait' but Benny was nodding and so she kept her thoughts to herself, rose from the sofa and left them to it.

They talked for hours; with Jack apologising, but he was unable to provide any sort of explanation for his actions, other than he had 'lost his head.' Jack wanted to try and start again, he loved Benny, and didn't want to lose him. Benny knew he'd been made a fool of, it felt as if Jack had built him up to be some kind of God-like man, and then trampled all over him, laughing. It was true, his confidence was stronger than ever, up until now, which was probably why Brian had suddenly been attracted to him. He wasn't interested; he could never really get the original Brian, with the boring suit and plastic shoes, out of his mind.

They seemed to be going round in circles and Benny said perhaps it was the end. Clara walked in, with a determined face, 'right you two, I need to lock up, its two o'clock in the morning, and some of us need our beauty sleep. Jack, Benny, you were made for each other. I spent forty years feeling lonely and afraid of loving someone. Don't make my mistakes. Forgive him Benny, and move on. I know it must be hard but if you don't, I think you might regret it for the rest of your life. Jack, if you ever even look at another man, you'll have me to answer to, and don't think just because I'm getting on that I'll not come and visit you from the grave if you mess this up.' This made them both smile.

Clara added that Benny was welcome to stay over, all the rooms were made up, and out she went. Jack nervously looked over to see what Benny was going to do.

'Everyone deserves a second chance but, that's all you get Jack, and call me 'mate' ever again and I'll swing for you, understand?' They went up the broad staircase, with Benny telling Jack all about his right hook at Isabella's and how he had saved the day. *I've missed him so much,* Jack thought.

CLARA

Dot thought she'd better look smart for this meeting with *Julian Clements, London Stage Director*, and Clara, who was always impeccably dressed. So, she styled her hair carefully and put her new suit on again, *now* she felt like she was at a business meeting, although she couldn't work out why Clara had invited her.

They met an hour before, at the theatre, and the weather couldn't have been less inviting. October was throwing its worst at them today; heavy bursts of the sort of rain that soaks you in ten seconds and gusty winds; her hair was messed up instantly, even Clara had to smooth herself down a little, once they had let themselves in. They switched on the house lights and both of them let out a sigh. A lot more had been done since last Monday; woodwork and metal fittings had been mended and polished, the silver mermaids, dotted around the auditorium, that Sindy had been repainting, sparkled with life and Clara detected the hand of Ruth Jackson on the windows, no-one could get glass to shine like that woman. She thought it involved the use of a towel, or maybe some sort of allegiance with the Devil, or perhaps both. The Mermaid Theatre was looking it's best, however; Clara mentioned her concerns to Dot.

'The one thing that lets us down here is the stage lighting; I know they work, but they're ancient and the operating system, is archaic. I think Mr Clements might change his mind when we go over that.'

'Would you like me to find out how much a new set would be? Perhaps we could organise some beetle drives, jumble sales and dances to help with the cost,' Dot said.

'I think you'll find that will be eye-popping and I'm not sure we could ever cover the outlay with ten years of pantomimes and that sort of thing. However, that's a good idea Dot, at least we would know the situation. Thank you.'

The door blew open and Julian Clements blew in, shaking himself and his umbrella in the foyer. 'Afternoon ladies, I can't say good. Is this weather usual in these parts? I'm quite the city gent, as you see,' and he did a twirl, 'but I think I'll need a 'seaside weather' wardrobe if this is the norm.'

'The weather comes straight off the sea here, so yes, possibly you will,' laughed Dot. 'Let me introduce Lady Clara Harrington, who owns both the pier and the Mermaid.'

She's a natural, Dot thought, as she shook hands with Julian.

'Please don't think me without manners, but I need to be back in London tonight for a premiere and so I would like to agree matters fairly quickly.'

'That makes three of us,' replied Clara. 'So, if you'd like to set out your requirements and suggested terms, to Dot and myself, we can get down to business.'

They walked through the whole theatre with Julian taking notes and then the thorny subject of lighting was mentioned.

'I am, shall I say, *tickled* by your antique lighting, which I can possibly use for a short while, however, with your permission and say, fifty percent of the cost, these will need replacing as I am sure you are both aware.'

Dot looked over at Clara and said, 'twenty-five percent, that's what we are prepared to contribute, Julian. From what I gather, you will be almost the sole user of the theatre, and as such, you will need to cover the majority of the outlay.'

'Well, Lady Harrington, your theatre manager certainly drives a hard bargain, but I like her and your theatre, so the answer is yes. After your Christmas production, for which I would ask you to reserve me fifty tickets, I immediately have a stage show planned. I am prepared to offer you a percentage of my takings or a single payment. Please take your time to consider this. I realise you will have other clients, but I would ask that I have first refusal on dates. I will have my lawyers draw up a contract, if that suits you, and we can begin.'

They shook hands, Julian braced himself for the pier, and almost jogged back, to his driver, who was waiting in the *Bentley*. '*They* are a pair of ladies who I am going to enjoy doing business with,' remarked Julian to his driver, as they purred off at a stately speed.

'Well Dot, if the cap fits, you should most certainly wear it.' Clara stated, as they were both literally jumping for joy. 'I would like you to take on that role that Julian has so presciently bestowed upon you. Shall we say £2,400 per annum, as a starting figure? Charles and I are keen to go travelling next year together, making up for lost time as it were. I love the theatre but some time for myself and that infuriating man, is what I would like for the future. Please say yes Dot, that would solve all my problems.'

'Do you really think I have the experience and knowledge for this, Clara? I did enjoy that meeting but, could I really be a theatre manager?' Dot was doubting herself as she had done for most of her life, when she suddenly decided it was time to stop. 'Actually, what the hell? Yes, please. Thank you. I won't let you down. This theatre has become my life now and so I might as well get paid for it. What on earth am I going to do with all that money?'

'I'm sure you'll think of something my dear, and thank you.'

CHARLES

They met at The Neptune to discuss Charles' idea; Rob, Samuel, Benny and Jack, even Patrick. They had briefly spoken about this during the wedding and agreed it could work well. A sort of men's 'Women's Institute', but with beer, cigarettes, cigar or pipe, as preferred. Twice a month to start with; there would be woodwork, which Samuel was going to instruct, cooking, which was Benny's department, do-it-yourself, which Rob and Pat were going to share, cars and maintenance, which seemed to belong to Charles, plus anything else that the boys wanted. Initially it would be just them, but newcomers would be welcome. They decided a small notice in Seabourne Matters might attract a few blokes. There were a lot of redundancies at the moment and money was tight, so they agreed it would be free, unless there were any costs involved. Wednesdays appeared to suit all and Charles drafted an advertisement.

Charles got 'home'; the joy of which he didn't ever think he would tire of, to find Clara looking at travel brochures. She was interested to hear of his plan, but this seemed to be at complete odds with her idea of them going away together for a good part of next year.

'But, my dear Charles, I have drawn up a comprehensive list of travel destinations, with ticket prices, hotels, everything. We can't let your 'boys club' interfere with our plans, can we?'

'*Your plans*, Clara darling. Although we talked about this, I didn't commit to being out of the country for that amount of time, I've only just got back and it's so very good to be home,' Charles replied, slapping the file of papers on the coffee table with a little more force than he meant to.

'Fine, forget it then.' Clara marched off to her bedroom, wondering if she had made the right choice with this high-handed, pig-headed, annoyance of a man.

BENNY AND JACK

It was odd for them at first, feeling apprehensive and jittery as they papered over the gaping crack between them; they were both tiptoeing around each other. Benny was thankful for his work, and also the fact that Jack had to go back to London the next day, it would give him some time to come to terms with everything. They talked, whilst Benny cooked, at the bakery, drinking mugs of coffee. Benny was adamant that Jack should go back and complete his work; after all, if he wasn't to be trusted, he needed to find out sooner rather than later. Jack knew he would never be such an idiot again, but wondered if the physical distance between them might widen the gap. It was the little things, like discussing the day, a kiss before going to sleep, coffee together in the mornings, that all made it work. However, as Benny stated, Jack had a job to do, just as he had a bakery to run. They *had* to make it work, and both agreed to set aside a little time each day to talk, until Jack was back in Seabourne.

Now that the wedding was over, Benny was holding a 'Halloween and Harvest' week at the bakery. He had lots of ideas and was going to decorate Benjamin's with pumpkins, autumn leaves and flowers. He had ordered thirty pumpkins which had arrived yesterday and he and Jack spent the whole day scooping the flesh out, separating the seeds; which Benny was going to roast in oil and salt. By the end of the day, they had slightly sore, orange hands, but lots of happy and scarily faced jack-o-lanterns. Benny had made spicy pumpkin soup, which he hoped would be popular, because otherwise he would be living off this all week. There were a variety of pies, decorated with tiny marzipan pumpkins, with the leaves and stalks trailing over the plate and onto the counter. Right in the centre he had made an enormous wheat sheaf loaf, with many ears of corn at the top, shining with an egg glaze and covered with rock salt. It all looked tempting and smelled incredible.

Jack left very early the next day, after promises, hugs, some tears, and leaving Benny a note and a gift, just under the covers, for him to see this evening.

SINDY AND PAUL

They arrived home, tanned and relaxed; a very confident and happy Mr and Mrs Harrington. Sindy wanted to see Betty first, and give her the beautiful flamenco dancing doll that they had chosen. Betty was looking pale but said she was keeping her pecker up. Sindy didn't doubt that, but asked about her scan date.

'I've not got it yet, my love, but I'm sure it won't be long now.' Betty lied, giving herself a bit more time. She hadn't had the results back yet; they were due later in the week. With Clara's help, Betty had prepared her back bedroom for them, it wasn't Sindy's original room, which was just a single. This one was quite grand, perfect for a married couple, with a fine old double bed, matching wardrobe and dressing table. It had a big bay window which let in lots of sunshine; Clara and Betty had washed the curtains and the candlewick bedspread, and bought a new rug; it looked really cosy. Sindy was delighted to see the room so welcoming and was touched at the effort Betty and Clara had gone to. They chatted about their honeymoon; the aeroplane was exciting; they had loved the incredibly warm and clear sea. Paul said it would be hard to get back into the cold water, he rather liked the Mediterranean. The food they weren't sure about, although they had tried everything, just to get the whole Spanish experience.

They popped round to see her mum and dad, who were very pleased with the duty-free cigarettes and Spanish brandy. Her mum made some tea and pointedly asked 'how she was keeping'. Sindy was looking remarkably well; the morning sickness had died down and she was glowing; people would start guessing soon. Patrick mentioned the boys club and thought Paul might like to come along to the first one; it made Sindy happy to see how much her dad was changing.

Next on their visiting list were Clara and Charles, who made a very fine show of being best friends, even though they were still mid-battle. Clara was delighted with the dainty Spanish fan that Sindy had found, Charles was even more pleased with a small box of cigars. Paul said he could never thank them enough for all they had done for him and Sindy. It was quite enough for Clara to see him so at ease with himself. They wanted to see Benny before the bakery closed and found him clearing up, so they were just in time.

'Hola, buenos dias,' Benny called as they walked in, and he offered them some of his new bakes to try, whilst performing an impromptu flamenco dance with a couple of vanilla cookies. Paul hoped the reason for this jolliness was because he and Jack had patched things up. They had bought him a Spanish confection called Turron, with almonds, which Benny hadn't tried before. Paul asked about doing more hours at the bakery, as he wanted to start saving and planning for their future. Benny grinned as he was hoping Paul could do more, he had really missed him this last week. Charles had been great, but not quite as speedy behind the counter as Paul.

Sindy had picked up some castanets for Lizzie to say thank you for being a bridesmaid, they would be seeing them later as Dot had arranged a costume fitting evening.

DOT

She was excited about this evening, as once they had their costumes, she knew their characters would really come alive. This was to be followed up by a sewing and alteration session which Sindy and Betty were up for, Clara as well, even Doreen had volunteered. Dot had never met Doreen before the wedding; however, she was fun, she had also said she'd do the stage make-up which would be very helpful. Dot was also looking forward to introducing Margaret to all her friends and telling them all about her own employment news.

Dot and Rob helped Clara and Charles with transporting all the boxes from Rutland Manor, down to the theatre. The evening turned out to be rather fun. Once she and Clara had assigned all the outfits, the boys had a laugh, just mincing about in the dame costumes, *what was it about men wanting to wear dresses and wigs?* Joyce had come along for some company and amusingly played a variety of tunes for everyone to dance around to. When she launched into "Play that funky music", followed by ELO's "Evil Woman" when Samuel (the wicked stepmother) came on stage, people were astonished that she had picked these up so quickly, and without written music. They had a couple of song practices and the hours flew by.

Margaret was really engaging with everyone, now she had got things off her chest, she was a joy to be around, helping with the costumes and encouraging people. Margaret couldn't wait until Monday, she said, to see the whole run through. Rob watched the evening unfold in his quiet way and was beyond happy for Dot. The Stage Manager job was the icing on the cake for her and he wondered if his now 'high flying' wife would just take off one day, hopefully not.

Isabella needed some help getting into the pantomime wedding dress for the final scene, and Dot popped into the dressing room. She looked breath-taking and they both said perhaps this should be her real wedding dress, but she couldn't do the back herself. Dot helped but once zipped up, she said it was a bit uncomfortable under her left arm, near her bust. They both pushed and prodded a bit to sort the problem out, which caused much laughter, but Isabella still complained of it not feeling right. Dot asked her if she had problems with her own underwear, but Isabella said she never wore anything tight and so hadn't noticed. Dot had had a scare some years ago, it had just been a benign cyst, and she offered to check her. Isabella couldn't stop laughing both from being ticklish and embarrassed, but Dot felt a small lump and showed her how to feel it. Yes, it was a definite lump. Dot advised her to pop in to the surgery and get it checked out straight away, it was probably nothing, but she didn't think Isabella should leave it.

ISABELLA AND WILL

When they got home, Isabella wanted to talk, which was useful, because Will very much needed to tell her about the letter. She had been full of life during the evening, but was suddenly very withdrawn after the wedding dress fitting. Will hoped it didn't mean she was having second thoughts.

'I have a lump, just to the side of my left boob,' Isabella blurted out, and Will was shaken from his own problems.

'Are you sure?' This was a silly response, but again, it just came out.

'Dot noticed it when we were trying on the dress, it's not very comfortable. I'm really worried Will, what if it's breast cancer? What will I do, who will look after Lizzie?' She burst into tears. Will gathered her up, kissing her tangled hair.

'We will get through this together and you are not to worry about a thing, but we must go to the doctors tomorrow morning.'

'Let's go to the one in Cliffbourne, Dot said it's much better there,' Isabella said and Will agreed, he'd known the doctor there for years. This was not the time to tell her that he had received a letter from Carol, his previous partner, asking could Will please meet up with her as she had a lot to say and *really* needed to see him. Will had thought he'd seen the last of her when she waved goodbye all those years ago, trying to look sad, but obviously being deliriously happy.

After dropping Lizzie off at school, they were at the surgery for opening time, and the rather sharp receptionist, found an appointment for them in fifteen minutes, if they would like to wait. She softened entirely when Isabella quietly told her the problem. Will waited outside as the doctor examined her. Yes, she needed a scan, the fact that it was a bit uncomfortable was a good sign, but it had to be checked. He would book her in as soon as possible. He also asked about her general health, took her blood pressure, weight, and then requested a urine test, which Isabella didn't understand, but forgot to ask the reason.

Will then needed to get to the station, as his colleague had been helping out for a whole week. Isabella said that was okay, she needed to bury herself in work and try to put the lump to the back of her mind. This was easier said than done, and within a few hours, she decided to go and see Dot, she really needed a friend to talk this through with. Will had been great, but there was no-one like a girlfriend with this sort of thing.

CLARA AND CHARLES

They had both carried this argument on too long, and it was time to settle things and make up, if only for Ruth's sake, who was more than ready to give both of them a clip round the ear.

Charles made his coffee and a pot of tea for Clara and they strolled into the sitting room.   Clara spoke first, 'Charles, I understand you have been away from home a very long time, and I realise it was possibly thoughtless of me to start planning trips without you. I'm sorry. Perhaps we can meet in the middle somewhere?'

'I think that is an excellent idea my darling, I don't have to go to all the club meetings, just now and again. I was looking at your brochures, the ones for a train journey caught my eye. How about we start our travelling with a trip on The Orient Express and see where the wind blows us after that? Sindy and Paul could move in here and keep the house going for us, until we return. What do you think?'

'That does sound very tempting, it's something I've always fancied doing. When were you thinking?' Clara was suitably impressed.

'Shall we book it in the Spring, it will be nice to have something to look forward to after the fun of the pantomime, and there is a certain romance to Paris in the Springtime.' Charles chuckled.

'Ah, so that's your game! You think my head will be turned by all that glamour and opulence, well, we'll have to see.'

They took a walk along the beach, holding hands and chatting through their plans, with Clara mentioning that Dot had accepted the role of theatre manager.

'That is good thinking, Clara my dear. Dot is one intelligent and capable woman; your precious Mermaid Theatre will be in very safe hands.'

As they walked back up the steps, looking forward to some lunch, Ruth met them halfway down, looking worried. 'It's Mr Harrington, the care home has just telephoned to say that he has taken quite a turn for the worst. They said can you come as soon as possible? They're not sure he's going to last very long now.'

Clara rang the bakery to let Paul know that his father was fading, and Charles said they could pick him up, as it was on the way. Charles had gone to school with Dennis, who he remembered as a fragile boy, even then. He'd clearly had a very sad life, which made Charles realise how lucky he was to have a second chance and that he should make the most of every single day. They sped to the home, just in time to see him fade away. There was a faint recognition in his eyes as he went to sleep and he murmured something about Paul and Jack.

Clara had visited him, once a week for years, but without any progress, and so she was pleased that there was a light in his eye for his youngest son, before he left them. Paul was numb, he hadn't visited Dennis that often and now he was crying guilty tears for a father he'd hardly known.

'Man up, old boy,' was Charles' advice in so many situations, and Clara just gave him a hug. Life had not been easy for young Paul, thank goodness Sindy was with him now and things were taking a turn for the better. They got home and telephoned Jack, who had just finished work. The phone went very quiet; like his brother, the visits had stopped when there seemed no point to them. Now, however there was a funeral to arrange and Jack said this was at least something he could do for his father. He talked it through with Benny on the telephone later that night and decided a further days' holiday was needed to get this sorted out.

BENNY AND JACK

When Benny got home from work on the day Jack left for London, tired from the rollercoaster of the last week, and exhausted from a customer filled day, he smiled when he found the envelope, together with a small, neatly wrapped package, with a piece of rosemary tucked into the knot. It was a long letter, of apology and hope for the future; it was Jack in paper and ink form, it even smelled of him. Benny realised that Jack meant what he had written, and opened the gift. It was a simple, heavy, silver chain, and Jack had said he hoped Benny would accept it as a token of his love, and a new start. Benny kissed it, put it on, and knew that he had to put this one, disloyal act, completely behind him now, otherwise it would keep on gnawing away at his insides until it won, which wasn't fair.

Jack arrived back home, and appeared to be wearing a three-piece suit made of guilt; for the father he had recently neglected, for his betrayal of Benny's love and because he should really be in London, working on his project. Benny grabbed a couple of towels, their swimming trunks and took him by the hand, making straight for the waves. Together they washed their worries and problems away in the cold, darkness. It was astonishing just how many negative feelings the sea could absorb and pound down to nothing, like grains of sand. As they walked home, shivering, Benny said they could work together to get the funeral organised. It was a sad end of an unhappy life, and Benny thought they should celebrate the legacy Dennis had left; his beautiful sons, Jack and Paul.

Benny was becoming quite knowledgeable about burials and

the rather morbid funeral director almost greeted him as an old friend, which they all found slightly spooky. Paul had joined them as he wanted to be involved and everything was simply planned for the Friday of that week. Benny and Paul opened up a little later that morning, and quickly got on with the business of the day, Jack came along with them and for a while he helped. He wanted to talk to both of them about his pantomime role, which he was enjoying immensely, but he had missed a lot and would probably miss more yet; he wondered whether Paul might take it on?

'Sure mate, I would probably make a better fist of it than you, anyway, he joked.' He had been standing in for Jack for quite a few weeks now and had learnt all his lines.

'Thanks for that little brother. You always know how to make me feel good,' Jack laughed. 'We just need to see what Dot thinks now.' It was a Monday and so they would get a chance to speak to her this evening. Of course, now that he had relinquished the role, Jack immediately felt sad that he wouldn't be involved, but there was still a lot to do in London and he was going to try and complete things in the next couple of weeks. Unfortunately, of course, he was not his own boss, and the final decision was always in the hands of Steve or the guys in London.

Jack explained his predicament to Dot that evening at rehearsals and she quite understood. Paul now threw himself into the role with lots more enthusiasm and Dot was pleased with the result, the costume actually fitted him a little better so perhaps it was meant to be. Jack left straight after rehearsals, with the songs and piano music ringing in his ears. He had missed a whole day and would miss another on Friday so he needed to put some extra hours in. As the train sped towards Waterloo, Jack considered how well the pantomime was going and how it had brought so many people together, giving them all new chances in their lives, focussing on the community, and mending relationships along the way.

It really was quite remarkable. Will and Benny had really been on form, they made the funniest ugly sisters Jack had seen. It was a pity Betty hadn't been there tonight; according to Clara, who was quieter than usual, Betty was a bit tired and sent her apologies.

BETTY

The nurse had phoned that morning and Clara had taken Betty to see the specialist. The news they received together, hand in hand, was what they had both been dreading. It was leukaemia and it was too late now to try any treatments. They had both known, and had simply kept this locked away until after the wedding. The specialist was a kind and straightforward woman; she said she could provide pain killing drugs up until the end, for which she couldn't give an exact date, but thought three months would be the most time that Betty would have where she would be able to function with a degree of normality. *Please let it be after the pantomime,* Betty thought. She had put so much into this and wanted to be able to sit there and laugh her head off and clap for all she was worth, as the curtains closed.

Clara took her up to Rutland Manor, Charles needed to be told and Betty wanted to do this herself. He was in the sitting room, enjoying the November sun, shining through a gap in the clouds, with his paper and a coffee, looking like he hadn't a care in the world, but his expression changed the second he saw them both walking in.

'So, Betty my darling, how long have you got? Don't, for one moment think I haven't noticed your gradual decline, I just wanted to give you the time to tell me when you were ready.'

'I'm afraid it's leukaemia, Charlie, and I have about three reasonable months left. I'm so sorry, we have only just had the diagnosis.'

'My darling Betty, you have nothing to be sorry about, I only wish I had returned sooner and then we would have had more time together.' Clara put the kettle on to give them a bit of time, just the two of them.

Betty was a surprisingly tough and practical woman; she quickly decided that if she had three months left, she damn well wasn't going to spoil them with feeling sorry for herself. This had already been the best year of her life, what with the swimming, the pantomime, Clara's friendship, Sindy's wedding and the baby, and most of all, Charles' return, and she was going to make the very best use of the time that was left to her. She would make plans now, to include everyone, before she was in too much pain to get these things done. People needed to know, because they would soon guess something was up, but she wasn't having anyone pitying her. A bloody good celebration of her life; that's what she wanted now, before her death, and then to go out with a big bang, and if she made it into 1977, then so much the better.

She knew that Sindy was going to be the most difficult; young people, with their unshakeable optimism, found it hard to accept the really harsh truths, Betty realised. She was comforted that Sindy had Paul, her baby, Patrick and Doreen, who had been so much better lately, and Clara and Charles there for her. It was late afternoon, and Sindy would be at home, getting the tea ready for them all. She needed to get this over with and so they went straight there, knowing Paul would be home by now.

Betty gave them both the news, as gently as she could. Sindy knew Betty was unwell but hadn't realised how serious it was. She was absolutely devastated and Betty had to be quite firm, telling her to think about the baby and calm down a little. Paul was very helpful, he understood how Betty wanted to live her last months, and said he would do everything he could to help. They both knew how hard this was on Sindy and he assured her that he would be there for her always.

No one ate much food, with everyone pushing it around their plates and Sindy sobbing quietly into her dinner. Betty got up and asked Charles to take her round to see Patrick and Doreen now, adding that from tomorrow, she wanted no more sad faces or crying, only happiness, fun and laughter for the next three months, after that, they could do what they liked.

DOT

Clara told Dot the news, and spoke of Betty's wishes for her remaining months. Dot was saddened but not surprised by the way Betty wanted to do this, she was such a strong and determined lady. *Good for her,* Dot thought and decided to make the most of every single remaining day of Betty's life. They could have some fireworks on the beach for bonfire night, and perhaps a small get together after each Monday night rehearsal, which could be brought forward an hour, so that Betty didn't get too tired. Dot decided to ask Charles to be a sort of shadow prompt, in case it got too much for Betty towards the end. She agreed to pass the sad news on to the others so that by the time Monday rehearsals came around, everyone would have got over their shock, and be able to put a jolly face on it, as requested. It was the least they could do for her. Clara and Charles thought these were great ideas and very soon word got round to everyone; Betty wouldn't have to mention it again, if she didn't want to.

Margaret had news, and Dot got home to find her buzzing with excitement. She'd seen a vacancy advertised in the local paper, for a purchasing director, at a large new fashion brand, not ten miles away. She'd telephoned and had an interview tomorrow. She was also going to look for a flat and did Dot want to come along with her? The thought of Margaret settling locally, filled her with happiness; it felt like all her dreams were coming true at the moment and she was worried in case she was receiving more luck than she was actually due in this troubled world. Rob would have laughed, but Margaret understood how she felt.

'Would it be okay for Kate to come and stay for a while,' Margaret asked, 'she can sleep on the sofa if you'd be more comfortable with that.'

Dot smiled, 'I don't think anyone would be more comfortable with that, least of all Kate. Have you sat on that sofa recently?' And they both agreed that perhaps a new one for Christmas would be nice. This sort of talk was dangerous; they both loved Christmas and were quite happy to go completely overboard, getting decorations out way too early and considering which shops sold the best mince pies; Benjamin's', obviously. Margaret remembered so many happy Christmas's when she was younger, and requested that she and Kate come home to Dot and Rob for a *proper* Christmas, like they had in the old days, with everything just as it used to be, including her dad's home-made bread sauce and stuffing. Dot just stood there listening, laughing and crying at the same time.

ISABELLA

Isabella had received the scan appointment, on Thursday of this week. She was glad it was soon because this was a strain on her, she didn't want to tell anyone else about it yet. Samuel sensed something was up, but Isabella couldn't confide in him at the moment. If it was just a cyst, it would be worrying him about nothing and if it was breast cancer, which had wickedly taken her mother, then, she realised they would all fall apart; she needed to be sure, one way or the other.

Will was being a bit odd and she couldn't quite put her finger on it. *He's probably worried about the lump in his own way,* and she guessed he didn't really know what to say. After picking up Lizzie from school, she decided a good brisk walk along the shore would help, and so they braved the salt laden gusts and battled along towards the pier. The fine sand was whisking up and rolling across the beach, carried by the senseless wind; they had to turn around in order to shield their eyes from it.

'Look, there's Daddy!' Lizzie's new name for Will; one day she had just started saying it and hearing this had made both Will and Isabella very happy indeed. She looked up to the pier, to see a couple, huddled against the wind, talking earnestly together. *Oh God, could this really be happening? Now? Just when she needed him the most?* Isabella turned away, out of his view. Luckily, he hadn't seen them and she didn't want him to, she needed to try and make some sense of this. He hadn't mentioned seeing anyone today and surely if he had a meeting, it would be at the station. There seemed to her, only one logical, if nightmarish, conclusion.

'Daddy's busy with a work friend,' was the best she could

come up with, and she didn't want Lizzie mentioning this to Will until she had time to think. 'Let's go to Benjamin's and get cake and hot chocolate, shall we?' Lizzie didn't need asking twice, and off they went, stamping the damp sand off their boots as they walked.

Benny was delighted to see them and Lizzie was soon sat in the special chair, cake in one hand and teddies in the other. He could see that Isabella had something big on her mind, Paul took over, and they went out the back to talk. Benny had been making huge saucepans of buttery, spicy mincemeat and the evocative smell of Christmas was enough to set Isabella off. After drying her eyes, she told Benny everything; the lump, the impending scan, and what she had just seen on the pier. He couldn't quite believe what he was hearing and he didn't know what to say, having so recently been the person who had been cheated on, he hadn't got any useful advice. He held her for a few moments, 'if you need me to come along to the scan, you know I will do that, I'm so very sorry you are going through all this at the moment.' And then he went on, 'are you sure it was a romantic encounter?' was all he said. He really didn't think Will was the type; if he was wrong, Will was going to have to answer to him, big time. He sent them home with one of Isabella's favourite cakes, and the certain knowledge that she could talk to him any time, day or night, if she needed to. He was just next door, after all, and they both meant the world to him.

PAUL

The next morning, Paul arrived early, as usual, to put the bread away and get busy with the rolls and sandwiches. The sunrise matched the shop colours this morning, flooding the beach with baby pinks and blues.

Every day, the bread was left outside, under cover, but not today. After looking around, Paul telephoned the little bakery to hear the news that they had gone under, the strikes, power cuts and everything else this last year was too much. Business closed. Paul ran round to Tesco's and looked at the Mother's Pride. *No*, he thought, and used his initiative. Soda bread, that's what Mrs Jackson had taught him to make, years ago when bread was short. Within half an hour, six loaves were baking in the oven, he had also popped to the local bakery, bought a dozen rolls and a very large bag of fresh yeast, plus some bread flour. He would try making bread himself.

Benny arrived to the homely smell of baking bread, and the sight of every available bowl, brimming with rising dough. Paul quickly filled him in and Benny was delighted with the way he'd handled this crisis. Customers were lured in with the smell coming out of the ovens, and Benny wondered why they hadn't thought of this before. Not only did the sandwiches fly off the shelves, but people were asking to buy whole loaves. Paul couldn't keep up but promised everyone that there would be more to go round tomorrow. It turned out that he was a natural baker as well as a brilliant salesman, and Benny realised they needed to find a bread flour producer, to keep them supplied. There was a mill about an hour away and they said they could supply as much as Benny could use, including wholemeal and other grains to mix in and they also sold yeast. *Bingo.*

Paul spent the last hour, whilst clearing up, discussing with Benny how he could flavour some loaves with herbs and spices, add other ingredients, and generally keep up with demand. He suggested that he would start getting in a couple of hours earlier, to make the breads, and perhaps leave a little earlier to help Sindy. This sounded good to Benny, who was also considering, perhaps another youngster to help in the afternoons, as trade was getting brisker with each day. At this rate they would need new premises, and he'd only been there a few months! Benny also had another idea for the bakery: Paul was an employee from Heaven, and he didn't want to lose him, ever. Benny felt he should make Paul a partner in the bakery, so that the profits were divided equally, after all, Paul was already working as if he had a share in the business. Benny decided to chat this through on the 'phone with Jack tonight, to see what he thought.

ISABELLA

Thursday morning rolled around, just as it does every week, completely oblivious of Isabella's anxiety about everything in her life. Over the years, she had learnt to keep things very much on the inside, and put on a brave face; today was no exception. She persuaded Will that she would be fine, she did not need him there, which hurt a lot, but Will realised this was a difficult day and if she didn't want him, then he would accept her decision. He went off to work, feeling shut out and lonely and thinking that there must be more to this.

The second the door closed, Isabella buried her head in the nearest cushion and screeched. *How could he have let her down?* Right, this was no time to cave in to her emotions, she needed to get over to Dot's house, as she was going to drive her to the hospital. They had become very close friends, firstly through sea swimming and then, the pantomime; Isabella felt she could tell Dot anything. On the way to The Memorial, Isabella explained to Dot what she had seen on the pier. Dot's reaction was very similar to Benny's, it seemed unbelievable, and Dot said Isabella must confront Will as soon as they both got home. The nurse walked through to the waiting room and called out for Miss Williams, and off she went. From the scan, the specialist said he thought it was most likely to be benign, but he took a small biopsy anyway; the results would be sent to her doctor, within a couple of days, they had a new machine and were getting results back very quickly.

'Why don't I pick Lizzie up from school tonight, and you and Will can talk this through. I'm sure it has got a happy ending.' Dot suggested.

WILL

After reading her letter, Will agreed to meet Carol on the pier, he didn't want to take her into his old flat, and certainly not Isabella's. She was bang on time and looked very well. He wondered what this was all about.

'Will, it's good to see you, how is life treating you?' she asked, gently.

Will was not feeling remotely pleasant towards her. 'What can you possibly want from me, Carol?'

Carol was quite taken aback, she remembered Will as being so kind. 'Nothing, actually, George and I just wanted to tell you something, and I said it should be done face to face, rather than on the telephone.'

Will softened, 'I'm sorry, go ahead, I'm all ears.'

'George and I are getting married, early next year. I am expecting his child and we are moving to Australia. I just wanted you to know.'

'Congratulations, Australia is a long way away, I hope you both like it there.' Then Will recalled that George had often talked of moving there, and they chatted about it for some minutes, whilst the wind whipped their faces.

Will finished the conversation with his news, I'm also getting married next year, but staying right here in Seabourne.'

'That's good to hear Will, I'm sorry about leaving you, but it seems it has ended happily for both of us. Goodbye and good luck with everything,' and she walked down the pier, being buffeted about by the gusts.

Will wanted to feel angry, but instead he was impressed that she had come all this way just to let him know. This, of course, made him slightly more cross. Still at least it wasn't bad news or some dreadful attempt to get him back. He needed to tell Isabella, but decided to wait until after the hospital. It was not important. He got to the station and tried to plough through the never-ending paperwork, but his thoughts were about Isabella. He had let her go to the hospital alone, against his better judgement, as he knew he should have been there with her. She was such a force to be reckoned with, at times. He was just thinking about her, when in she stormed, looking very much as she had done in the summer, the first time he had laid eyes on her. Beautiful and exceptionally angry.

'Can we talk, please Will?'

'Of course, my love, how did it go this morning? Do you have any news?'

'Do *you* have any news? That's what I would like to know.' Isabella replied.

Will was confused, he wasn't generally slow to understand things. 'I'm sorry, I'm not sure what we're talking about here. Please tell me what they said at the hospital, I've been worrying about you.' He gently took her hand and they went into an interview room to talk.

'So, been seeing anyone new lately?' Isabella asked and suddenly Will realised.

'You saw me on the pier, why didn't you come over and say hello?' he asked, not understanding how it had looked. 'It was only Carol, you know, the one who went off with my brother, George. They are moving to Australia, getting married and having a baby. She wanted to let me know, face to face.'

'Why didn't you tell me? I've been worried sick that you had found another woman.'

'Why on earth would I want another woman? I have the

most beautiful, wonderful girl alive. You are my world. Have you absolutely no idea of how very much I love you? I didn't tell you as I hadn't a clue about what she wanted at first, and I wasn't going to worry you unnecessarily. My darling, I wish you had come over; I would have been so proud to introduce you.' They looked at each other, Isabella calming down now. Will put his arms around her and they talked about the scan. Will said it sounded positive but they would both feel much better when they had the results, hopefully.

DOT

Once Dot had dropped Isabella off, she turned her attention to tomorrow, fireworks night. She picked up a couple of big boxes with lots of Roman Candles, (her favourite), and popped them in a metal tin for safety, together with twenty packs of sparklers. Rob, Patrick and Charles were in charge of not blowing them all sky high at once. It was dark now by six o'clock and all the dippers were coming along, some bringing friends and neighbours. There was going to be a night sea swim for anyone who was brave enough. Benny was in charge of food; he was going to serve home-made sausage rolls, hot spicy soup, ginger cake and cinder toffee. Jack, who was home anyway for his father's funeral, said he would like to let a big rocket off for Dennis and also said he'd bring beer and wine. Rob promised some chairs, together with blankets, in case anyone got chilly. Margaret was picking Kate up tomorrow, and Dot was looking forward to meeting her.

The sky was bright, clear and cold on Friday evening, with just a slip of a moon, to oversee the evening. Samuel brought the music as usual, including some old-fashioned stuff for Betty, and people were in the mood to let their hair down. Betty was having a good day and was joining in with all the oohs and aahh's. The smell of gunpowder filled the air as roman candles followed traffic lights, the jumping jacks raced after unwary spectators, rockets shot up into the air, lighting up the sky (with Standard Fireworks). Then they enjoyed the Catherine wheels shakily struggling to whirl round and the never-ending fun of trying to light sulky sparklers. Eventually, Rob got out his pipe lighter, which got them going. Finally, Paul and Jack lit the touchpaper on a massive rocket, both of them remembering the good times with their father, when they were younger as the showers of coloured sparks fell from the sky.

Betty, Joyce and Clara sang along to Glenn Miller, as he worked his way through various hits, with Charles remarking that they put the Beverley Sisters to shame. Even Paul and Sindy were trying to dance to these war time songs, much to the amusement of their elders. Dot and Doreen were enjoying more than a couple of Babychams with Doreen telling Dot about her friend, Rani, who she wanted to introduce to Samuel. 'I wish you good luck with that,' laughed Dot.

Isabella and Will watched Lizzie and her dancing friends, writing their names, again and again with their sparklers, and chatted quietly to themselves. Fireworks done, the swimmers 'manned-up' as Charles was keen to say, and all ran in together, holding hands. Jack took photos, this was going to be a great collection. The velvet sea was burning cold, even those who had been weekly swimming, squeaked when the gentle waves hit them, agreeing that the sea temperature must have dropped considerably. A small bonfire was lit on the beach and there was applause when Guy Fawkes (made by Lizzie and her mates at school) was chucked, traditionally, on the top.

Margaret and Kate were, quite simply, perfect together. Dot introduced them to most of the dippers and they also joined in the swim, 'I honestly don't know how you do this Mum,' Margaret said, shivering and laughing at the same time.

'You get used to it darling, and it makes a great start, or in this case, end to the day, well done you two for trying it. You'll soon be addicted.'

CLARA AND CHARLES

They had watched Betty's enjoyment of the bonfire night, with love and sadness as this would be her last. It had been a great idea and they agreed with Dot to have as many get togethers as Betty could manage; they all hoped she would live long enough to enjoy Christmas and *Cinderella*.

Charles had planned his first boys club meeting for the following Wednesday. They had agreed to meet at the theatre, it had cost nothing (just this once, Dot had joked), there would be seats for everyone and they could organise the next few meetings.

With the panto and the theatre very much in Dot's capable hands, Clara turned her attention to Christmas, which she hadn't enjoyed celebrating for a very long time. Before the war, her family had gone to town on celebrations and Clara was planning a comeback.

Together, they had driven round to the Christmas Tree Farm, to see if old Mr Snowball, (yes, that really was his name) was still alive and selling trees. It was young Mr Snowball now, although he looked so much like his father, the two were interchangeable. Of course, he would get the biggest tree, Clara could reserve it if she wanted. He glanced at the rather flashy, totally inappropriate car and suggested they all drive out to see it, in *the Landrover!* Clara broke a nail as soon as she climbed aboard, it was smelly, filthy, tractor like, and Charles decided then and there, that this old tank of a car was the new love of his life. Despite their transport arrangements, the tree was a showstopper, and Mr Snowball was happy to cut and deliver it just before Christmas. The turkey farm was the next stop and an unfortunate, fine specimen was selected for their table.

Clara wanted to buy some nice modern Christmas lights, as her ancient set had stopped working decades ago. They popped into Turner's on the way home, Patrick had just received his lights order and Clara bought six of the twelve boxes. Doreen offered them tea and they chatted about Christmas this year. Patrick said he would very much like to make it a special day for Betty and Clara offered a big Christmas day lunch at Rutland Manor. *They* (this pleased Charles) could easily fit twenty people around the dining table, which would include the whole gang. They all agreed that if Betty was up to it, she'd love it. At least two more turkeys would be needed.

As they walked through the town, they bumped into the solicitor, who hailed them down and said he'd been trying to reach either of the Mr Harringtons on the phone, without success. Clara didn't realise that Dennis had left a will, but apparently the boys needed to go and see him. It had become a busy morning, coffee was needed, and so they dropped by Benjamin's.

Paul had produced the most amazing loaves of bread, which had taken pride of place in the window; Clara was so proud of him. This time, it was Paul who needed to talk and so they sat at a table and Benny took over, smiling to himself. They both had news. Ladies first, Clara said he needed to get in touch with the solicitor and Paul told them both about Benny's offer for him to be a partner. He didn't need to put anything into the business, Benny had just said he should be enjoying the fruits of his hard work and enjoy a share in the profits.

ISABELLA AND WILL

The surgery had rung, Isabella's results were back. No, they would not discuss them on the phone, she had to make an appointment to come in. This didn't sound like good news, however Will reminded Isabella that most of the receptionists there were 'jobsworths' and not to worry, they were going in today. But, by the time they reached the doctor's room, Isabella was certainly worrying. Dr Skudder immediately reassured her that it was not breast cancer. He was rather cross that whichever receptionist had called, hadn't put her mind at rest on the phone. He would have a word about that later. Isabella had a cyst, nothing at all sinister. It would very probably go down by itself but she could have it removed, after Christmas now, if she wanted to.

'Thank you, doctor.' They were keen to get out of there and celebrate and quickly got up to leave.

'Not just yet if you please,' and he asked them to sit down a while, as he had more news.

'Please don't think I'm prying, but you are a couple, enjoying a 'full' relationship, I assume?' Dr Skudder had known Will for quite some years, and felt he could tease him a little, since they seemed to have no idea. 'Well, PC Johnson, it's time to make an honest woman of her now,' he joked. 'Congratulations, you are going to be new parents.'

Will's face slowly lit up. 'That's amazing news.' He turned to Isabella, 'did you have any idea?' and she shook her head.

'No idea whatsoever,' she managed to say. *Oh, my goodness, Dad is going to explode with excitement,* she thought, and then her mind turned to Lizzie. She was going to love having a little brother or sister.

'I'm going to be a father. I'm going to be a father.' Will couldn't stop saying it. They had never talked about it, but they'd both assumed this would be on the cards for the future.

Thank goodness it's early days, Isabella thought. An obviously expectant Cinderella would have been a turn up for the books, even if it *was* 1976.

It was Monday, so rehearsals tonight and ideally, Isabella would have liked to keep things quiet until a little further on. One look at Will's face told her that it would be cruel to make him keep this secret for hours, let alone months and so she suggested they go and tell Samuel first. The rest of their friends could hear about it later this evening. Samuel was working on the outside of the theatre, painting and making good. When he saw them both together, in the middle of the day, he assumed something was wrong and jumped the last few steps down the ladder.

The silly grin on Will's face told him otherwise. He knew that type of grin and drew them both into his arms, asking what was up.

'Dad, Lizzie is going to have a little brother or sister, and we wanted you to be the first to know.'

'That is the most wonderful news, my angel. Congratulations to both of you.' And now there were two grown men dancing round on the pier, sporting silly grins.

SINDY AND PAUL

They both had appointments on Monday afternoon. Paul was due at the solicitors to hear the Will being read and at the same time, Sindy had her first appointment to see the midwife at the hospital. They kissed and hugged and wished each other good luck. Paul bumped into Jack rushing out of the station, worried that he was going to be late. He had just an hour before he needed to be on the train back to London and he wanted to see Benny, if only for five minutes.

They walked into the solicitors, tidying themselves up, as seemed appropriate, and certainly weren't prepared for what they heard. Dennis had set up two savings accounts for them when they were born, no-one knew about it and he had forgotten about these along with his whole life. They had matured and the Prudential had finally contacted the solicitor. Jack would receive the sum of £4,500 and Paul, the sum of £2,000 as his savings account was started much later. They couldn't believe their good fortune. Jack immediately knew what he was going to do, it had been in his mind for a week or so, and now he had the funds to do it. He couldn't wait to tell Benny. Paul thought it would be sensible to buy their own place, this would be a great deposit and he couldn't wait to tell Sindy.

Sindy had asked Doreen to go with her to the hospital, which cemented their new-found closeness. The midwife was an efficient, middle-aged lady who immediately made Sindy feel at home whilst she performed various tests and made lots of notes. Finally, she laid her, rather cold, stethoscope on Sindy's tummy and listened, for what seemed like a long time.

'Would you like to hear the heartbeats?' she asked, casually.

'Yes please,' Sindy replied, 'but you said heartbeats, I think your stethoscope must have gone a bit wrong.'

'No dear, it's working just fine. There are two heartbeats because there are two babies, that's why it has taken me so long with all the details.'

Sindy was a bit overwhelmed to say the least, but Doreen said that Paul was going to make a brilliant dad, and that Doreen and Pat would always be there for her, and that getting it all over and done with in one go was the way forward.

Doreen dropped Isabella off at Benjamin's so that she could tell Paul. Jack and Paul had just returned and there was a wonderful, muddled explosion of news, with no-one quite listening to, or believing what the others were saying. Once things had quietened down a bit, Benny suggested some new camomile tea, that he was trying out. It was supposed to be calming; they certainly needed something to bring them all down off the ceiling.

BENNY AND JACK

Jack decided to stay in Seabourne, with Benny; it just felt right today. He telephoned the London office and before he had time to say that he thought he might have a stomach bug, the receptionist said that she had been trying to get hold of him, and had left messages. The meeting this afternoon had been cancelled as the Lead Architect was not well, it would be rescheduled for later in the week. *Well, that's handy,* Jack thought, and they embraced warmly. Benny smiled as he realised the old Jack was firmly back now.

The rest of them decided that the baby announcements should be made tonight at rehearsals, which were only about an hour away. Paul, Benny and Jack put together pies, biscuits, and some sandwiches, with yet more bottles of Champagne, and they all decided, that particularly for Betty, tonight should have a proper party atmosphere, after the slightly more serious business of rehearsing had finished.

Once it was just the two of them, Jack set out his ideas. 'I've made a lot of contacts in London and the South-east now, and although I am enjoying working for Steve, I think it's time I branched out on my own. Not London, I hasten to add, but in Seabourne. I can work from anywhere, and I can travel now and again, but I want my base to be here, not too far from you.'

This was exciting news and Benny listened, whilst wrapping things up, and selecting some nice cakes for the evening.

'This money I've got is enough to start my own design business, the only reason I hadn't seriously considered it before was lack of funds.'

'I'm so very pleased for you Jack, but how do you think Steve will take the news?' Benny was a bit worried in case there would be one too many architects in Seabourne.

'Steve and I do pretty different stuff, which is why I got the London work, so I don't think he'll be too troubled. I have worked there for over ten years now; he's probably seen this coming lately.'

'Then, I'm thrilled for you, congratulations. So, it's back to Goddard and Smith to find some premises soon, and they both laughed. Benny then told Jack about his suggestion to Paul to be a partner in Benjamin's. 'As you know, he works so hard and has the right attitude. I can't lose him, and now he has a growing family, he's really got something to work for.' This was a typically kind, Bennyish thing to do, and Jack loved him for it.

Benny suddenly noticed the time, heavens, they needed to get to the theatre.

DOT

As soon as she walked into the theatre, Dot felt an atmosphere that was fit to burst with what? Excitement? Information? Just plain silliness? She couldn't decide, but whatever it was, they needed to get it out of their system before the rehearsals started, that much was clear. This week, Dot had invited Doreen who also brought Pat as they did a lot more together these days. He was enjoying looking round the beautiful auditorium. Dot jumped up on stage.

'It seems to me that there are a lot of people here tonight, who need to get something off their chest, I hope it's all good news, guys. Clara, do you want to go first?'

Charles laughed; Dot was such an astute woman. The room hushed. 'Charles and I just wanted to invite all our friends up to Rutland Manor on Christmas day to have Christmas dinner with us. Everyone is invited, we thought it would be good to be together and it would make us very happy. Thank you, Dot, that's our news,' finished Clara. Everyone clapped.

Will was next, he got up on stage, with a few (knowledgeable) people sniggering and whooping. 'Isabella is expecting a baby, she hasn't got breast cancer and we are just so grateful.' He jumped off into the auditorium and there were cheers, and shouts of 'congratulations.' They had told Lizzie their news earlier and said she would be the best big sister ever. Samuel clapped Will on the back and said he would make a perfect dad. After some minutes, the calm returned, with folk looking around to see who else had something to say.

Paul, obviously, had to do something silly, 'I'll see your one baby and raise it by one more.' Every single person looked across to Sindy who was smiling and said, 'yes, I'm expecting twins.'

The hall erupted and Dot hoped there would be shouts and applause similar on opening night. Joyce, who was sitting at the piano, struck up "Congratulations."

Pat went over to Sindy and gave her a hug, 'well, that's going to keep us all busy, you don't do things by half do you?'

Pat shook Paul by the hand, 'nice to see you've got some lead in your pencil lad.' He went over to Doreen, 'you don't look old enough to be a granny,' he teased.

'I never will,' she laughed. She looked over at Samuel, on his own, apart from Lizzie, and decided to bring her friend, Rani to the next rehearsal. She was a widow, and a kind woman and loved dancing more than anything. They would be perfect for each other.

Jack poured Champagne and Benny handed out food; a party had begun. Charles looked over at Clara, realising that she already knew part of this. 'As we aren't actually married yet, I see no reason why you should keep secrets from me, but, what wonderful news. Now I understand about the wedding.'

'I only knew about one baby,' Clara laughed, 'but in future, I will keep you updated with all the family gossip.' Charles liked the sound of that.

Betty was tickled pink, there had been twins in Ted's family, but she had completely forgotten until now. She had started on the painkilling drugs, they made her a bit sleepy but at least it meant she could enjoy evenings like these, and she certainly meant to enjoy herself tonight. She had a glass of Champagne in one hand and a plate, loaded with cakes on her lap, good friends and family surrounding her, what more could she want? *She thought to herself.*

Rob, Margaret and Kate chatted together and enjoyed all

the treats. Margaret was spellbound by her mum's ability to take charge of a situation, and with such elegance. She could get people doing what she wanted, with just a smile. She was going to make an amazing theatre manager. Margaret realised she had underestimated Dot for years, and suddenly, without any warning, jumped on the stage to make her own announcement.

'I think most of you know me by now, I'm Margaret Baker, Dot and Rob's daughter. I just wanted to say that I've not been the easiest of daughters but I am so bloody proud of my mum. She's just amazing. I love you, Mum. I love you too, Dad. Also, it's time I said I love you to someone else,' and she looked over at Kate, who nodded. 'I love you too, Kate, but in a different way.' This announcement was followed by laughter, more clapping and cheers. Dot was in pieces, and thought that they could probably skip a rehearsal, just this week.

CHARLES

His days used to be mainly strolling down to the shops, to get his croissant for breakfast and then back again, to select some cheese and bread for supper, with an awful lot of quietness in between. Now, he had reunited with his only family, lived with a beautiful, human hurricane, and his days included weddings, babies on the way, men in women's clothes, singing, sea swimming, so much life. He was finally alive!

As he walked down to the theatre on Wednesday evening for the first boys club, thinking that the five or six of them would be rattling around in the big auditorium, he was pleasantly surprised when he saw about twenty chaps, milling around on the pier, talking about the idea and what might be in store for them. Charles showed them all in and welcomed everyone. All ages had braved the cold night and pitched up, ranging from a couple of old boys; even older than himself, right through to some youngsters, like Paul, who didn't have much to do with their time. This was incredible, they all got talking, exchanging ideas, so many had skills or experiences to share; most of whom didn't realise they would interest other men.

One chap, Bill, sat at the piano and enjoyed playing classical music, there were a couple of fishermen, who said they would happily teach others their sport. Beer flowed, but conversation flowed even more freely, with all of them agreeing that it was a good job their Mrs's weren't there to hear all the chatter and gossip. At half time (football was one of the main topics of conversation, with the F.A. Cup winners, Southampton, being a local team), there was lots of praise for the winning goal from Bobby Stokes, together with the cakes, and pies that Benny had brought in. Jack and Patrick made teas and coffees. Charles had suggested this, as he didn't want all the guys going home, the worse for alcohol. The girls and women in their lives would soon put a stop to this, if it just became about drinking. He wanted to keep a happy medium. They all praised Benny's food, the next meeting was going to be about cooking. If they each brought twenty pence in, they would go home with a tasty Victoria sandwich, and a lot of brownie points to boot.

All it had taken was a tiny advertisement, to get these men together, chatting, laughing and sharing their worries about the world, some of them lonely, bored, or just plain frightened of what the future had in store for them. The hours shot by, and at the end of the evening, they had the next few months organised, with loads of offers to help. Rob and Samuel were highly praised on their restoration work at the theatre, and most said they would be getting pantomime tickets for their families for Christmas. Manly slapping of backs and nods were exchanged, a lot of new friendships having begun. Charles walked home to Rutland Manor, feeling like he'd started something good. *They must think of a name for this group as the old boys' club just didn't cut the mustard.*

BENNY AND JACK

One of the reasons they had thoroughly enjoyed the evening was that they had just been accepted by a random selection of men, for who they were, and Jack thought, perhaps times were finally changing. No credit taken away from Charles though, because it was his brilliant idea and a lot of fun. Benny was looking forward to his baking session in a couple of weeks' time at Benjamin's.

Jack was on the first train up to Waterloo, as things were wrapping up with the project for him; it had been incredible to be involved with this level of work. Looking in his briefcase, he was touched by the note, sandwich and pastry Benny had put in there the night before, 'for the journey'. He was in sharp, but there was already a note on his desk to go to the top floor, and see the boss.

'Jack, can you do one more week for us here?' Andrew, the guy in charge was saying before Jack had even sat down, on one of the trendy racing car seats in the impossibly sleek office.

'No problem boss,' Jack replied. His own plans were firmly set in his mind, and another week in London wouldn't affect that.

'Also, we've been super-impressed with your work here, over the last few weeks. Trevor and I would like to offer you a full-time position with us.'

Wow, Jack had *not* seen that one coming. 'That is a huge honour, Andrew, thank you.'

Whilst Andrew was talking through all that would be involved, including the sizeable pay check and benefits, Jack was steadying himself for his response. *Yes, this is a huge honour, but it's going to wreck my life with Benny, no two ways about it. I can't be too clever with this, but let's see if I can turn it around slightly,* Jack thought.

'Andrew, I am immensely flattered by your offer, and please don't think me ungrateful, but; I am planning to start my own design company, where I live, on the South coast. Would it be too bold to ask if I might work freelance for you? I don't want to take business from Steve, who has been supportive of me throughout my career, but I feel I need to branch out on my own.'

'I have to confess, this does not surprise me one bit, although we would have loved to have secured you all to ourselves,' joked Andrew. 'I'll talk this over with Trevor and let you know in a couple of days; I wouldn't have thought it will be a problem though.'

This would be the most incredible kick-start to my new business, Jack thought. 'Thank you, Andrew, I would really appreciate that.'

Jack's week continued positively; Trevor agreed, there was a suggestion of an architectural award for the job that Jack had been working on, and in the evenings, he planned his new business venture.

Benny's week had been so busy that by the following Friday lunchtime he finally accepted, he needed another pair of hands and put an advertisement in the window, for someone to work in the afternoons, and possibly on Saturdays. Paul had been suggesting this for a couple of weeks. As he was sticking it in the window, an attractive, middle-aged Indian lady stopped to read it and smiled, they were both smiling at each other through the glass. She laughed and he beckoned her in, unconsciously realising that she was the one. He could just see it in her soft eyes and intelligent face. She had no experience but was keen to learn, and could start as soon as he wanted.

Paul came in from his lunchbreak with Sindy, and was very pleased to meet Rani. They hit it off straight away.

Within a week, Rani had made friends with all the customers, charming men and women alike. She was a very spiritual lady with tattoos and lots of jewellery, who connected particularly well with Isabella, Benny noticed. She originated from Trinidad, just like Samuel, but her father had been white and her mother, Indian. Paul loved her, she was an amazing addition to their team. It was Friday afternoon, and they were all just clearing up, when Samuel, who Benny hadn't seen at the bakery for a while, popped in for a late lunch. He'd not met Rani before and the chemical reaction between them in the first few seconds of him walking through the door was palpable. Neither one of them were socially awkward; however, Samuel looked dumbstruck, and Rani blushed, knocked a cup of tea over, and hurried out the back to get a clean cloth, with a jangling of bracelets and beads and the feint aroma of patchouli.

ISABELLA AND WILL

They were enjoying a lazy Saturday morning, Will had the weekend off, Sindy was reading a baby book (things had changed even since Lizzie was born) and now that Lizzie was of course, the big girl, she was making them breakfast in bed, which involved a lot of very small, slightly sticky, plastic crockery and some dubious looking food, which Will made a convincing job of pretending to eat.

This serenity was slightly at odds, however, with the list of things which were on their 'to discuss and get done' list. Wedding plans were dancing around in Isabella's head, she wanted to be married before baby arrived but wasn't sure if it was just too much to fit in. Will was keen to start the adoption process for Lizzie, but uppermost on both of their minds was to find a bigger, family home for them all, before baby arrived. At the last rehearsal, Betty, who was not looking so good that night, asked if they would take Diesel on, when the time came. She knew they were the right people, Diesel had spent more time with them lately, than with her; they loved him just as much, and of course they agreed. They would need a house with a nice big garden, for him to really run around, not to mention, for their two children to play in.

'Not sure why we're lying in this bed, drinking pretend coffee when we should be getting busy,' Will joked. 'I'm popping over to Benjamin's for some real caffeine, pastries and perhaps a pie for all of us, for lunch.' That sounded good to Isabella, she was always starving these days, and had no morning sickness at all. On his way back, he popped into the estate agents, and picked up some house particulars. They sorted them into 'how much Lizzie liked them' order. On the top was a lovely Victorian semi, with a rambling, slightly overgrown garden and Isabella thought it was marvellous. There were three bedrooms, one which would be perfect for a nursery. They needed to get their flats on the market.

Isabella had a 'magic fairies' dance rehearsal and costume fitting in the afternoon, the little ones hadn't been on the stage yet, and would need to get used to it. As the mums filed in with their daughters, there were gasps at just how smart the theatre looked now. Each mum had made a little white costume, and Isabella had been busy fashioning wings out of net and coat hangers, "Blue Peter" style. Once they were all dressed, there was not a dry eye in the house. The "Bibbidi bobbidi boo" dance was practiced quite a few times, with Joyce, starting patiently again, and again, and again, always with an indulgent smile on her face. Joyce also had an idea for the ballroom scene; as the guests were dancing, how about the little ones join in as well? She played "Some Day My Prince Will Come", whilst Isabella helped them to pair up and perform an approximation of a waltz. They looked adorable, Dot and Clara walked in half way through and heartily gave it the thumbs up.

JACK, PAUL AND BENNY

Working back in Seabourne, Jack quickly realised, was a lot more conducive to his productivity. He had told Steve, and although he hadn't wanted to see him go, he quite understood, and they parted company as friends. Jack's involvement in the project was finished, and so he took one more week to wrap things up and left; with both of them promising to forward the boring jobs, which they didn't fancy, to the other.

So, he was on his own. Exciting and daunting at the same time, he had been working on ideas for his design company. There were a number of jobs in the pipeline for early in the new year and now he needed to turn his plans into reality. He and Benny lived mainly in Benny's flat now; there were no ghosts of a lost family there. Paul was at Betty's, and Jack knew it was time to sell, as his father was not coming back. It was a big, family house, with a forest of a garden, and was in dire need of refurbishment. Dad hadn't done anything there for over twenty years and for Jack and Paul, it was just like a bedsit, with them both coming and going, and no-one giving it any love or attention. If they divided the profits, he could buy an office outright, perhaps with a small flat above, and really afford to invest in his business. Time to chat this through with his brother.

It was day one on the advent calendars, and it seemed like everyone in Seabourne had decided to order pies, puddings and cakes. And of course, there is nothing like a small queue forming out of a shop door, to encourage more to join and place their orders, just in case Benjamin's ran out of the richly fruited delicacies that could not be done without, at Christmastime. Jack actually laughed as he slipped past customers, giving him a look, to go and chat with Paul. That was not going to happen for a while, so he made them all coffees, donned an apron and helped, where he could. Once Rani arrived later, they had time to talk.

'Mate, I have been wanting to ask you the same thing, but I was worried you wouldn't want to let the house go, memories and all that.' Paul was quite relieved.

'Let's get it on the market and then you guys can think about a family home yourselves.' Jack said, as Benny sat down to join them for a quick break.

'You know Will and Isabella are looking for somewhere with a big garden, and yours is like a jungle. Why don't you see if they're interested?' Benny added.

'It would need gutting and starting again, but hey, why not? That's a brilliant idea Benny.' Jack could see Samuel and Rob turning it into an incredible home, although old and with too many sad memories for him, new eyes and life could really transform it. Benny thought the office and flat idea a good one, and as Jack pretty much lived with him now anyway, better to get on with it.

Shortly after Rani's arrival, Samuel *just popped in,* as he often did now, and so they chatted through their ideas for the house with him. As the theatre was finished, and work was a little quiet, he said he'd nip round and take a look, and perhaps take Rob with him. No-one had to commit to anything; he loved nosing around old houses. Rani served him with one of her special spicy chicken sandwiches with coriander, and a special smile on the side. There was something quite wonderful developing here.

It seemed like the world and his wife were descending on

Benjamin's today, and who should walk through the door next but Doreen, in search of a nice white loaf. She stopped in her tracks. There was Rani, her friend, chatting as bold as you like, with Samuel, without any intervention from her at all! It was obviously meant to be, she could see they were both fascinated with each other, and she would always claim that it had been her idea in the first place.

SINDY AND PAUL

Diesel seemed a bit restless on Sunday morning, keen to get down to the waves, so Paul and Sindy made their way to the sea, with an over-excited greyhound dancing about in the wind, chasing the occasional squawking gull. The two babies were certainly announcing their presence; she was looking more than healthy now. She'd borrowed a bigger swimsuit to cover the tiny bump, and also her Prince Charming costume had needed some alterations. Doreen was a magician with a needle, and had put in some extra panels and darts, so that the sparkling tunic would keep her secret from the audience.

With so much going on, swimming each Sunday was perfect; however, they all missed the calming, refreshing and grounding influence of the sea during the week. It wasn't the best of weather today; the wind was blowing the cold rain straight in off the sea, but all the dippers braved it, even for a few minutes, and huddled round their hot drinks afterwards, congregating like penguins under the tiny bit of shelter that the pier offered.

Benny had brought mince pies, saying it was never too early. Jack was telling Clara and Charles about his new venture, which he was going to call 'Harrington Designs', and that he would probably need a young, apprentice designer before too long.

'Have you not seen the one, right under your nose?' Clara asked with her usual directness. 'Just add another 'Harrington' to your business name, and you're there,' she added.

'But Paul already...' Jack suddenly realised that Clara wasn't talking about Paul. What an oversight he had nearly made. Without further ado, Jack approached Sindy and told her of his plans.

'Obviously, you are going to have a lot on your plate soon, but you are such a talented artist and I would be pleased if you would consider an apprentice position with me, perhaps going to college to study, as well, if you wanted to.' Jack said.

Before Sindy could answer, Charles was keen to add, 'Sindy, your talent is undeniable, and I would be happy to help you further it, in any way I can, whether that's babysitting or helping with the cost of college.'

Sindy was quite taken aback; no-one had taken her doodles quite this seriously before. 'Thank you, Jack, Uncle Charles, I will take you both up on those offers immediately. I can think of nothing I would rather do as a job than use my pencil, I won't let you down.'

Paul had come over and was nodding vigorously with all that was being said. 'We have loads of support, and I can do my bit with the babies.'

Sindy smiled, but suddenly her eyes filled with tears. Betty, who had been such an amazing nan, and her best friend, would never meet them. In that moment, Sindy decided that she would like to name one of the twins, Betty, if there was a girl. Clara came over and wrapped her arms around her.

'Clara, I would like to call one of the babies Betty Clara Doreen Harrington, if we have a girl, what do you think?' Sindy asked.

'And if there's a boy in there, I would like to call him Peter Charles Patrick Harrington, if that's all right with you two,' Paul added. He had decided against his fathers' name, as most of his memories were of a ghost of a man. Clara beamed. It was perfectly all right with her.

ISABELLA AND WILL

Samuel and Rob had gone round to Jack and Paul's house, and couldn't believe their eyes. It was the most perfectly preserved 1930's semi that they had seen. Yes, there was a lot of work to be done to make it habitable for a young family; a new kitchen and bathroom, damp work and total redecoration, but once that was all done, it would be a great place to live. Jack had tried to clean up a bit on the Saturday that Samuel was coming back with Isabella, Will and Lizzie, to have a look. The space was incredible, Isabella loved the high ceilings, picture rails and all the fireplaces. The hall was really big, with a lovely old -fashioned stairway, she could just picture where they would put the Christmas tree next year, and that decided it for her. The garden was something else, and Lizzie said she would be like an explorer, in the wilderness, which amused everyone. It had been valued and they could just about afford it. Samuel would do most of the work and Rob could get a lot of the fittings at cost, so that would help. They shook hands, and the deal was agreed.

Their flats were now on the market although the estate agent didn't think there would be much interest this side of Christmas. They finished a bit of last-minute shopping while they were in town and popped into Benjamin's for some cakes to enjoy when they got home. On their way out, they bumped into the estate agent.

'PC Johnson, I've been ringing you all morning, I have five people who want to view your flat today, and someone to see Miss Williams' flat. They're in the office now, if it's convenient, can I take them straight round, they're very keen?'

Luckily, they had tidied up before leaving and it was looking very festive, with a lovely tree and decorations, and they agreed. They decided to take their cakes down to the beach for a windy picnic. For a while Lizzie enjoyed running around on the sand, chasing the amusing blobs of sea foam which were blowing about wildly, but the rain started and Will suggested they pop into the station until it stopped.

Will had one foot in the door when he spied the Chief Inspector coming out of the office. *Damn. Now I'll never get away.* The Chief was famous for finding 'little jobs' that needed doing, regardless if it was your first day off in weeks.

'Morning Sir,' Will said, while trying to apologise to Isabella with just his eyes.

'It is a good morning actually PC Johnson, and are you going to introduce me to your guests? I'm assuming you haven't just arrested them and brought them in for questioning, again?' The Chief joked. *Crikey, it must be nearly Christmas,* Will thought. Chief Burrows never made jokes.

'I have two pieces of news for you, Will. Firstly, I have front row seats at your Pantomime. I am bringing my whole family, including my cherished mother-in-law, who is quite a pantomime connoisseur, so it had better be top rate, lad.'

Oh God. 'Yes sir, absolutely sir, won't let you down.' *I'd better tell him now.* 'Just so that you know, I am playing the part of an ugly sister, so will be wearing a dress etc. Strictly for the show, you understand.'

'What you do in your spare time is not my concern, PC Johnson. Now there is another matter I wanted to discuss with you. Come into my office.

DOT

The week before Christmas was her favourite time: Clara had invited Dot to join her and Charles on a shopping trip to London tomorrow, in the sports car, and Dot couldn't wait. Seeing the lights in Oxford Street, and enjoying the splendour of Fortnum and Mason, were on top of her list, she was also hoping to get a nice pipe for Rob in Jermyn Street. She loved all the racing around, wrapping presents, buying too much food, the anticipation of the day itself, and of course, this year there was the added pleasure of sharing all this with Margaret and Kate, not to mention the excitement of *Cinderella*. Dot enjoyed Boxing Day with all the cold meats, pickles and salads, but after that, the year seemed to fizzle out, like the end of a sparkler. As she was walking down for the Sunday morning swim, she wished there was a pantomime to look forward to every year, and then remembered there probably would be with her new job. It hadn't really kicked in yet, but already there was plenty in the diary for next year with Julian Clements and other enquiries as well.

She was just thinking about Margaret and Kate when they caught up with her on the way down to the beach.

'Hello you two, how are things?' They barely had time to catch up the last couple of days.

'We've got lots of news for you Mum,' Margaret said, giving her a hug. I got that purchasing director job and they want me to start in the new year. I'm so excited.'

'Congratulations darling, I'm really pleased for you and I know Dad will be thrilled.'

'But I'm sorry Mum, the job will be mainly based in London and so that's where I'm going to look for a flat, but I'll be coming back here probably at least once a week, would it be okay to stay with you guys?'

Dot was pleased for her; London was Margaret's home now; she had her life there and her friends.

' Of course, it will. We'll be glad to see you whenever you're down this way, you know that my love.'

Kate was smiling and added 'I've asked Margaret to move in with me and she has agreed. After two years, we are going to be a proper couple.'

'I couldn't be more delighted for you both, come here.' And Dot wrapped her arms around them. 'Let's celebrate all this wonderful news with a dip in the freezing grey sea, shall we?' Dot asked. Laughing, they continued down to the beach.

Dot was pleased to see Samuel, arm in arm with Rani, she was such an infectious lady and quietly these two people, who had both suffered a great loss in their lives, were finding comfort in each other. Samuel had always been an upbeat man, but now he had an air of warm hope surrounding him. Isabella and Lizzie were chatting away to them both. She looked over at Rob, who had also noticed Samuel's new found happiness and they nodded and smiled.

Most of the dippers had braved the cold and were charging into the still, icy water. Somehow it felt so much colder when there were no waves which was difficult to understand. It was down to six degrees and they didn't stay in long. Their minds were recharged in less than a minute and they all came out sporting the funny red/brown skin that looks like a suntan but is the complete opposite. Much rubbing of arms and jumping around was needed, together with strategically placed hot water bottles and layer upon layer of clothes. There were a good variety of bobble hats being sported now and Jack was taken with all the colours. His camera was out as usual and he decided this collection would be called 'The Shades of Winter.'

THE BROTHER'S CLUB

The cake making had been a roaring success, with all the men joking that perhaps their womenfolk made a bit too much of this baking thing. Anyone could do it! Benny smiled, *yes, with my constant help to avoid disaster*, he thought. Tonight, they had decided to have a vote on their name. This involved a lot of joking, silly ideas, and laughs, but ended with Samuel's suggestion of The Brother's Club and this week they were back at the theatre. As it was nearly Christmas, Bill was going to play some carols, Benny had brought mince pies and Jack had said if they all brought a bottle of cheap red plonk, he would show them how to make mulled wine, which they could take home for Christmas. There was a useful kitchen area behind the bar and they all got busy. The smells of orange, clove and cinnamon, together with the red wine, was making them all feel very Christmassy and a lot of it got consumed whilst it was still steaming and just too tempting to be bottled up. Charles was interested to see how, without the girls there, they felt comfortable to let their feelings out, whether masculine or not, and enjoy things that might be dismissed as daft in everyday life and he remembered this was also the case with the men in the war.

Last time Paul asked if anyone could help him wrap his Christmas gifts; he'd got a special bottle of perfume for Sindy but was rubbish at wrapping it up. Patrick put his hand up; he was very used to paper and Sellotape, and said it was all a matter of sharp angles.

'Bring your presents down, next time,' he'd said and I'll bring the paper and expertise. They all laughed and agreed.

John from the newsagents, opined that the ladies like bows and things, and added he would bring some from his shop. Job done. The meeting for just after Christmas was at Rob's yard, so they had better all wear some warm stuff; Rob would provide coffee and Samuel was going to show them how to use his lathe and turn some wood. Benny thought he might bring a first aid kit, just in case.

CHRISTMAS EVE

The morning started exceptionally early at Benjamin's, with the smells of Benny's hot spicy mince pies, competing with the homely aroma of Paul's Christmas loaves, both, trying to be the most alluring to the customers. Dressed in matching festive jumpers and wearing them with pride, they could hardly move for boxes of Christmas orders, which would be picked up by sleep deprived parents, hung over youngsters and grandparents who had done it all before, so many times and still enjoyed every minute of it.

Rani came in around mid-morning, jingling more than usual, and looking stunning with her unruly curls bursting from a merry festive hat finished off with a tinkling bell. Samuel gave her a chaste peck on the cheek and said he'd see her later. She restocked the shelves as the cakes and pies appeared to have grown wings. Today the customers left with their shopping, a festive drink to keep them warm and a Christmas gift to say thank you for their support. Paul had the idea of a lucky dip box, filled with lots of little wrapped goodies, including miniature Christmas cakes, mince pies, sweet and sticky Christmas buns, plus gingerbread and stollen. Grown up people were getting so much child-like pleasure in unwrapping their unexpected gift, to see what their surprise was.

Jack had designed a $1/12^{th}$ scale model gingerbread 'Rutland Manor'; Benny had baked it and he'd been working on the decoration for days. It was a Christmas present for Clara and Charles and was now taking centre stage in the bakery.

There were delicate windows made of boiled sweets, marzipan figures, and the whole thing was covered in snow. People were taking photos of it, and asking how much would one be and could Benny possibly do this for them for tomorrow? Laughing, he said he'd take orders for next year, if they would like to bring him a photo of their home.

Meanwhile, in the slightly bigger Rutland Manor, there was a mountain of vegetables to peel, turkeys which needed stuffing and sauces being stirred on the aga. Ruth had lists everywhere, and although she gratefully accepted help, there was no mistaking who was the captain of this particular ship today. Betty was doing well with the sprouts, sitting on a nice high, comfortable chair, with everything she needed to hand, in particular a large glass of Harvey's Bristol Cream. Clara was perfecting the dining table. Charles had brought down her cherished Spode Christmas tree crockery from the attic; she hadn't used it in years and it was such a pleasure to set it all out, together with fine linens and shining glasses. There would be at least twenty tomorrow; the table was looking glorious, with all the greenery that they had collected, arranged in the centre. Just as she was admiring her work, Charles came in, told her to open her hands and close her eyes, and presented her with two lightweight, but big boxes.

As Clara opened her eyes, she gasped with excitement. 'You really shouldn't have, you naughty, extravagant, delightful man,' and Charles was rewarded, with a Christmas kiss. During their trip to London, he had spent some time in Fortnum and Mason, and had bought the most elaborately expensive crackers that Clara had ever seen, they even matched her table. He was looking so pleased with himself.

'Thank you so much, these are perfection,' she whispered, as they stood, under the mistletoe, just holding hands and surveying the scene.

Sindy was busy at Turners in the morning, Pat had made

a large order several weeks ago, which had unexpectedly just arrived the night before. Unfortunately, on the evening he'd been filling in the order forms, he'd possibly had one too many Spanish brandies, and that had rather affected his decision making. Most of his usual stock had been fine, but there had been some half price torches in the catalogue which Pat thought would be very useful, and so he'd ordered 10, although his biro had run out and he'd had to go over the amount quite a few times. The packing clerk at the warehouse had thought 110 torches to be quite a lot, so he mentioned it to his boss, who said they wanted to get rid of them, so not to query this. Patrick didn't want to appear foolish and realised sending them back would be difficult, so he and Sindy found spaces for them all, eventually.

Doreen was very much looking forward to tomorrow; someone else cooking the dinner and such pleasant company, sounded like Christmas to her. She'd bought Clara and Charles an attractive silver photo frame, to say thank you. Once Sindy had finished work, she went home to make Paul a romantic dinner, just the two of them, as Betty was staying at Clara's. She knew Paul would be exhausted after his busy day. They had bought a little tinsel tree and a set of fairy lights from Woolies for their room. Most of the other dippers had given them a few decorations, remembering you never have very many to start with.

Samuel had taken Lizzie and Diesel out for a long beach walk, to tire them both out and also give Isabella and Will some wrapping-up time. On her list to Santa had been a Sindy doll, Spirograph and Twister. She'd asked for more grown-up toys this year, as she was soon going to be a big sister.

Dot was enjoying wrapping presents today, she was thrilled with the gifts she'd bought for Margaret and also Kate; who was easy going and easy to love, she could quite see why Margaret had fallen for her. She had bought Rob a new briar root pipe, he'd been mentioning it for ages and she had been pleased to find one during her trip to London. Jim, their son was coming on Boxing Day, she was looking forward to seeing him, it had been years. Sitting happily on the carpet, amidst a tangle of ribbons and paper, Dot suddenly realised the carol concert at the church would be starting soon, they'd better get their skates on.

On their way to the church, Benny and Jack dropped into Rutland Manor, with their gift.

'That is, without doubt, the finest gingerbread house I have ever seen,' opined Clara, giving them both a squeeze.

'Thank you, chaps, you have both excelled yourselves. It looks much too good to eat, but knowing you Benny, it will taste even better than it looks,' Charles said as he placed it in the cool hallway, where everyone would see it. *How thoughtful those boys were.* 'Fancy a quick one to keep the cold out?'

The organist played all the old favourites, plus a few new ones like 'Little Donkey'. Clara was glad to hear the descant in 'Hark the Herald Angels Sing', it wasn't the same without it. Samuel always liked 'O little Town of Bethlehem', and was not disappointed. Isabella had agreed with the vicar to do 'The Holly and The Ivy' as a solo, chiefly because he said he'd heard so many people screeching through it, it would be wonderful to hear it sung beautifully, and she did. The evening finished with 'Away in a Manger, sung by the school children. Joyce had arranged it in the round, and it was mesmerising. The Vicar thanked God for Benny's mince pies and hot drinks.

On the way out of the church, people commented on the raw weather, saying it felt like snow on the way, Rani said she could taste it in the air, was it going to be a white Christmas?

CHRISTMAS DAY

No prizes for guessing who was first up on this hushed, blanketed, still very dark day, and yes, he had visited and left an enticingly bulging stocking at the end of her bed. Will was next to wake, hearing Lizzie's squeals of excitement. He would never forget his first experience of Christmas with a true believer, and the three of them merrily unwrapped their way through the early morning.

Rutland Manor was next to stir and Charles and Clara rushed out into the transformed garden in their dressing gowns and jumpers. They knew they needed to follow all Ruth's instructions for putting the turkeys in the aga, but, as the first soft snowball hit the back of Clara's sweater, it was obvious that there were more important things to be done on this magical morning. Clara returned fire and the next twenty minutes were spent with attacks, counter attacks, pulling branches to form unexpected avalanches on each other, and finally making snow angels. They snapped out of being eight-year-olds pretty damn quickly when they saw Ruth and her husband coming up the drive in his old 4 by 4. When Ruth had pulled the curtains on the morning, she realised what would probably be happening and smiled, remembering that if you want something done properly... etc. They all pulled together and Christmas day was back on track. They joined Betty, who had been enjoying the whole show from the warm kitchen window, laughing at their antics.

For once, Benny hadn't needed to set his alarm, *bliss*, but he woke at the crack of dawn anyway. He made a coffee and tried not to wake Jack, but when he opened a window and saw the snow sparkling in the street lights, he also took a trip back to childhood.

'Happy Christmas, beautiful' he woke a very sleepy Jack and together, they threw on some wellies, coats and hats, and went rushing down, through the silent snowy streets to the pier. The strangely light, snow-covered beach made an amazing contrast with the dark sea, and Jack, who always had his camera slung over his shoulder, was happily snapping away. They had forgotten their gloves and when their fingers got too cold, they walked merrily back home, with Benny wondering just how many dippers would brave the Christmas morning swim.

Paul had wanted to make their first Christmas together really special. He'd saved up and bought Sindy a bottle of Chanel No 5, and really hoped she was going to like it. Clara had said you couldn't go wrong with Chanel, so he'd wrapped it carefully, and put it under the tree. He was up way before her and made breakfast in bed, her favourite; boiled eggs with soldiers. It seemed cold in the house, and after lighting the fire, he took her tray up. Sindy felt very spoiled as she smelled her luxurious gift and they both enjoyed breakfast without even opening the curtains. Eventually, not being an early riser himself, Diesel stirred to see what all the noise was about and they opened the front door to see the sun just starting to rise and a world covered with snow. Diesel rushed out into the garden first, and tried eating it, rolling in it, eventually deciding that the warm fire was calling. Sindy and Paul had other ideas and a snowman soon emerged.

No one was up early in the Baker household. They had all enjoyed talking far into the night about long-ago Christmas's while listening to carols on the radio. However, they had made a pact at midnight that no matter what shape they were in, they would all swim on Christmas morning, and so sleepily and rather hung-over, Dot opened the front door. A good six inches of snow fell into the hall.

'What are your plans now, Mrs Seabourne Dipper? You can't be a fair-weather swimmer you know,' teased Rob, adding a couple more jumpers, a hat and scarf to his swimming bag.

'We've absolutely got to get down there' Margaret called from the top of the stairs. She hadn't enjoyed snow for years and was going to make the most of it today.

By ten-thirty nearly everyone was at the beach, shivering, snowballing, eating and drinking, even Betty was in her chair, covered up with so many blankets and hats that she could hardly be seen, but her laugh was the giveaway. Finally, all the swimmers were down to their swimsuits and they leapt along the snowy sand and pebbles, laughing and shouting. Betty called out one, two, three, and they all rushed in to the freezing water, yelling, screaming and some actually managed a 'Merry Christmas'.

Most people rushed straight back out again, with a few of the boys and men having to show how brave they were, including Samuel, who felt he had to impress Rani, and Rob who wanted to stay in a few second longer than Dot, so that he could tease her about it later. More hot drinks were handed out and the happy scene soon dissolved with people heading home for hot baths. Clara and Charles had walked down, this was not the weather for the sports car, and with glowing cheeks, they trudged happily back through the snow to the comforting smells of Christmas Day.

Benny and Jack were first to arrive. Benny had brought the puddings, which needed a good couple of hours steaming. Clara was looking stunning in a red velvet trouser suit and Charles had gone to town, with a very dashing gold smoking jacket, teamed up with smart black cords. The towering tree in the hallway, covered with gold and silver tinsel, decorations and lights brought back childhood memories for anyone who brushed past, with that evocative pine fragrance. Clara and Charles quickly made everyone feel at home; the fire was roaring, Champagne and sherry were flowing and Joyce was sitting happily at the piano in the lounge, tinkling out carols and Christmas tunes, with Betty singing along. She was soon joined by Isabella and Rani and a festive sing song had begun. Samuel, Will and Lizzie were playing with an ancient train set that Charles had found in the attic.

Dot, Rob, Margaret and Kate arrived with gifts, bottles of whisky and chocolates. They decided to open presents after lunch and, of course, the Queen's speech. Doreen and Pat picked up Sindy, Paul and Diesel, and brought them safely to Rutland Manor. It was turning into a beautifully sunny day and the snow sparkled on the gabled roof tops, with morning shadows stretching across the lawn. Doreen was enjoying a very large glass of sherry, on an empty stomach, and joking about Patrick's torch order. This amused most people, who said they would know where to go if they needed one, and the new and improved Patrick just laughed it off, with the others. Once they had all started heading towards the dining room and the kitchen, Diesel hopped on to the cosiest looking sofa, and stretched out properly for a nice long nap.

Dinner was served, with everyone pitching in. Charles was carrying the turkey, Samuel the sauces. Rob, Paul and Margaret were in charge of the many platefuls of golden, crispy roast potatoes and Patrick, Joyce and Rani carried the vegetables. Benny and Jack were pouring the Chateauneuf-du-Pape, whilst Mr Green, Ruth and her husband, were enjoying being served, Army style. Dot and Kate carried the jugs of gravy and stuffing, and Betty was happily directing operations from the comfort of her chair. Finally, they all sat down and remembered the people who couldn't be there. Crackers were marvelled at, and finally pulled, with Dot saving all the fancy decorations, for next year, and they started their meal. Half-way through Christmas dinner Clara thought, *something is missing,* and came back in from the kitchen with the pigs in blankets. *How could they have been almost forgotten?*

No one had any room for pudding which didn't stop them having a slice with lots of cream when Benny brought them in, flaming with brandy. Gathering around the television, they enjoyed some port and mints, watching the Queen's Christmas message. Clara thought she looked lovely in her bright yellow blouse and Dot said the theme of good spreading outwards, with every little bit helping, was really nice. Gifts of all shapes and sizes were exchanged with the usual mountains of wrapping paper forming. Samuel had carved an exquisite mermaid out of walnut for Clara, Patrick had bought Charles a very nice box of cigars and everyone had brought something for Lizzie to unwrap; Isabella and Will were quite overwhelmed.

Sindy had quietly saved the best till last. Once she had finished restoring the original *Cinderella* poster, she mentioned it to everyone except Clara and Charles (who couldn't possibly be trusted to keep the secret). Samuel had framed it and after wrapping it, Sindy had written "To the Mermaid, who will always be the star of every show, with much love from your friends," and everyone had signed the card. As she opened it, Clara was astonished to see the poster looked exactly as it had done, forty years ago. She was speechless. She looked around her home, filled with friends, family and laughter and began to explain.

'Thank you so much Sindy, everyone. Before the war, the stage was my life, with any free time, being spent in the sea. Swimming was my passion then, and Peter, my late husband nicknamed me 'The Mermaid'. It stuck and became my stage name until, well you probably realise.' She stopped for a moment, then continued, 'when Peter built the theatre, there was really only one name it could be and for years it was my pride and joy. After the war, it was just a reminder of all that I had once been and everything that I had lost. And now, thanks to all of you, and especially you Dot, all that love, fun and excitement has come flowing back, like the best wave.

Thank you, my friends.' Charles who had stood watching her with tears in his eyes, poured her a large glass of brandy and wrapped his arms around her, to cheers and whoops and here heres' from everyone.

Doreen and Dot came in with a tray full of snowballs, the alcoholic kind, which the ladies enjoyed whilst the boys went into the drawing room to smoke and drink too much whisky.

Jack went out to get more logs for the fire and announced that it was snowing again and had been for some hours, by the look of the path and driveway. It really wasn't the weather to be going home, either on foot or by car and so Clara suggested they stay over; she (meaning Charles) could find some blankets and sleeping bags in the attic. Everyone thought this to be a wonderful idea and continued drinking, playing charades, cards and monopoly (which got quite competitive) until the early hours of Boxing Day.

Kate and Margaret were up first and decided to approach the washing up. Enjoying the peace and warmth of the kitchen, they talked about their future as they ploughed through the glasses, plates, and finally the saucepans. It didn't feel like a chore after such a perfect day and they got through it quickly. When Ruth came in, rubbing her head slightly, she was delighted to see what her 'Christmas Angels' had done and thanked them warmly. Together they organised a Boxing Day brunch for all who felt like eating, and set it out in the dining room, along with jugs of water and Alka-seltzers. Slowly, the others woke and stumbled into the kitchen in search of coffee and teas, with everyone agreeing this had been the best Christmas ever.

DRESS REHEARSAL

The lazy, indulgent days after Christmas went by; finishing up the festive food, eating the least tempting chocolates, which had stayed at the bottom of the tin, thinking about diets and going for long beach walks. Most of the cast had a few slightly nervous looks at scripts, wondering if they were going to remember their lines once on stage, with the bright lights shining on them. Clara was up with the lark today, she also wanted to run through her lines, check all was in order at the theatre, and look in on Betty on the way. Betty had been getting slowly worse; however, she was still managing to get about, on a mixture of sheer grit, the occasional glass of sherry, determination and strong painkillers.

Dot and Charles were already at the theatre, checking the lighting, and oiling the trap door. The ugly sisters were going to be 'pushing' Cinderella down it, when Prince Charming came knocking to see who the glass slipper would fit. It had gone well so far in rehearsals, but it wouldn't hurt to check it once more. Clara made sure all the costumes were named and in appearance order. Dress rehearsal would start early tonight, so that problems could be ironed out and no-one was too late home. Although everything should run like clockwork, Dot secretly hoped it wouldn't go perfectly – that was a sure sign of problems on the opening night.

Later in the day, Doreen came with bags full of make-up, false eyelashes, brushes, rollers and lots of hairspray and hair pins. She wanted it all set out ready. Benny and Jack brought boxes of supplies for the evening; rehearsing, they had found out, was hungry work and the bakery was very quiet at the moment. Jack was going to work in the foyer, then double up as stage manager; the cast needed calling for when they were due on stage, otherwise everyone tended to stand in the wings and get in the way of the others. Charles and Betty were joint prompts; if she didn't feel up to it at any time, he would take over. She was more than happy with that arrangement; just having him sitting next to her, and smiling, was a bonus she never thought she would enjoy.

Joyce arrived next, and sat chatting and playing her way through the afternoon, sometimes pantomime songs, classical, and also jazz when the mood took her. The excited magic fairies slowly started arriving with their mums and people began to get into costume. Half an hour before the rehearsal, Dot called for everyone to be backstage, and a bit quieter so that it would feel like the real thing. Make-up was done, with Samuel, Will and Benny all trying to outdo each other with their fancy faces. Five minutes was called and the hush was replaced by Joyce playing a medley of the tunes to come.

First on stage was Cinderella in her rags in the kitchen, singing and telling her woes to Buttons. Isabella's beautiful voice was effortless and this scene went well, with Buttons having the traditional box of sweeties that he would be taking to his granny (asking the audience to shout if anyone should try and take one, let's have a practice, and of course, all the other characters do try and take one). Enter the wicked stepmother and her ugly daughters. Dot, sat in the front row, almost crying with laughter as the three boys flounced their way through the first half, appearing outrageously nasty and ridiculously dame-like at the same time. She had chosen well with these three but, the show was stolen by Clara, who shone as the fairy godmother, her stage presence being immense. Charles was spellbound! The transforming magic was weaved on the pumpkin and the mice, with the magic fairies enchanting everyone. Dot had learned a clever 'double' trick whereby she had a second Cinderella (Kate was up for this) in rags with her back to the audience while walking off stage, so that the real Cinderella comes in magically dressed for the ball in a few seconds. It worked a treat and Dot hoped it would be just as good tomorrow.

They all relaxed and chatted in the interval and Dot praised everyone, there was almost nothing to change. *This is going too well,* both Clara and Dot thought to themselves.

The second half went just as smoothly, Dot couldn't fault them. Sindy made a captivating Prince Charming delivering her lines with the slightest hint of amusement. It worked brilliantly. Rob performed his forest ghost scene well; it didn't need to be too scary, but included many 'it's behind yous', and was just long enough to change the set behind the curtains.

The wedding finale was joyous, with everyone giving their best and enjoying the walk down at the end, which they hadn't practiced before. Dot looked over to Doreen and Patrick who had watched it all from start to finish, to see their reaction and was more than rewarded.

They all left, with everything tidy and ready for tomorrow evening. Jack opened the door for everyone to go home and was surprised and blown back by the gusty wind, which had got up while they had been busy inside; it looked like a stormy evening was on its way. As they walked back up the pier feeling tired but elated, Dot and Clara exchanged looks which said; yes, it has gone too well, but we've worked hard. Tomorrow will be great.

FRIDAY 31ST DECEMBER.THE OPENING NIGHT

Yesterday had been a long one and most of the cast slept a little later than usual. At one point Benny rolled over in bed, waking himself up saying 'no, Prince Charming, there are no other ladies living in this house,' and glanced over to see that it was still very dark outside. *Must be early,* he thought, and went straight back to sleep.

Paul and Sindy had been awake for a while in the night, she couldn't get comfortable, and once they finally got back to sleep, they also slept through the storm. Dot and Rob were first to wake up and Rob said as it was her first night, *he* would put the kettle on. He wandered down to the kitchen, filled the kettle right up; there would be a lot of tea needed this morning, and flicked the switch. Nothing. Perhaps the fuse had gone. He rummaged about, looking for the right fuse in amongst tape measures, old paintbrushes, drawing pins and bits of string, and realised he needed to put the light on in order to do this. Again, nothing. Main fuse box then. No luck. Right. He looked out of the window; it must be about seven o'clock. Total darkness, not even a street light. *Oh NO.* This situation required tea and so he went out to his shed, brought the gas ring and camping kettle into the kitchen and got on with it. By this time Dot was up, in her dressing gown saying that everywhere was a bit cold and perhaps they should check the central heating. Seeing what Rob was doing, she realised.

Ruth had got up early as usual and, once she had assessed the situation, guessed that without its ancient radiators creaking away, Rutland Manor would be getting quite cold and the residents would probably be getting pretty frosty as well. This was a setback that no-one could have foreseen, and of course, Clara would not be happy. On her way, she saw fallen branches and quite a few power lines down. Everywhere she looked, there was evidence of last night's storm.

Clara greeted her with a hug, and together they set about lighting fires in all the rooms, Charles made several pots of coffee on the Aga, which thankfully was solid fuel, and they sat down together, around the table to put their thinking caps on. They all agreed this was no time to panic, somehow the show must go on. Charles said he would grab Rob and go down to the theatre and look at the situation. Luckily there were no trees blocking his way, and miraculously the theatre seemed to have escaped the storm's wrath; it seemed to be more inland that the damage had occurred. They popped into see Will, who was already snowed under with phone calls and people wondering what they should do. He had contacted the electricity board who said that power was down all across Seabourne and Cliffbourne and would be out for at least 24 hours, possibly more. They had every available man working on it.

As the hours ticked by, most of the dippers gravitated towards Rutland Manor, to see what was going to happen. By mid-morning, everyone was there; Charles was making bacon sandwiches, Benny was serving tea and toast; there were big decisions to be made. Pat Turner was the hero of the hour. He had 110 torches, all with batteries, ready for use! Rob had a couple of heavy-duty lamps, with a small but noisy petrol generator, which could be used if necessary. Everyone had candles and nightlights in jars (in a seaside town, power cuts were not that unusual) and together they wondered if this would be enough.

Sindy had the idea of putting notices up in as many windows and busy places as possible, saying that *Cinderella* will be going ahead tonight and could people bring all the torches and candles that they could spare? Everyone thought that was a great idea and they all joined in, cutting up an unused roll of wallpaper to make lots of posters. Lizzie had brought her colouring pencils and the new felt tips that Father Christmas had given her. Isabella thought they would help keep her busy, but didn't realise just how useful they would be.

As usual, Benny decided that food would ease the situation; Jack drove him and Rani to the bakery to get all the ingredients they could fit in his car, and together all who weren't drawing posters, got busy in the kitchen making food that could be given to the audience, to make up for the lack of lighting. Jack also suggested that a free drink on arrival wouldn't go amiss. They had made a good profit with ticket sales and could afford to be generous.

By late afternoon, they had taken a mountain of delicious looking snacks to the theatre, all the torches and candles that they could muster, and plenty of alcohol to ease the situation. There was no more that could be done. The latest update was that power wouldn't return until tomorrow at the very earliest.

In complete contrast to the previous night, the full moon shone brightly, creating a wonderful beam across the sea, and those magical moonlit waves as they crested the shoreline. Everything was ready back-stage and the paying customers slowly began to arrive. People had been amazing, carrying torches, lanterns, gas and oil lamps, in fact every kind of light you could imagine. Charles just hoped the fire officer was busy elsewhere that evening.

It was difficult backstage, but they managed. People were seated, and Jack made an announcement, thanking everyone for their help, and would they please switch off the torches now until the curtains opened. 'You are all our lighting technicians, thank you, and enjoy the show.' With that, Joyce started the overture with a flourish, and the curtains swished open. What the torches lacked in power was more than made up for, by the enthusiasm from the audience. Cinderella was applauded for her song, Buttons caused a sensation with every character trying to take the sweets, with the children yelling: 'Buttons, someone's stealing your goodies' at the tops of their voices.

People roared with laughter, when at first, Willameana (aka PC Johnson) entered in a pink hooped dress with matching wig, handcuff earrings and wearing his police hat on the very top (he hoped Chief Burrows would take this in good part). The problem with having no stage lights was that you could see much more of the audience, and their reaction. But they needn't have worried, people were in stitches. Bernice (previously known as Benny) swaggered in next, looking like a vision in yellow and purple, with a tray of buns, which he merrily threw into the audience. The time flew by and it seemed like minutes before Clara, glittering in a full-length turquoise and silver gown, was using her magic wand, she had only just walked on stage and the applause erupted. The fairy dance charmed everyone, young and old and the little ones were beaming.

Dot ventured out in the interval to hear the reactions. The free drinks and food were going down well, but the talk was all about *Cinderella*. Everyone was amazed at just how professional and funny it was, even without lights. Dot thought she would burst with pride and rushed backstage to let them all know. Within minutes, the second half had begun, the glass slipper had been lost and found and Prince Charming was going door to door to find its owner. The 'royal knock on the door', was the cue for the sisters to push Cinderella into the cellar, via the trap door, which tonight, would not open. They tried and tried; it was completely stuck.

The audience started laughing, and then Samuel had a good idea. 'Is there anyone with building skills backstage, we could really use a BUILDER right about now, to fix this' he yelled in his stepmother voice. Rob, who had his overalls on, under the ghost outfit, got the gist, and went on as the local pantomime builder, which caused a huge round of applause and laughter. With his magic can of WD40, which, he informed the audience, could be purchased at Turners' Hardware store for a vastly inflated price now, he sorted it, made a low bow and sauntered off stage. *I did that rather well,* he thought, and quite fancied a part in the next one.

In no time at all, the walk down began with everyone taking their bows, amidst cheers and whistles, followed by the final song, which the audience joined in, with gusto. The applause started with Chief Burrows and his party instigating a standing ovation. One by one, everyone got up, cheering, clapping and still singing. Eventually the final bows were taken and the curtains closed. No-one seemed in a hurry to go home and Jack had to almost push them through the door, out into the moonlight. By this time, Will had removed his make-up, changed and decided to help Jack with the last knockings. Just as he thought nearly everyone had gone, the Chief tapped him on the shoulder. 'I hope you will perform your new role at Cliffbourne, with as much enthusiasm as you have clearly done this evening, Inspector Williams.' Just at that precise moment, the lights all flickered a couple of times but then went straight off again, but it was hopeful.

SATURDAY 1ST JANUARY 1977 – MATINEE AND LAST NIGHT

Power was restored later that evening, which, although the first night had gone well, relieved everyone. Batteries had begun to fail during the second half, and candles were burning dangerously low. But! It had worked, people were raving about it everywhere; there was panto chatter in Tesco's, a queue had formed at Benjamin's to see if there were any available tickets, people couldn't decide whether Pat Turner was the saviour of the show with his torches, or if it was in fact Rob Baker, with his WD40. Some folk who came last night, wanted to see it again. Clara and Charles enjoyed a coffee in Benjamin's listening to all the praise. Dot was loving chatting the whole evening over at home with Rob. It had been such hard work but what incredible fun. Margaret and Kate were still asleep but they had enjoyed every minute of last night.

The matinee performance would be different this afternoon, they always were, and it took a lot of energy to run through the whole thing twice. Two o'clock rolled around very quickly and everyone was buoyed by the addition of the lights. This time, the trap door didn't stick, however the children screamed and shouted so much at the outrage of Cinderella being shoved down the cellar, they had to stop for a few moments, as no-one could hear anything that was being said. The youngsters gasped at the magic that the Fairy Godmother had performed and all their hands shot up when the question was asked: 'Are there any children in the audience who would like to help us with our song?' Just about managing the mob, Dot and Rani helped eight of them up on stage. The song was successfully sung, with the left side of the audience, being better than the right. Oh no they weren't, etc., and off they went with a little prize for being the best.

The second half went off without a hitch, with the children particularly enjoying the 'If I were not in pantomime, something else I would like to be, song.' There was something about silly slapstick that kids, and adults loved every time. Finally, the last of the audience left, singing praises and the songs, whilst walking back into town.

The characters came out into the auditorium, it wasn't worth changing for a couple of hours, and all enjoyed a much-needed tea. This time, they had brought their own, as Benny was completely out of ingredients, cakes, pastries and every edible thing. The little fairies, including Lizzie, played in the dressing room, some of the men had a smoke, and in no time at all, it was showtime, for the last time. Dot was nervous as Mr Clements and his party were coming this evening, she hoped it would show just how professional the Mermaid could look. There was a light-hearted feeling backstage, with lots of chatter, and Dot, while congratulating them all on a brilliant job, nearly finished, had to remind them to keep quiet during the performance. It was surprising how sound carried.

Julian Clements arrived early and sat chatting to Dot about how it was going. The press were also there tonight, to take photos and do an article. Suddenly there seemed a lot of pressure in the air. People were beginning to take their seats, programmes were going like hot cakes and following that wonderful dark hush, the curtains opened on the last night of *Cinderella*.

Everyone was on top form, the boys did a lot of naughty ad-libbing, including Samuel, arriving on stage tonight, not from stage left, but on the ariel rope, completely unbeknown to Dot. People did laugh though, the sight of him flying about, singing "Down at the Old Bull and Bush" with his working boots on, stripey coloured tights, bloomers showing, skirts billowing, brought the house down. Cinderella who was doing her best to look sad and downtrodden, was trying very, very hard to keep a straight face. Dot, who was wondering when they might get back to script, looked across to Julian, who was actually crying with laughter.

Normal pantomime service eventually resumed, with the evening going well, even if there were a few more last night japes. This evening there was a lot more audience participation with the 'it's behind you', and 'oh yes you did's', going on forever. At the end of the walkdown, Clara made a little speech, thanking everyone for their help and inviting Dot to come up onto the stage. Lizzie presented her with a huge bouquet of flowers, from the cast. Dot thanked everyone again and the final curtains swished across. That was it, done. Months of planning, writing, refurbishing, all finished in the blink of an eye.

Once everyone was changed, an impromptu party got underway. It was late, but people were as high as kites on adrenaline and needed some down time. Julian stayed as well, he was so impressed with Dot's production and he was also keen to know a little more about Isabella. Her voice, he said was pitch perfect, and so natural. Whilst walking up to the Bentley, he said that she could contact him if she ever wanted to go professional, and gave her his card. That really was the icing on Isabella's cake.

Charles asked for quiet as Clara wanted to say a few words. 'I just want to say a huge thank you, firstly to you Dot, because without you, none of this would have happened, and to everyone who made this production possible. My life has been transformed over the last few months and I am so very grateful.' Jack had supplied their celebratory drink of choice and everyone toasted Clara and Dot and then The Mermaid Theatre.

After many more 'congratulations' and 'you were wonderful darling's' they slowly peeled off with Clara happily closing the door of The Mermaid Theatre, knowing that this would certainly not be the last time.

EPILOGUE

After realising how bright and inviting Benjamin's looked, Doreen and Patrick decided to completely re-brand Turners, painting it in peach and cream, which tickled Betty no end. Trade was even brisker, and they had to employ a youngster, now that Sindy had her hands full. They also had a new focus in their life; their grandchildren, whom they shamelessly doted on. Making up for the past; Doreen joked that Pat was trying to win a 'best granddad of the year' trophy.

Samuel and Rani's relationship grew slowly into what they both needed: someone to rely on, love and look after. They remained in their own homes, with both of them saying they had lived on their own for too long now to change completely, they liked their own space at times. However, the time they spent together was spiritual and wonderful, filled with incense, bangles, dream-catchers and crystals, and Samuel thanked his lucky stars for the day she walked into Benjamin's. Rani was never trying to replace Vera, Isabella's mother, but she became her closest friend (after Benny of course), and made an amazingly cool grandmother.

Betty had managed to enjoy and celebrate Christmas with the brother she thought she would never see again. She had achieved her aim to laugh her way through *Cinderella*, if quietly, in the wings, a set of prompting lines on her lap, with Charles by her side. They had made a good team, and Clara had said a very special thank you to her at the end of the production. She got to see the new coat of paint on the shop front, but with an extra surprise. The re-brand had included a new name: 'BETTY'S ' was painted in huge gold letters on the front. They had a little opening party, with sherry and chocolate cake, and all the gang were there, including Diesel.

Betty said goodnight to her friends on the 25th January 1977, and as requested, her send-off was a 'bloody good celebration' of her life.

Sindy struggled with Betty's death, everyone did. She had been such an inspiration, always seeing what others had missed, finding a laugh in situations that didn't initially appear funny, and her laughter seemed to ring out, long after she had left, especially in the wings of The Mermaid Theatre. Time was the only healer and Sindy got busy with her apprenticeship with Jack, who was often reminded that he'd not hired a 'yes' woman. Sindy and Paul got their wish: Betty and Peter were born, weighing a healthy 6lb each, in the summer of 1977. Although both of their jobs were demanding, they had so much help from their friends, who advised them to enjoy every minute of it, because it goes so very fast, that they managed to juggle their young lives, and keep their heads just above the water.

Isabella, Will and Lizzie had adopted Diesel just before Christmas, this suited everyone and he soon bonded with them all, once he had shown them which sofa he preferred. The sale of their flats, refurbishment and everything went smoothly. There was a fair amount to do when they moved in, but they were all thrilled with the space and particularly the garden. Lizzie's bedroom was first to be decorated, she was a big girl, nearly seven and she wanted purple, not pink, actually, and there was a carefully neutral room waiting for her little brother or sister. Isabella continued teaching until she couldn't really move around that well, due to her bump, but was happy to have some time to enjoy her home and family. Their wedding was planned for after the baby, and Lizzie was thrilled to be a bridesmaid again. Inspector Johnson's life was busy, but he enjoyed the work at Cliffbourne and couldn't wait for the arrival of his first child.

Benjamin's Bakery went from strength to strength; they decided that a bigger premises would soon be on the cards. Paul's baking really took off; he did a couple of courses in London and came back with some very fancy ideas. Benny loved them.

Harrington and Harrington Designs was slow initially, but once he had work on his drawing board, enquiries flowed in. The window was a huge attraction. Jack had enlarged a lot of the photos and collections he'd taken throughout the previous year; of the dippers and their surroundings and placed them in the window. So many people stopped and smiled, while walking through the town.

Dot's career did take off, but she was never tempted to fly away. The Mermaid Theatre took up a lot of her time, and she absolutely loved it. She and Clara had agreed to take a percentage of Julian's profits for his productions. What a brilliant decision! He was making a fortune, as well as pulling in huge audiences into The Mermaid; they didn't need to advertise. Dot always had time for swimming, however, and was on the beach every morning, generally before the rest of them, twirling round and enjoying the waves. Rob and Samuel formed a lasting friendship which helped him to chat about John. Samuel would have loved him, he said as they worked away quietly together, pencils behind their ears, and workshop coffee on the side.

Charles felt Betty's death very deeply and for a long time, he just couldn't get past the fact that he had missed so much. However, Clara with her usual directness, eventually gave him his own advice, 'man up, old boy,' because it would have been what Betty wanted. They had the rest of their lives to enjoy together; fast cars, (Clara did get a new, very fast, Ford Granada), flashy clothes, (they both loved a bit of theatrical showing off) and, of course, travelling.

As they drove up to Victoria Station to catch The Pullman

down to Dover, Clara smiled at the extravagant set of matching luggage Charles had bought for them both. They enjoyed a very dainty lunch on the train, which boded well for things to come. The Orient Express swept into the station, its brown and cream coaches gleaming with the prospect of luxury and excitement. The guard opened the door for them and Clara was amazed by the opulence of the carriage and their cabin. Finally, after much champagne and ceremony, the doors clunked shut, the whistle was blown, and they moved off, at a stately speed, out of the station to start their adventure together.

THE END

ABOUT THE AUTHOR

H F Burgess

I have a love of sea swimming and have been doing this year round for the past couple of years. It is extremely beneficial for all aspects of health. Pantomime is also one of my joys and I have been involved in writing and producing amateur ones. The wonderful friends that I have made whilst enjoying both these pastimes, inspired me to write my first book, combining both.

Printed in Great Britain
by Amazon